GALAXY JONES
AND THE SPACE PIRATES

GALAXY JONES

AND THE SPACE PIRATES

BRIANA MCDONALD

Simon & Schuster Books for Young Readers
NEW YORK   LONDON   TORONTO   SYDNEY   NEW DELHI

SIMON & SCHUSTER BOOKS FOR YOUNG READERS
An imprint of Simon & Schuster Children's Publishing Division
1230 Avenue of the Americas, New York, New York 10020

For information about special discounts for bulk purchases, please contact Simon & Schuster Special Sales at 1-866-506-1949 or business@simonandschuster.com.
The Simon & Schuster Speakers Bureau can bring authors to your live event. For more information or to book an event, contact the Simon & Schuster Speakers Bureau at 1-866-248-3049 or visit our website at www.simonspeakers.com.
Interior design by Hilary Zarycky
The text for this book was set in Adobe Jenson Pro.
Manufactured in the United States of America
0923 BVG
First Edition
2 4 6 8 10 9 7 5 3 1
Library of Congress Cataloging-in-Publication Data
Names: McDonald, Briana, author.
Title: Galaxy Jones and the space pirates / Briana McDonald.
Description: First edition. | New York : Simon & Schuster Books for Young Readers, 2023. | Audience: Ages 8–12. | Audience: Grades 4–6. | Summary: Galaxy Jones ventures across the universe with Prince Weston in order to save her family and friends from ruthless space pirates.
Identifiers: LCCN 2022058829 (print) | LCCN 2022058830 (ebook)
ISBN 9781534498297 (hardcover) | ISBN 9781534498310 (ebook)
Subjects: CYAC: Outer space—Fiction. | Pirates—Fiction. | Lost and found possessions—Fiction. | Friendship—Fiction. | LCGFT: Space operas (Fiction) | Novels.
Classification: LCC PZ7.1.M434353 Gal 2023 (print) | LCC PZ7.1.M434353 (ebook) | DDC [Fic]—dc23
LC record available at https://lccn.loc.gov/2022058829
LC ebook record available at https://lccn.loc.gov/2022058830

To Shannon, for making my world brighter, sillier,
and better just by being in it.

CHAPTER ONE

A photo of Ron's face illuminates my phone as I video call him. A small green dot dances above his name as it rings, calling out to him across the empty distance in our outside corner of the solar system. The photo is a couple years old, cropped from a selfie we took back when we met up weekly at my parents' inn or his mom's astronaut ice cream factory. Now we have video calls instead, since the distance between our homes is too far for frequent visits.

My phone beeps as the call connects. A pixelated image of Ron's slim, freckled face fills the screen.

I almost drop my phone out the window as I snatch it up from the sill. "Ron! You're there!"

"I'm here." He grins, then tilts the phone so I can see the room behind him. The wonky deep-space service makes his video shift in delayed, choppy movements, but the image is familiar enough for me to figure it out. He's on the first floor of the factory, by the welcome desk. There's no sign of customers, but his mother is hunched there, shifting through an important-looking stack of papers. The room is flooded with cardboard boxes full of product. "I'm always here, Lexi."

Here feels like a different solar system at this point. I tug at the thick, hemp rope that ties his window to mine, all those hundreds of miles and miles away. Sometimes I wonder if the rope is stretching, too, as the universe expands. Here on the outskirts of deep space, the metric expansion of the universe increases the distance between objects at a steadily increasing pace. And as much as I wish our homes were gravitationally bound to each other, with each passing day the distance between the rocks we call home grows and grows as dark space expands between us.

I envision the rope stretching in unison with the expanding universe, growing longer and thinner as the days pass. Kind of like Ron is, from the look of him on my screen. "Do you think you can come by this weekend?"

He groans. "I'm going to be jammed in the delivery pod with Mom and about thirty boxes of ice cream this weekend. We're going to be more compressed than a white dwarf." He runs a hand through his strawberry hair. "I don't know why she doesn't make my sisters go with her—"

"Probably because they're five," I interrupt with a laugh.

"Only bright side is that I'll be able to pick up some more interesting ingredients from the specialty stores that don't have deep-space shipping," he says. I start to frown at the thought of the central system having anything special that we don't when he adds, "But if we have to cram any more central system deliveries into one weekend"—desperation rises in his voice—"Mom's going to have to run me through the ice cream dehydrator for me to even *fit* in the pod."

I sigh and press my knuckles to my cheeks. Out my window, past our O-Zone and out in the starry sea of sky, the astronaut ice cream factory floats at the end of our rope. When we were kids, astronaut ice cream was all we ate: freeze-dried chips of ice cream—pink, brown, and white—as we went on adventures in our solar system.

It used to be *our* solar system. Now it feels like it belongs to space. Nothing but black, expanding space.

"At least drop some ice cream here on your way," I say, voice smaller, more hopeful than I want it to sound. "I'm sure our guests would love to have some."

Ron's blue eyes light up. "You have guests?"

My stomach feels like a ton of asteroids dropped into my intestines. "We could, by this weekend."

The sparkle in his eye falters. I tug at a loose curl by my ear. "But it sounds like you guys have a lot of orders. That's good, right? Other than you getting squished."

"Yes, other than the small fact that my organs are being compressed by blocks of cardboard." He chomps his too-big front tooth on his lower lip. "The trips are getting longer, which Mom says is expensive. But no one wants to pay more for astronaut ice cream, let alone the long-distance trip to the factory. So . . ."

I prop my phone by the window and stand upright in the frame, hands planted on my hips so he can see my full power pose. "So nothing! This is our solar system. We're gonna stick by it, no matter what. People will see what it's worth," I say, chin tilted up.

I want it to be true—*need* it to be true. The outer system is the only home I've ever known, and no matter what changes, I want to keep it that way.

Ron leans closer to his screen, squinting at my pixelated image on his phone. "Soon, people will be coming here in droves. Staying at the inn and touring the ice cream factory. It'll be even *better* than it was before." I smile, properly uplifted, and take the phone into my hands. "And we'll even be able to afford a super-speed pod that can fly us back and forth along the length of the rope," I say. "I'll see you every day."

He pretends to wince. "Every day?"

"We'll go riding on comets!" I declare, fist held to my chest. "We'll rescue lost ships from black holes, and fight space pirates! Like we pretended to as kids."

Like that time we watched a comet through my dad's telescope when an astronomer from a university in the central solar system—where the capital and all the cities are—stayed at the inn to view it as it passed. Or exporters from an agricultural planet told us about the time they had to use an escape pod when their supply ship got sucked toward a black hole. Or when we'd huddle on the downstairs couch on chilly days, snuggled into thick blankets while sipping hot chocolate with moon-mellows while begging older guests from the central system to tell stories about their travels and run-ins with space pirates, like the infamous Great Astro Bonny.

Thinking about all of it sends a rush of warmth through my chest, strong as a supernova. On slow, empty days at the inn like this, those memories are like fuel propelling me onward. A reminder of how things could—no, *should* be.

"We'll be *flooded* with tourists, even better than before," I say. "And this time, they won't just be bringing the stories to us. Deep space will be full of adventures of its own."

His eyes go wide. The corner of his mouth inches to a smile, raising his freckles into tiny constellations. "You really think deep space could be like that again someday?"

"We tied a rope across the outer system to hold our homes together," I remind him. "We can do *anything*."

That's when a shout comes from downstairs in Dad's high, singsong voice. "Lexi! You've got to see this!"

Ron smirks on the screen. "Your dad space watching again?"

"Hey," I say, eyebrow raised, "last week his telescope caught a double-moon eclipse. So this could be good."

"Photos or it didn't happen."

I wave and press end call. Then I burst out of my room and into the long, second-story hallway. I rush past closed doors and vacant rooms, each numbered for our nonexistent guests. This place used to be *brimming* with space travelers— explorers, vacationers, politicians, and visiting families who came on the space train, back when our stop was still in service. Now, other than the occasional central system delivery driver, it's usually just my footsteps echoing down the hall and the carpeted stairs.

I run into the open-concept dining and living room, quickly, so the familiar uneasiness that comes from the silence doesn't kick in.

Dad stands by the bay window, the end of the telescope pressed against the glass. He's hunched over, fluffy black hair poking up around his ears and all the way down to the tip of his collar. He doesn't look up as I approach but waves his hand for me to come.

I crawl onto the couch by the window and lean over the back cushions. Dad grips the telescope and his wide-rimmed glasses clink against its lens. "Look, hon. I think we have guests."

I nearly fall over the edge of the couch. "Guests?" I gasp, and tug at his shirt, trying to get my view.

Papa calls from the kitchen. "Last time you think you saw a guest, it was just a deep-space minerals collector who needed directions."

"And I directed him to stay over," Dad retorts, "so it still counts."

I crawl over the back of the couch and nudge Dad out of the way. "Let me see."

"They're still too far off to see much," Dad says, stepping to the side to give me room, "but it looks like a pretty big ship."

I peer through the lens, one eye shut and the other squinting hard. A giant, white dot expands on the horizon, appearing to grow in size as it comes closer. Dad's sight is bad even with his glasses, so I have to zoom out a bit to gain focus. That's when the sharp image of the ship comes into view.

A miniature castle with strong jets on the back zooms through the black space, toward our hotel. Giant flags wave at the tips of each tower, and smooth gold shutters shimmer in the starlight. There's even a small patch of grass at the front of the ship, with a fence to keep passengers from toppling into deep space. A fluffy brown dog with an O-Zone bulb floating around his head rolls on the grass by the front steps.

My eyes turn to slits. I know that dog. Everyone this side of the Milky Way knows that dog. But I, unlike any other sucker in the solar system, am *not* happy to see it.

"It's not guests," I declare, shoving the telescope back. "At least not for us!"

A crease forms between Dad's brows. "What do you mean?" He leans back toward the telescope. I cross my arms, lower lip jutting out, and watch for his response.

His eyes go wide and he steps back. "Paul? You're gonna want to see this."

Papa appears in the kitchen doorway, wearing a pale-blue apron and puffy kitchen mitts. There's flour in his short black hair. "If this is another eclipse, Derek, I swear . . ."

"It's the royal family," Dad says, tapping the telescope. With each passing millisecond, he taps harder and faster. Papa picks up the pace, rushing toward us while tearing off his mitts. "They're back. They've come back."

Papa presses a hand to Dad's back and lifts the telescope up toward him with the other. I maintain my firm posture, arms twisted together like an angry pretzel. "And this time we won't let them in," I say. "We know better now. They are the absolute loudest, rudest, messiest, worst-est guests in the entire galaxy!"

"Yes, hon." Dad ruffles my hair but doesn't look at me, his eyes fixed on Papa's expression. "But they're also the richest."

I tilt my nose up. "Well, we don't need *their* money."

Papa shakes his head. "Oh, yes, we do." He struggles with the knot of his apron and turns to Dad. "There's lasagna about to go in the oven. Get out the good parmesan, sprinkle some on, and put it in for forty. I'll take a duster to the third-story rooms, and Lexi"—he gives me a serious look—"puff the couch cushions, wipe the windows, and put on your purple dress."

Dad's already off, running toward the kitchen so fast he nearly knocks the dining room chairs over. Papa rolls his apron into a ball and starts toward the staircase. I leap over the couch and jump in front of him.

"You can't be serious about this," I say, blocking his way to the stairs. "Don't you remember what happened last time?"

Papa veers to the left, making to step around me. I jump onto the top step and grip both sides of the banister, creating a human shield.

"After they left, you closed the inn for a whole week! Dad opened that bottle of double-gravity-pressed wine, and I got to try a sip. You even took the gifts they left behind—" Papa cringes and his eyes fall shut, his hand pressed against his temple. I straighten up, say the words louder, "And we went out to the black hole and had a tossing contest. Remember?"

His hand remains against his temple, head bent down. I think I've won, until he says, "You need to puff those cushions."

I point to the couch I crawled over, pillows dented from my feet and throw blanket dangling off the edge. "I kind of did."

His dark brow knits together. "Galaxy Jones, I'm serious."

I drop my arms to my side and look at my mismatched

socks. "That's redundant, because you only say my full name when you are serious."

Papa sighs. He presses his hand against the dark waves of my hair, thumb against my cheek. "Things were different back then. At the time, I saw them as just another guest. But they weren't." His chest rises and falls and his jaw shifts left, right, as he debates his next words. "The money we made from their stay . . . we didn't realize it then, but it ended up keeping us afloat for years. During the slow seasons, and then when every season started to feel like a slow season."

Even while I'm standing on a step, Papa is a half foot taller than me. He leans down, forehead tilted toward mine. "We're doing everything we can to stay here, in this neighborhood."

So you can be closer to Ron, he doesn't say, though I know that's part of it. When our neighbors' houses and businesses started to drift farther and farther from ours, and the central system tourists looking for a getaway in deep space became few and far between, I spotted more and more moving ships passing by our window. Some hooking to shops and homes before heading toward the central system and a new location. Some smaller moving pods, stuffed with boxes by old classmates and neighbors who'd rent a few rooms on whatever central system planet still had occupancy.

The central system has always been more populated, the planets clustered closer together than any parts of deep space. So, even as the universe stretches and expands, businesses still thrive in the central system. Schools are close enough together that kids can attend in person. And everything—from food deliveries to getting a space plumber when a pipe bursts—is faster and easier and cheaper there.

But as our deep-space neighbors' homes and shops were roped to ships and tugged away, chipping a piece of our neighborhood off with each one, I saw an opportunity. A way to tie the factory and inn together here, in deep space, using the same method those ships used to leave it behind.

Because someday, deep space would be as lively and bustling as it once was. And until then, Ron and I had to stick together—had to keep our family's legacies alive, keep our spot in deep space for when that day did come.

That's what we told our parents, at least. But sometimes I wonder how much it cost our parents to buy all that rope and tie our homes together. Right now, I think I'll be too afraid to ever ask.

"I know," I say, before he can say any more. His expression softens, and I quickly add, "But please don't make me be nice to Prince Weston." Papa starts to roll his eyes. I drop my voice, as serious sounding as I can. "Papa, he's my interstellar *nemesis.*"

He laughs. As though it's a joke. My throat feels tight, like it's stuffed with space dust.

It's been nearly four years since I've seen the royals. As a kid, they were just faces on the news, or names my fathers mentioned when discussing politics. Like, "Did you hear the Queen funded a study on interplanetary water pipelines?" or "the King suggested reducing the number of train stops due to the universe's recent growth spurt—do you think this will affect our stop?" (Spoiler alert: it did.)

I never thought much of them. They lived in the central part of our solar system, on a tiny planet close to most of our citizens. Last time they passed through, they had to stay over on their way for a meeting with another system's royalty. We had other guests at the time, too, but I don't remember a thing about them. All I remember is the King and Queen bossing my fathers around like they were servants. And how they'd kick our other guests out of the dining room so they could spread their papers all over it and talk, in their pompous voices, about their Important Meeting. I remember the royal court digging through our cabinets and closets as though they lived here, too. Even the dog was a menace, getting sick on our carpets while the royal guards accused our home of being "a wobbly space rock" before forcing me—*me*—to clean it up.

But more than anything, I remember the total torment I suffered from Prince Weston.

There was the time he walked through the door and kicked off his shoes so hard they flew right into my gut. Or the time he purposefully spilled a cup of hot tea on my lap and blamed it on the "two-star turbulence." Or how he'd shout from his room every night, demanding he be brought this or that, and when I stopped responding, tied a bell to a chain and dangled it down from his window to mine. He always needed something *just* as I was about to sit down, and had an opinion about everything I owned. And then he suggested his parents ban astronaut ice cream—yes, actually *ban ice cream*—because it was quote-unquote *archaic* and *unhealthy*, but mostly just to tick me off.

By his last day, standing outside by the front gates, he'd gazed off into the starry sky and reminded me for the thousandth time how eager he was to return to "real civilization." I offered to push him off the hotel and give him a head start on his travels.

Thankfully, my fathers didn't hear *that*.

"Look," Papa says, syllables interrupted by soft chuckles. "He's a guest, so you have to be nice to him." I open my mouth to object, and he holds up a finger. "*But* you can be twice as mean about him behind his back, if you're decent in person. Understood?"

I groan. "Understood."

Papa plants a quick kiss on my scalp and moves up the stairs. I linger at the first step, nails picking a loose chip of paint on the banister. Pots and pans clang where Dad is in the kitchen, and the telescope remains pointed toward the sky. By now, they're close enough that I can see the approaching ship with just my eyes.

"Papa?" I call, gaze fixed on the window.

I hear his steps slow. "Yes, hon?"

My throat feels drier than dehydrated Neapolitan ice cream as I ask, "Why do you think they're here?"

After a beat of silence, I look up the stairs. For a split second, I see the laughter leave Papa's eyes.

"I don't know, hon," he says, voice tight. "Just go fix the cushions, okay?"

I trudge toward the couch, focus returned to the approaching orb of light on the horizon. Regardless of what they're coming for, it's going to be a terrible stay. But as I think more about it, I can't help but wonder what would bring the royal family all the way out here, to the farthest corner of our system.

I fold the throw blanket, smooth out the corners. No matter what they're here for, I decide, I'm ready for the challenge.

CHAPTER TWO

The doorbell rings.

Dad and Papa exchange a glance, both hovering by the doorway. Dad nods toward the door and Papa smooths nonexistent wrinkles from his shirt.

He reaches for the knob just as the door flies open.

"It is *so* cold out there!" a shriek comes, followed by the Queen herself, draped in a dozen ornate shawls and scarves. Her dark hair is twisted to the top of her head, loose curls cascading past her pale, crinkled face. She steps through the threshold, head high and shoulders back, and flings her outermost shawl into Papa's arms.

"Outer space tends to be cold," I mutter, and Dad shoots me a warning glance. Then he smiles warmly at the Queen.

"Welcome, welcome," he says as she strolls past, eyes accessing the entryway. She's closely followed by the King—a wrinkled, white-haired man Dad once joked that "gravity did not treat well"—and three stern-faced members of the royal guard. Comet, the dog with an O-Zone bulb floating protectively around his head, bounds in after them. I glare at him as he dashes past, wondering how it is that his orb can keep oxygen in but send his vomit out.

Dad and Papa are talking in their host voices, collecting coats and guiding the crowd inside. I remain by the door, avoiding eye contact with the royal guards and court as they filter in, and await the inevitable.

Someone remains on the porch, purposefully prolonging his entrance to build as much melodrama as possible. He clears his throat, loud and deep, like a trumpet announcing his arrival.

I scowl, jaw so tight it could shave my teeth down to space dust. That's when one gold-colored, shiny shoe lands on the welcome mat. Then, after a dramatic beat, the shoe's owner follows, nose angled toward our chandelier and shoulders squared so his cloak puffs out around his body.

Prince Weston. His blond, wavy hair jutting in all directions yet somehow looking like perfect rays of sunlight. His small, stubby nose curled up, pink lips pulled into a smug grin. Not even half an inch taller than me, but trying to appear so in his wedged shoes and with his chin tilted up.

And that cloak. That stupid, red-and-gold cloak that clips under his white collar and hangs down to his elbows.

"Nice cape," I say, in a voice that lets him know I don't think it's nice at all.

He adjusts it at his neck. "It's a *cloak*. With locally sourced gold on the trim."

He wiggles his shoulders so the light catches the gold, making it twinkle. Not subtle at all.

"You look like an off-brand superhero."

He frowns. "You look like the daughter of two failing business owners."

I grasp his cloak and tug so hard that he lets out a quiet yelp and stumbles toward me. "Want me to take that for you? I know some great black holes around here that can take care of that incessant twinkling—"

He grabs my wrist, tries to twist off my grip with his totally inferior strength. "Sure, if you promise to go with it—"

"Galaxy!"

We rip apart and put on our best grins as the adults turn around. Papa glares at me from across the room, thankfully the only one to have seen our scuffle.

Weston unclips his cloak and whips it off his shoulders. "She was just about to take my cloak for me," he says, voice laced with fake warmth. "She's just as wonderful of a host as I remember."

The Queen and King smile, then turn back to my fathers. The second the attention shifts from us, Weston rolls up his cloak and throws it right at my face.

"Thanks, Lexi," he says, with cavity-inducing sweetness. I peel the cloak from my face and glare as he saunters away.

"Take a seat anywhere you'd like," Dad is saying, gesturing to the dining table. "We have some dinner cooking now, and—"

The Queen pulls out a chair and plops down, untangling herself from another shawl. "We brought our own tea this time. If you follow the brewing instructions, I'm sure you won't mess it up."

Dad forces a grin and follows two guards into the kitchen. As I hang up Weston's cloak, I whip out my phone, head back to the table, and text Ron.

Royal family here for Mars knows what reason. Send help.

He replies with a kitten emoji, which I decide to count as help. There's not much Ron can do from the other end of a miles-long rope. But it makes me miss the last time the royals were here, which is something I'd *never* thought I'd say. But at least, back then, I had Ron just a meteorite's skip away.

Even when there were enough kids living in deep space that we didn't have online school, Ron was the one I'd call for everything, and vice versa. He'd rush over, wide-eyed and eager, every time Dad spotted something new with his telescope. I'd spend hours with him at the factory, experimenting with new ice cream flavors until our aprons didn't have a clean spot left. We'd help each other with our families' work, too; when a guest rolled up to the inn with five or more suitcases (translation: *rich*), I'd invite Ron over so we could chat about the factory within earshot and land him a new customer. And when the inn flooded with guests, Ron would scrub dishes and fold sheets to make sure work was done in time to chat with the visitors after dinner and collect stories from their travels.

Last time the royal family tortured me with their stay, Ron was there every day to get me through it. We'd hop from rock to rock outside the inn, far enough that I could vent about our guests without them—or my fathers—hearing. Ron would tie a throw blanket around his neck like a cloak and do Weston impersonations for me, the ice cream factory floating within visible distance on the horizon behind him. When Dad and Papa were focused on catering to the royals' every need, and our other guests were too focused on the royals to bother with me, it was *Ron* who got me through. Because no matter how mad Weston made me, Ron made me laugh harder.

Not having Ron here now leaves a crater-sized gap in the scene. Thinking about it sends a hard throb in my chest. While I'm glad the rope keeps the factory from drifting away farther, sometimes I wish I had a gravitational pull that could yank him back to my side, where he belongs in moments like this. Facing them without him not only feels wrong—it feels downright impossible.

Because now it's just me. And this cat emoji. And a taller, brattier Weston.

I shuffle back to the dining room, moving in half steps as though I can prevent arriving. The King sits beside the Queen and gestures toward Papa. "While we wait for the tea, perhaps you can start bringing things up to our rooms?"

The Queen runs her palms over the tablecloth. "And it seems this time there's enough space for us! Thank goodness you have no other business." She laughs, high and cheery, and I want nothing more than to wrap her scarf around her face so she can't say another word.

Papa is composed as ever, hard smile in place. "Of course. If the guards would like to give me a hand—"

"And Lexi can show me up to my room!"

Weston stands, hands on his hips, beaming at me with that devious twinkle in his blue eyes. I square my jaw.

"I'm so tired from the trip," he says, blinking innocently, "and would love a place to rest my head. And Lexi is *so* hospitable."

Papa looks like he's resisting a laugh. I ignore him and glare holes into Weston.

Time alone with Weston means jabs and pranks and oodles of self-restraint. But considering the royals are waiting on tea, and suitcases, and whatever else they make up to boss my fathers around, I'm not going to find out why they're here anytime soon. Going upstairs with Weston is my best shot at figuring out what's going on.

And if he doesn't want to tell me, I can lock him in his room until he answers.

Just the thought alone makes me feel warmer inside. I return his smile and skip toward the stairs. "After me, Your Highness."

He nods cordially. "Thank you, Your Hostess."

I take the stairs two at a time, Weston at my heels. He walks slowly and purposefully behind me, shoes clanking gently against the floorboards. On the second floor, I see Papa closed my bedroom door and polished the room numbers. I head to the end of the hall, toward the second staircase. Not a single photo or painting is off-kilter, and a pot of fake flowers has been placed on the stairwell's windowsill.

I wait at the landing for Weston to catch up, shooting a glance out the window. Dark space stretches like a fitted sheet over the horizon, no sign of the factory, or even the rocks Ron and I jumped across last time, laughing about the royals.

Swallowing, I look at the hundreds of miles of rope that connects my house to Ron's and imagine that he's part of this and I don't have to face Weston and his family alone.

"You're slow," I say when Weston finally reaches the second set of stairs. "What, are you used to being carried on a royal litter?"

"A *what?*" he snaps, trudging up the second flight. "My parents don't waste their gold on royal lifters. I can lift myself."

"Barely," I mutter. "And it's a royal *litter*. The box Earth kings and queens were carried in." He finally reaches me and I position my smug smile right in front of his face. "How do I know this and you don't?"

His hand grips the banister and he leans, slanted, against the railing. "I imagine you have plenty of time to read between guests," he says. "Years, perhaps?"

I groan and stomp up the final flight, to the third floor. "I'm not giving you the room above mine this time. If you need something during the night, you can go and fetch it yourself. I'm not your dog."

"Good," he snaps, rushing after me. "I already have a dog, and he smells better than you."

I whip around and get right up in his face, his upturned nose inches from my flaring nostrils. "Why are you here, anyway?"

He grins, as though he's been waiting for this. I ball my fists by my sides and stand my ground, ready for whatever comes next.

Probably.

"Business," he says, pretending to check his nails.

I swat his hand down. "What possible business could you have in *deep space?*"

He cocks an eyebrow, and hot shame pools in my cheeks. I'm an innkeeper; I'm *supposed* to be flaunting the various attractions of deep space, and directing my guests to enjoy other businesses, too—like the ice cream factory. But so many people and businesses have flocked to the central system that there's not much left for me to recommend to guests. Instead, I'm hopeful that they'll come with stories for *me*, so that I can live vicariously through them.

Back when Ron and I were little kids, it felt like we could embody the stories our guests and customers shared with us, or that we read about famous pirates—like the Great Astro Bonny—in books and the news. Dressing up and reenacting those tales together, it felt as though we, too, could explore the universe and go on epic adventures someday.

But the universe expanded and travelers willing to wander this deep gradually dwindled, taking their stories and promise of adventure with them. Directed by the Great Astro Bonny, space pirates began to loot and conquer entire planets, quickly becoming a constant, terrifying threat in the central system when they used to be nothing more than vagabonds and rapscallions who lived outside the confines of the norm.

The universe may be literally expanding, but it felt like my world had shrunk until all that was left was folding sheets, checking the guest log, prepping the continental breakfast, and everything else I had to help my fathers with for the inn to survive. For *us* to survive, out here in the loneliest corner of deep space.

But this was my *home*. The only one I'd ever known, and the one I was determined to stick by, no matter what. And despite the smug look Weston's giving me now, I'm not about to let him think that I'm anything *but* proud of where I'm from, and dedicated to making sure spoiled central system city kids like him don't forget what makes deep space great.

"Or do you not even know why you're here?" I ask, hoping to regain the higher ground. "Did your parents only bring you so they'd have someone to babysit the dog?"

Something flashes behind Weston's eyes, and I know I've hit a nerve. But I'm not sure *what* nerve, and I don't feel the surge of triumph I was hoping for. Without Ron's calm smiles and gentle laughter backing me up, I just sound like a bully.

"First of all, his name is *Comet* and he does not need babysitting." Weston kneels down and lifts the dog up into his arms. He cradles him against his chest, and Comet looks up at me with deep-brown eyes, laying the guilt trip on thick. "One, because he's an old man, *not* a baby. And two, because he's just as much a part of the family as anyone else."

Comet pants happily in his arms and I feel bad enough that I actually, truly consider *apologizing to Prince Weston*, despite the fact that it goes against every instinct in my body. But, thankfully, his knack for monologuing saves me.

"Second: my parents have some business with the next solar system over. It concerns an alliance of our interstellar armies for support getting the space pirating under control."

He barrels on, though my brain is stuck on the mention of *space pirates*. "Your inn is just a layover."

"Wait, what do you mean, *getting the space pirates under control?*" I ask, eyes wide as full moons. "Does the royal guard *not* have them under control? Have they taken over more planets?" I hate that I'm letting any fear slip into my voice as I add, "Are they coming *here?*"

Weston's face goes as pale as the surface of an ice planet. He opens and closes his mouth, as though the O-Zone around the inn had been turned off and he suddenly lacked proper oxygen.

It is *not* a comforting look, to say the least.

"I don't know!" he yells, so sudden and so loud that Comet wriggles free from his grip. The flash of frustration behind his eyes catches me off guard. Not because I'm not used to Prince Weston being grumpy and short-fused. But unlike before, I'm not sure what part of what I said affected him so deeply.

And not knowing when it comes to the threat of *space pirates* leaves me unsettled.

His ears turn an embarrassed pink. Weston rushes to do what I did earlier, attempting to regain the higher ground, as he snaps, "What, do you not even get the *news* out here? Astro Bonny's crews have been seizing villages and planets for *years* now."

I squirm uncomfortably, pressing my fingertips against the stair railing for support. Space pirates have never been *good* or *righteous* people. But before the space pirates started to take over the solar system in the calculated, aggressive way they do now, Astro Bonny was like a celebrity in our universe. Sure, she ransacked and pillaged like any pirate does: but she never targeted innocent people or villages or planets to strip them of their goods and take over. Instead, she was always on the hunt for the rarest and strangest space-techno, determined to be the most powerful and mysterious woman in all of deep space.

Being reminded of how far off her legacy has veered from what I'd read about as a little girl always came with a strange pang of disappointment. And talking to Weston now, it's also a cold reminder of how little I really understand about our solar system.

"Of *course* I do," I snap. "I'm probably less sheltered than you, considering I actually go to tele-school instead of holing up in a lonely castle with a tutor."

It's a flimsy argument. To me, space pirates were something figurative, part of a reality outside my own. They were characters in books Dad would read at night, snuggling me close to his chest during the scary parts before the hero saved the day. Or peripheral figures in the stories Papa would tell me about his early childhood in the central system, appearing in passing. When Ron and I were younger, we'd take the giant waffle cones from the factory and pretend to duel like pirates. We'd even tuck napkins into our collars like extra-wrinkly cravats.

But as the guests faded away and Ron and I outgrew bedtime stories and dress-up—and as Astro Bonny's legacy turned from inspiration to a painful warning—it was almost as if the pirates left our world along with everyone else. Sure, I'd heard about the ongoing struggle the central system had with pirating—from the morning news Papa plays alongside his morning coffee. But with Weston standing in front of me now, cheeks flushed and fingers curling and uncurling by his sides, I feel like there's something I'm missing. Like clues to a silent warning passing right beneath my nose.

I inhale sharply to steady myself. If one thing's for certain, it's that Prince Weston is *not* a reliable source of information. For all I know, this ambiguous talk of space pirates is just a game, Weston's way of messing with me to pass the time during his stay at the inn.

I make a mental note to mention it to my fathers later. But for now, I focus on what I know best: innkeeping. I straighten my shoulders, imagining the weight of Weston's presence rolling right off my back.

I march up to the first door on my right and swing it open, gesturing widely at the dresser, closet, and neatly tucked bed. "This one's you," I say through clenched teeth. "Dinner will be served within the hour. Bathroom is third left down the hall. Continental breakfast will be at nine sharp, and any special requests are due before eight tonight."

He opens his mouth and I immediately add, "And you can direct them to my parents."

With that, I storm back down the stairs, heart drumming wildly in my chest, wishing for the first time in months that not even one of our guest beds were filled.

I don't have alone time with my fathers until the royals declare they're taking over the conference room (aka: the storage closet by the living room that we stuffed a table in a few years back as a marketing tactic). The royal guards filter off with them, only one or two guards remaining in the living room and by the doorway. Weston takes Comet out to pee, and the kitchen and dining room are finally royal-free for the first time in hours.

I stack dirty plates in my arms and hurry into the kitchen. Dad is bent over the sink, suds trailing up his forearms, while Papa frantically skims his recipe book, likely planning tomorrow's breakfast for our unexpected guests.

Dad smiles when he sees me. "Dump those right in the sink, hon. There's a clean dish towel in the second drawer if you could start drying these ones."

It feels like falling into an old routine with the three of us cramped in the kitchen, excitedly prepping things for guests. I may be less than thrilled about *who* those guests are, but a giant smile bursts across my face like a supernova as I grab a dishcloth and slide up next to Dad by the sink.

Papa glances up from his recipe book, one eyebrow raised. "You seem happier than I thought you'd be," he remarks with a gentle smile. "Are the royals too busy to bother you this time around?"

His question lands like double gravity on my shoulders. Even my smile falters under the pressure as I think about what's keeping the royals so *busy* this time around.

"Weston said that they're here because things are getting really bad with the space pirates," I say. I scrub a plate in hard circles, imagining I could wipe my fears away as easily as the water on china. "Like . . . Astro Bonny's lackeys, and all that."

A flare of hot shame rises inside me at the mention of Astro Bonny. I admired her for so long, I almost feel guilty by association.

Papa lowers his recipe book onto the kitchen table and sits up a bit straighter. "Weston said that to you?"

Dad drops the mug he's washing, letting it clatter loudly in the overfilled sink. "Lexi, hon, you have *nothing* to worry about," he says in a rush, eyes wide between his thick glasses' frames. "They're just here for a stopover on their way to another system—they're not here because there are any pirates in deep space."

"And he never should have insinuated there are," Papa adds a bit gruffly.

Part of me wants to lean in to the fact that Papa is *finally* as annoyed with Weston as I've been most of my life. But with Dad and Papa frantic to reassure me, I'm almost more afraid of how little I know about what's going on in the central system than I am of the pirates themselves.

Well, not really. Pirates *are* terrifying, given their knack for taking prisoners, sieging planets, and using planks and hooks and cutlasses to get their way.

But *still*.

I turn back to my plate with intense focus, as if I hadn't picked up on my fathers' anxiety. "Do you think people will move back to the outer system, since the pirates are causing so much trouble in the central system?"

Dad makes an aborted attempt to press his hand against my arm, recoiling at the last moment as he remembers the clumps of soapy bubbles on his hand. "I don't think so, love. There are more risks out there, for sure. But most of the people who left here left because they didn't have sustainable work anymore. They . . . might not have a choice."

What he doesn't say is that we're not much different. That the royals are the first guests to come to the inn in ages, and we probably would have left for the central system, too, if it wasn't for me and my rope and my stubborn love for the place I call home.

Deep space is safer, too, I remind myself. *Dad and Papa wouldn't leave, even if you offered it.*

Safe is the word I'd overhear Dad use when he and Papa talked in those low, whispery voices when they had conversations about the inn and money, the kinds I wasn't supposed to overhear.

"Lexi's happy here," Dad would say, making my chest swell with an unlikely mix of relief and guilt. "And with everything going on out in the central system . . . it's starting to look like it did when *we* were kids. So, staying here is probably safer, too."

The conversation usually ended there. And we stayed, here, in the peace and still of deep space, so far from the rest of the world that it couldn't touch us. So far that guests no longer brought epic stories of the central system and pirates, because guests no longer came at all.

I swallow and place my dry plate to the side, reaching for a set of spoons. A lump rises in my throat at the thought of asking them directly, because a big part of me doesn't want to know the answer.

"The royals will get the pirates under control," Dad continues, voice calm and soothing. "That's why they're here now. Everything will be okay."

Papa rises from the table and crosses the room. He grips his recipe book in one hand and places the other gently between my shoulder blades. "You don't need to worry about any of that, Lexi. Just focus on not fighting with Weston—"

I shoot Papa an incredulous glance.

"*Publicly*," he corrects, rolling his eyes. Dad shakes his head and lets out a soft chuckle.

Papa runs his hand up my back before ruffling my bangs lightly. "The royals will take care of the space pirates. But even so, your Dad and I will always, *always* keep you safe," he says in that soft, serious tone of his. "You have nothing to be afraid of."

I lean back, Papa tall and steady behind me and Dad pressed warm against my side. My eyes slip shut and I imagine what he's saying is true: that out here in deep space, nothing bad can reach us. So long as I stay at the inn and keep my focus on our guests, I have nothing else to worry about.

Space pirates, royals, and battles over planets: those are all worries for someone else. Galaxy Jones is an innkeeper, first and foremost. And even if there used to be some small part of me that dreamed of epic adventures through the solar system, it faded to nothing as soon as the wicked intentions behind Astro Bonny's escapades became clear.

"Now, back to those dishes," Papa says, giving me a soft nudge toward the counter. He plants a quick kiss on Dad's temple and adds, "You too. We don't want to give our guests any reason to cheap out on a tip."

I grin and hurriedly dry the next damp plate, feeling as though all the planets in the solar system are properly aligned again. Not matter how the universe expands, or what's happening in the central system, or whatever drama Weston and his family bring to our door, I'll always have this. And that, I decide, is all that matters.

Once the dishes and breakfast meal prep are done, I make a beeline for up the stairs and to my room. I don't have any new texts from Ron, which makes sense considering he's prepping for a big delivery. I fight the pang of disappointment that comes from my blank phone screen and open my window, absently running my fingertips over the coarse fabric of the rope outside.

The touch sends a ripple through the first few feet of the rope and it sways slightly, as though stirred by a breeze. But even if I grabbed the rope with both fists and shook it until my arms throbbed, the motion would never reach Ron. There are hundreds of miles of rope between us. And though I'm grateful to our parents for installing the rope so another few hundred miles couldn't wiggle their way in, the rope doesn't undo the distance created by the metric expansion of space.

With a small jump of surprise, I spot Prince Weston on the patch of fake grass by his docked ship. He stands in the center of the yard, watching Comet as he waddles across the grass and relieves himself against the empty mailbox. It's a scene I've watched a dozen times before—except last time all three of us were younger, so Weston used it as an opportunity to chase Comet around with squeaky toys and practice the bark command to interrupt my sleep. Now the old dog patters toward Weston and settles on a patch of dirt by his foot, tired from the day. I expect Weston to carry him back inside, but instead he lowers onto the ground beside him, knees pressed tight to his chest.

I crinkle my nose, confused. The second the royals had given us privacy I'd rushed to ask my parents what they thought of what Weston had said. With a huge meeting planned with the nearby solar system, didn't Weston have a lot to discuss with his parents, too?

Seeing Weston sit on our lawn against the dark, endless backdrop of empty space, I wonder if the loneliness I feel while holding the rope is echoing in him now.

Whatever atom-sized sliver of empathy I felt for Weston in that moment is gone when his familiar knocking comes at my door hours later, jolting me from a peaceful sleep. I throw off my comforter with a dramatic groan and stomp to swing open the door.

Sure enough, Weston is standing right there, Comet at his heels. The whites of his eyes are bright against the dark of the hallway, but heavy, red-rimmed lids tell me he's as exhausted as I feel.

I try to brace myself for whatever nonsense he's about to spew, but nothing can prepare me for what he asks next.

"Can I see your pirate stuff?"

I stare at him blankly, half-asleep and fully confused. "My *pirate* stuff?"

My grip on the door falters and Weston stumbles inside, his O-Zoned–headed dog at his heels like Velcro. "You know, that junk you and that ice cream kid used to play with all the time."

An embarrassed flush rises to my cheeks. "Why would you need any of *that?*" The prince stalks around my room, hands held on his hips as he scans my bookshelf as though looking for something specific. "Are your parents' armies so desperate that they're ready to send you out to fight with my Styrofoam cutlass?"

Weston runs his fingertip over the spines of my school textbooks, brows knit with concentration. "My parents don't need to ask for my help with things like that."

I scowl. Weston *knows* that my parents make me work at the inn because they need my help for our business to survive— for *us* to survive. I imagine hot gas spewing out my ears as I snap, "Great, then you shouldn't need my help either. *Get out.*"

Weston groans and moves to get Comet. We both turn at the same time to see why the dog has been so suspiciously quiet since Weston barged in. He's planted on the rug by the edge of my bed, gnawing idly on the corner of an old photobook that I keep hidden in the gap between my bed and the floor.

All my self-righteous anger fades into white-hot humiliation. It's not an old photo album with embarrassing photos my fathers took of me as a baby—it's *worse.* Somehow, Weston's dog managed to make a chew toy out of my super-secret, super-embarrassing copy of *The Great Space Pirate Astro Bonny Unofficial Photobiography.*

I want to scream for him to drop it, want to lunge forward and snatch it from the dog and shove the book back into hiding. But panic grips every muscle and I stand frozen in place, staring in horror as Weston reads the title on the front cover and takes in the photo of Astro Bonny positioned triumphantly at the helm of her ship, a mischievous, self-assured smirk on her face.

Dad bought me the photobook. Having grown up in the central system near some of the worse space pirates, Papa was never interested in Astro Bonny's legacy; but Dad not so secretly loved learning about the strange space-techno she collected on her travels. Like the atom-splitting laser she used on her former righthand man turned archnemesis, Calico Jack, when he tried to take control of her ship. Or the ultra-rare items that it was rumored she'd found, from watches that bent time like wormholes and keys that opened doors to the multiverse.

But while Dad was just interested in the legends surrounding her space-techno, I was obsessed with reading the stories about her epic battles, escapades, and discoveries. As our guests dwindled, so did my access to stories from other planets and their citizens' adventures. After a while, returning to Astro Bonny's book was all I had.

I swallow, a sticky, hot sweat breaking out across my forehead. This book is the last, most damning relic of my space pirate obsession, and of the silly fantasies I played at as a little girl. And right now it's laid out in the open for my interstellar nemesis to see.

Weston's eyes widen. "Comet, you're a *genius* as always, buddy." He snatches the book off the ground, and Comet's tail wags behind him proudly. "This is *exactly* the kind of thing I was looking for."

Weston makes for the door, as if this conversation is over. I plant myself firmly in front of it and lean back so it slams shut with a click. "Are you an Astro Bonny fanboy now?"

He crinkles his nose. "What? No way."

The way he spits the words makes my stomach churn with shame. I steal a glance at the cover, studying Astro Bonny's sturdy posture. I try to mimic her pose, as though embodying her courage can make me strong enough to fight off Weston's taunts. "So, then why do you need my book?"

Weston shoots a glance at Comet, as though he's going to offer talking points to get him out of this conversation. But the dog just pants happily in response.

"Research," he says lamely.

I cross my arms over my chest. "I thought you said your parents didn't need your help with the space pirates?"

"They *don't*." His chin wobbles a bit as he says it. Which is weird, considering he *just* mocked me for working at the inn, as if it was better that his parents kept him out of their affairs.

I feel my usual Weston-directed anger slip from my features. Weston watches my expression change, and I swear I see a flash of something uncharacteristically vulnerable behind his eyes. But the walls quickly come back up, his eyes going hard and his lips curling into a tight line.

"Look, space pirates are *not* just cute little characters from your books. It's Astro Bonny and her lackeys who are terrorizing the entire solar system, taking over planets and tossing anyone who fights back into the nearest sun."

He shakes the book as he speaks, and my eyes follow the photo of Astro Bonny back and forth, the motion making it look as though her cutlass is swinging along with Weston's movement.

"But you wouldn't understand that," he says, face getting that familiar, cool look that warns me he's about to regain the upper hand, "because you've been safely tucked away in deep space, where there's nothing good enough for even a *pirate* to want to steal."

Comet lowers back on his hind legs and releases a soft moan. Probably because he needs a walk, but I pretend it's because he's disappointed in Weston being such a jerk.

I don't know why Weston is suddenly so desperate for a book on Astro Bonny, or why someone as rich and spoiled as him had to get it from me. But right now I just want him out of my room—and I want the book gone, too, like it should have been ages ago.

I *knew* Astro Bonny and her apprentices were the ones leading all the attacks in the central system. But some part of me was so desperate to hold on to the *idea* of her—who I used to think she was, and what she used to make me feel *I* could be—that I hadn't been able to get rid of the book myself.

"Go ahead, take it," I say, swinging the door open so fast it stubs Weston's toes. "I hope your dog enjoys his new chew toy."

Weston ducks his head as he hurries past me, Comet

lagging at his heels. Before I slam the door shut behind him, I catch him clasping the book tight to his side, as though anxious whatever it is he needs from it could slip through his fingers.

Despite having read that book a hundred times, I have no idea what Weston could want with it. But as the last piece of my idolization of Great Astro Bonny is carried off down the hall, I decide to let it—and let *her*—go.

CHAPTER THREE

I'm groggy and puffy-eyed when Papa wakes me up the next morning, setting a plate of freshly baked mini muffins on my bedside table while he rattles off our to-do list. I spent more time than I'm proud to admit lying awake in bed after Weston left, acting out imaginary arguments with him in my head, where I always had the quickest, wittiest comeback to gain the upper ground without stooping to his level. Right now part of me wants to bury myself beneath my blankets and fake a cold until the royals leave. But the sickening thought of letting Weston *win* like that sends a shot of adrenaline through my body that jolts me out of bed.

"Your dad and I have breakfast covered," Papa is saying, "and I know you have tele-school later today, so you don't have to come downstairs—so long as you can keep things tidy up here between classes."

Tele-school is all prerecorded today—it is more often than not lately, considering the service issues involved in broadcasting live to deep space. But I'm too relieved at the thought of avoiding the royal family to mention that.

"Sounds good," I say. "Make sure Dad doesn't mess up the Queen's precious tea."

I spot a smirk tug at the corner of Papa's lips, though he tries to conceal it. "Vacuum the hallways and then you're off the hook, Lexi. And we're downstairs if you need anything."

I waste no time getting dressed, pulling my purple dress from the night before back on since I only wore it for a few hours and don't have another royal-worthy option. I rush out of my room and to the supply closet, drawing out the hand-held super-vacuum Dad bought a few years back during one of his space-techno shopping sprees. The sooner I finish my one chore of the day, the sooner I can hide from our guests.

My fathers' voices carry from downstairs, their familiar host-tones telling me that the royals must be down for breakfast already. Confident that the coast is clear, I quickly sprint to the third floor. I run the vacuum over the carpet in a hurried state Papa would definitely not approve of. But it's worth it to finish our guests' floor without having to actually deal with any of our guests.

My relief has a shorter life span than a supernova, though; just as I make it to the second-floor landing, the sound of a familiar, haughty throat-clearing sends a buzz through all my nerve endings. I turn around to see Prince Weston making his way down the stairs after me, his usual smug grin on his face.

Part of me feels bad that his parents started breakfast without him. But any sympathy dissolves the second he asks, "Didn't you wear that yesterday?"

That question makes every inch of my skin tingle and

burn like the surface of a star. I only *have* one nice dress, because I usually don't have to dress up for guests. And even if I did, we don't have enough guests now for it to matter—and we don't have enough guests for me to *afford* more than one nice dress. And I don't need a literal *prince* questioning me for that, especially when there is quite literally no one as spoiled as him in the entire solar system.

"Considering you ransacked my room like an amateur pirate last night, I don't think you're the most qualified person to critique my things," I snap.

I switch the vacuum on and run it over the stair landing, hoping the deafening whir of the machinery will tell Weston this interaction is over. But, as usual, he's too determined to push my buttons to take a hint.

"The book didn't even have anything useful in it," he says, shifting back and forth on his feet. "I don't know why you bothered keeping that thing for so long."

I still have no idea what Weston could possibly have been looking for in that book—especially when his parents didn't invite him to their conference yesterday and probably won't be including him in the meeting with the other solar system's royals once they arrive at their destination, either.

But none of that is my concern right now. My only concern is the inn and the prince-sized pest that's taking up space in my hallway. I snap the vacuum off and drop it to the carpet, spinning around to face him with my hands on my hips. "Great. So no need for you to stay here for so long, either. You've got business in the next system—so when do you leave?"

The corners of his lips curl into a big smile. Like he's just struck locally sourced gold. "We're never leaving, Lexi. Your inn *is* our business. Forever."

The blood runs out of my cheeks. It seems like the room is tilting, as though the inn is about to slip off its rock and into deep space.

My voice is smaller than I want it to be. But in this moment, I don't care. "What do you mean, you're not leaving?"

"The voyage from our central system to their main planet is too long without a stopover," he explains, nonchalant. "We need a place to stop on the way."

My fists shake by my sides. I hope he thinks it's from anger rather than fear. "A place to stop is not a forever home."

"No," he says, glancing past me at the ceilings, the doorways, the wallpaper, as though appraising the house for himself. "But if we're stopping over, we'll need privacy. And while this inn certainly isn't as crowded as it used to be . . ."—he looks back at me, grin taunting—"there are still a few occupants we'll need to be rid of."

I step toward him, despite the way my throat rattles like a loose pipe, or how something damp and warm pricks at the corner of my eyes. I swallow hard, force my words out steady as I can. "The inn's not for sale."

Weston shrugs. "Considering the lack of foot traffic here, for your family's sake, I truly hope that it is."

I don't respond, and there's silence. Silence from every empty room in the house, every bed and chair that's been unoccupied for months. Silence outside the window, across the dark expanse of sky where the trains no longer run and tourists no longer travel and family no longer pops by. Silence all the miles along the rope that ties my home to Ron's, silence past the floating rocks and bored asteroids and hungry black holes.

Silence where there used to be sound, before the universe expanded until we didn't quite fit here anymore.

I shake my head. "They can't sell. They can't sell." I say the words like a soft chant, mostly for myself. "They can't sell. They can't . . ."

I stumble back, as though I can run from this. As though I can turn back time to before we opened the door, before the royals set their GPS our way, before the world stretched and everything I was used to slipped away.

The room turns in my vision, and I wonder for a second if our inn really *does* have turbulence. The white walls wiggle at the edges and my legs feel like al dente noodles beneath me. Weston's smile falters and as I stagger back, he steps forward. When he speaks, his voice sounds faraway, like I'm hearing it underwater.

"Hey, you're not going to faint on me," he says, words slow and stretched in my mind, "are you? Because I don't want to—"

There's a heavy crash and my knees give out beneath me. I tumble onto the carpeted floor, the fabric rough and prickly against my bare arms. My eyes squeeze shut and I'm certain I've blacked out when I feel a heavy weight pressed against me.

My eyes fly open and everything is back in focus. Including Weston, toppled over on the floor with his body sprawled over my legs.

I pump my knees. "Ew, get *off!*"

"Don't *ew* me!" he snaps, pushing up from the floor. "Believe me, I'd rather have fallen back down the stairs than on top of *you.*"

I leap to my feet, smoothing out my purple dress. "Why did you fall, anyway? Suddenly get a conscience and were overwhelmed by the weight?"

He rolls his eyes. "What do you mean, why did I fall? Didn't you feel that crash?"

As he says it, I notice the paintings dangling unevenly along the wall. A small crack lines the stairwell window, as though formed by an impact.

"But your parents aren't moving your ship," I say, slow and unsteady.

"And you never get visitors," he adds, eyes widening.

In unison, we sprint to the window by the landing, bumping our elbows and tripping over one another's feet with every step. I tear back the curtains and we press our noses to the glass, breaths fogging its glossy surface.

A second ship rests on the edge of our lawn, next to the royals'. It's shaped like a water ship rather than a spaceship, the kind I've seen in books about water planets, or on the ride I went on as a toddler when we visited the water park by the purified springs lab that supplies our corner of the solar system with water. Large black flags hang still from a crow's nest, and giant black masts jut from the center of the ship.

People in dark cloaks rush around the ship's wooden landing, one pair hoisting an anchor over the edge and into our inn's yard. A pair of inky-haired twins, not much older than me or Weston, stand by the figurehead. They're dressed in the same uniform as the rest of the crew but with tricorn black hats atop their heads, decorated with a symbol I recognize from textbooks and stories I heard from guests growing up: an alien skull with crossed bones behind it.

"Space pirates," I breathe, barely believing the words as I say them.

It's like watching pages from my Astro Bonny photobook come to life—except I am *not* prepared for a reenactment of those pages unless it involves Ron and me in costume.

My head spins and the floor feels as unsteady beneath me as it did when I fell a moment ago. This *can't* be happening. Just yesterday, Weston assured me space pirates wanted nothing to do with deep space. My fathers promised we were safe here, so long as we stayed at the inn. The inn was supposed to be safe from everything—but *especially* space pirates.

Weston goes pale beside me. His fingertips tremble against the glass and he gets the same look Comet used to before throwing up.

"Not just any space pirates," he says. "The Odette Twins."

He swallows, throat bobbing. The name is unfamiliar, and I wonder if the neighbor kids who moved away over the years would recognize it. I used to know everything that was happening out there from my guests and the stories and souvenirs they brought to the inn. Back then, surrounded by people and their stories, I felt like I was a part of it too.

But even back when the inn flooded with guests, we never had pirates drop by.

Space pirating happened to other places. Other *people*. We were always safe here, out in the astro-boonies. Too distant for the pirates to reach. Too obscure for them to care.

Until now, at least.

Weston looks so scared I almost feel bad. I step on his foot to snap him—and me—out of it. "All pirates are bad," I remind him. "These two can't be worse than anyone else."

"Not all pirates are the children of Astro Bonny's co-pirate, Mary Read," he says, and as if *that* wasn't enough to capture my attention, he adds, "And not all pirates want to kill me."

My eyes go wide. Mary Read was Astro Bonny's right-hand woman and copilot after Calico Jack's infamous betrayal—and from the little bits about her in my book, and what I've overhead when Papa has the news on, she was just as ruthless and fearless as Great Astro Bonny herself.

Mary Read was killed in a battle with the royal guard a couple years back, when things first started to get really bad with the space pirates again. I remember my fathers and teachers saying it was a huge victory against the pirates, but knowing she has children as merciless as her—children who are now part of Astro Bonny's plan to take over—fills me with ice-cold dread.

I grab Weston's elbow and yank him away from the window, to the farther corner of the stairwell.

"What do you mean, want to kill you?" I whisper. "You mean they want to kill you like I want to kill you? Because I'd get that."

He frowns, the scared look faltering for a moment. "No, like, they *really* want to kill me. And unlike you, they could probably take me."

I want nothing more than to grab his pearly white collar and take him up to the challenge. But I inhale a steadying breath, pretend I'm doing Sunday morning yoga with Dad, and ask, "Why do these pirates want to kill you, in particular? Beyond the obvious reasons."

I gesture up and down at his entire being. He huffs.

"Because I stole from them."

Forget yoga. I grab his collar and yank him toward me. "What do you mean, you *stole* from space pirates? Let alone space pirates whose mother worked for *Great Astro Bonny?*"

The words taste strange on my tongue, surreal and grand in a way that feels more like a story I'd imagine as a kid rather than something that could happen this close to me. But as amazing as it feels to be this close to something involving the offspring of Great Astro Bonny's most iconic follower, that closeness comes with more *danger* than *grandiosity* in this context.

I remember Weston's strange expression yesterday when I asked about space pirates, and that restless, overtired look in his eyes when he'd taken my photobook in the middle of the night. "So you stole from space pirates, and then you stole my book?" I squint my eyes with suspicion. "That's a lot of looting for someone who isn't a space pirate himself."

Weston manages to roll his eyes despite the way his entire body is shaking with anxiety. "I stole your book because I hoped it would have something useful about Mary Read or her kids in there. But just like everything else in this inn, it was completely *useless*."

The pieces of the story slowly slide together, and it's as clear as any story guests have told me in the past. Except those times, I sat safely by the hearth or at the dining room table as the guest recounted their tale: beginning, middle, and end. This story is still *happening*, and happening *here*, in my home. And this time, there's no safety of a guaranteed happy ending.

"And you let them follow you here, to my house?" My voice drops. "To my fathers?"

He shakes his head frantically. "Your parents will be fine. They're only after me."

I remember the way Weston sat outside last night, separate from the King and Queen. They must not know about his situation, either. Even the mention of space pirates spurred a conversation between me and my fathers. I can't imagine being *hunted* by space pirates and not telling my parents. "Just give them back what you stole."

"I can't."

I tighten my grip on his collar. "Why not?"

He runs his hands through his blond waves, sending a few jutting upright. "Because . . . ."

His lower lip trembles. I give his collar a tug.

"*Because?*"

A hot flush rises to his cheeks, like his skin is reflecting the crimson color of his vest. "Because I dropped it in deep space."

My palms feel sweaty against the smooth fabric of his shirt.

The easiest solution is gone, and I have no idea what other solution there possibly could be to get these space pirates off our rock, away from the inn. I'm choked with helpless fear, my mind swarmed with worry but empty of any solutions.

I tighten my grip to hide the way my hand trembles. "What are we going to do now?" He shakes his head dumbly, lips parted wordlessly. "What even was it?"

That snaps him back into focus. His eyes go sharp. The whites are wide, not with anger.

With fear.

"I can't tell you."

I can't imagine this prissy prince stealing from pirates, let alone what he'd want badly enough to even try. Weston's family is swimming in space coins. They're rich enough to just *buy* our inn on a whim, to have a space to drop in a few nights a year while traveling somewhere else.

What could he possibly want from a pirate that he couldn't buy for himself?

I release his collar with a shove. "My fathers are in danger because of you," I snap, voice hot with fury despite the way it trembles. Because we're supposed to be *safe* out here, in deep space. And the thought that something could happen to tear my family apart—that Dad or Papa could get hurt—fills me with a depth of terror I didn't even know was possible.

I peer back down the stairs. Voices come from the first floor, too far away to make them out. But I recognize the sounds of my fathers', and the Queen's shrill tone. The sound of hard, banging footsteps, a pot being knocked to the ground.

I press my palms to my knees and rise to my feet. Whatever's happening down there, I have to stop it.

"What are you doing?" Weston whispers. I ignore him, taking the stairs two at a time. "You can't just confront a bunch of pirates. They won't leave if you ask them to."

"Neither do you," I grumble, carrying on. I reach the second floor's landing and cross the hall toward the main stairs. The voices are louder now, more distinct. I slow my steps, my shoes quiet on the carpet.

Around the corner I'll see real, live pirates, as though sprung from the pages of my book. Fear wiggles up my throat, and my windpipe goes tight.

A hand grabs my arm and yanks me back. I almost let out a yelp, but Weston clasps his palm over my mouth.

"If you're going to sneak up on pirates, at least don't be stupid about it," he whispers.

I wriggle in his grip, pulling my lips from his hand. "Says the guy who got caught."

"In my defense, I didn't get caught until now."

"Shh!" I press my finger to my lips, and he throws his arms up in exasperation. Then, quieter this time—because I hate to admit it, he's kind of right—I head to the edge of the stairs.

I duck in the shadows by the banister and peer through the wooden slats, down at the dining room. As the royal guards circle around them, the Queen remains seated, twirling a small spoon in a cup of steaming tea, while the King stands upright beside her, chest out and lower lip bulging. Dad is by the kitchen doorway, frozen with a tray of mini muffins in hand,

and Papa is by the foot of the stairs, tall and upright as though nothing is happening. I realize that, oddly enough, Weston's mom and my papa have a similar reaction to stress.

The source of the stress stands in the foyer: the Odette Twins and their crew, tracking dirt on the carpet beneath their boots.

The twins stand front and center. The girl has smooth, dark hair trailing in two tight pigtails by her shoulders, and her hat is pushed down hard on her forehead, its brim creating a curve by her brow that resembles a scowl. Her brother wears his hat lopsided on his short black hair, revealing his too-big ears and mirroring his lopsided smile. They both wear the same uniform: black coats hanging down to their knees, unbuttoned to expose puffy white shirts and tight vests, and grimy brown boots. Their belts hang heavy with weapons—especially the sword in its sheath, which I can't take my eyes from.

I do *not* want pirates in my house. And definitely not armed pirates who happen to be looking right at my parents.

When I told Ron I hoped deep space would be full again soon, I was *not* picturing a space-pirate invasion. But if my parents and the inn are in danger, I have no choice but to act. I may not have experience with space pirates outside of dress-up games with Ron, but Galaxy Jones doesn't sit by and let the universe dictate what happens to her home. I roped the inn to the factory to fight the expansion of space, so I can channel my previous obsession with Astro Bonny, kick these pirates out of my living room, and rescue my parents, too.

I think. I *hope.*

I lean forward, nose poking through the stair railing. Weston tugs me back into the shadows and we watch, wide-eyed and out of view.

" . . . looking for something," the boy is saying, running his gloved finger over the back of a vacant chair. "We thought we saw it go in this direction."

Behind him, an older crew member with a scraggly beard runs his arm along the top of our china cabinet. His wrist sends a flowerpot toppling onto the ground with a crash. The Queen jumps and Dad flinches. Papa's stony expression doesn't waver.

The girl pirate steps toward the edge of the table. The other pirates watch attentively—her brother, nodding to each step with a loose and open smile, and their lackeys studying her every move as though on standby—waiting for her to call for them to attack. Even though she's my age, they all watch and wait as though *she's* the leader. And looking at her now—with her self-assured step and thin-lipped, sinister grin—I start to see why.

Briefly, I wonder what her story would be if she were just another guest. What she'd tell me by the fireplace while drinking cocoa, explaining how—despite being a kid just like me—she ended up as the leader of a wicked pirate gang.

She slides her sword out of her sheath. The light catches the sword's shiny surface, momentarily blinding me. I blink fast, dark spots dancing in my vision. The girl tugs the end of the dining room tablecloth toward her, making the dishware clatter and a spoon fall on the King's shoes. She runs the cloth over her sword, polishing it so its point is in plain view.

"Something important was taken from us," she says, voice as smooth and sharp as her weapon. I shoot a glance over at Weston, who recoils slightly at her words. I can't imagine what a prince *and* a pirate could want badly enough to chase across space.

But it's been a while since any guests stopped by with the latest space-techno and high-end gadgets, and even longer since Dad could afford to order them for his personal projects. Like the active galactic nuclei light bulbs he bought to illuminate the inn's sign with the brightest power in the universe, or the gravitational lens mirrors he set up to make the smaller rooms appear to be twice as big. But most of those things are broken down or collecting space dust in one of Dad's drawers, their updated models and any improved creations now just thumbnails on internet ads we scroll past without a second glance.

Whatever Weston and the pirates are after, it's probably well outside of my price range.

"It may take us a while to find it." The girl smiles cruelly. "But I'm sure you won't mind if we stay here for a bit."

Taking her words as an invitation, a short and bulky crew member tosses himself on the couch. A spring snaps beneath his weight.

I grit my teeth. "There's no way we can afford to fix all of this."

"That won't be your problem anymore," Weston reminds me.

I press my forehead against the banister, its sharp edge poking my skin. Depending on how long the pirates stay, the damage could be irreparable. And we can barely afford to keep the inn running as it is. But I can't let the royals take our inn. It's our *home*. The place I grew up with Ron. The only place in the solar system I've ever known.

"It's still my problem so long as my fathers and I are here," I say, shutting Weston up.

Downstairs, the girl pirate saunters around the room, picking up coasters and putting them back askew and rubbing her dirty shoes all over the carpet. "You can consider this our new base," she says.

Her brother nods, hat tilting so it looks like it could slide right off his head. "Indefinitely."

"You can all stay, though," she says with a soft snicker. "We'll need people here to scrub our shoes and wipe our decks."

The Queen straightens up, aghast. "You'll find that you can't, in fact, stay here," she tells the twins down the brim of her nose. "We have a vested interest in this inn."

Dad blinks. "You do?"

I can't watch this. So long as we just sit here, crouched by the stairs, those dirt-crusted villains will be flashing their weapons and breaking my house. And they'll be doing that *indefinitely*.

Weston wrings his hands. "This is *bad*."

"Yes," I agree. "But I've got a solution."

I pinch his ear between my fingers and rise to my feet. Weston squeals and scrambles up after me. "What are you—"

I nod to the scene downstairs. I see Dad's hands shake. Mini muffins tumble off the tray and onto the ground. Comet dashes over, oblivious to the tension, and laps one up.

Seeing my carefree, jovial dad so uncharacteristically *scared* forms a planet-sized lump in my throat. Everything about the scene downstairs is *wrong*, and each nerve in my body tingles with the need to *fix it*. "Me and my parents have nothing to do with this drama," I say. Then, hard and fast before I second-guess the words, I add, "so I'm turning you in."

Weston blinks, dumbfounded. He swats my hand from his ear and rises to his full height. Which is basically my height, so we're standing eye-to-eye, our pinched, angry brows mirror images of each other. "You're turning me in to *pirates?*"

"You *stole* from them! And something valuable, obviously. Something they need back."

"They stole it from someone first." He rubs his red ear. "That's why they're called pirates. Because they *pirate* things."

"So this shouldn't be a problem, then, since you're now a pirate yourself. Prince Pirate: it suits you."

My shoe presses down on the top step. Weston grasps at my wrists. "Lexi, come on. You know they'll eat me alive."

Weston's chin wobbles. Downstairs, his mother is explaining to my parents her plans to buy the inn. But here, on the second-story landing, Weston is watching me with shimmering, desperate eyes, small and shaking in the halls he so recently declared would soon be his own.

That's when an idea hits with full force. I bounce on the balls of my feet, unable to get the words out fast enough. "I can help you," I start. Weston's muscles relax and he pumps a small fist toward the ceiling. "*If*," I say, loud and forceful, "you agree to return whatever you stole from the twins, so they'll release my fathers." He frowns, but nods with understanding. Until I add, "*And* when we get back, you need to convince your parents not to buy the inn."

Like melting butter, his shoulders slump. "What? We need this place," he says, as if my home—my *life*—was about as valuable as a disposable appliance. "And what makes you think they'd listen to me?"

His question means he's considering it. I'm inching closer to victory. "You're their spoiled little boy. They'd do anything for you. Including rewarding me for your rescue by letting my family keep the inn."

"I'm not spoiled!" For a moment I catch a glimpse of his familiar smirk. "I'm just persuasive. And charming."

"So . . . *spoiled,*" I say, syllables punctuated by a soft laugh. "Persuade them, charm them—I don't care. Just . . . if I do this for you, you can't let them buy this house."

Something clangs downstairs. I look down to see the girl pirate spinning a teacup on the edge of her sword while the others watch with glee.

Weston gestures toward the scene. "I don't get how you can possibly see *saving my life* as equivalent to keeping a failing old inn."

The cup spins off the edge of her sword and shatters against the dining room wall. The brown tea mars the pale pink wallpaper and water drips in thin lines toward the carpet.

Years ago, Ron and I once broke a lamp in the dining room, four times the size of that cup. There was glass everywhere, tiny shards tucked into the carpet. We'd stood in our bare feet, surrounded by the wreckage. Ron's lower lip trembled and I was sure he was about to cry.

Papa rushed in, yanking on his sneakers. The glass crinkled beneath the soles of his shoes and he carried us, one at a time, to the safety of the living room.

"This inn *is* my life," I say, voice low. "It's my Dad and Papa's lives, too. I don't expect you to understand it. But if you don't want me to turn you in to those glass-breaking, dirt-tracking pirates, you have to respect it."

Weston reaches for my wrist, and this time I don't yank it back. His fingers wrap around my skin and he tugs me, gentler this time, from the stairs. We stand in the shadows by the first guest room, the pirates and our families distant murmurs. He stares at his shoes, polished so deep, his eyes reflect back up at us.

He inhales a steadying breath. "I'll do what you say. Just tell me you have a plan."

For the first time in what's felt like hours, I smile. "Oh, Weston. You'll soon learn that Galaxy Jones *always* has a plan."

I don't know what to do to save my home in the long term. I don't know how to get the train stop opened back up, dropping vacationers and explorers a throw from my doorstep. I don't know how to make our neighborhood full and lively like it once was, clusters of houses and businesses floating in the same tight orbit. I don't know how to stop the universe from stretching everything out farther and farther, until everything slips away and I'm left floating, alone, on a rock in the dark depths of space.

But I know that for any of those questions to matter, I have to protect this house. And that means stopping these space pirates before they destroy it—or hurt my family. I'll do anything to rescue the inn. Even pretending to get along with Prince Weston.

CHAPTER FOUR

As soon as I know I've won Weston over, I spring to action. I tear my hands from his grip and sprint back upstairs, toward the window. After a moment of confused blinking and emotional whiplash, Weston scrambles after me.

"What are you doing?" he whispers, low and frantic. "You said you *have* a plan, but somehow, in the span of five seconds, you forgot to share it with me."

I yank the window open and a gust of cool air greets me. "I'm going to go find that thing you lost," I declare. Because, yes, Galaxy Jones always has a plan. But sometimes she doesn't know her plan until she's saying it aloud. "We're going to get it back, return it to the pirates, and then you'll be off their hit list. And after that—"

"I talk my parents into rewarding you with the inn," he recites, rolling his eyes. "I've got it, I've got it."

Below the window, the lawn is empty, the two parked ships vacant on our lot. I take a deep breath and hoist my leg out the window.

I straddle the windowpane, one foot dangling out above

the yard, the other pointed toward the safe carpet inside our house. Weston hovers inside, arms wrapped protectively over his midsection, and watches me with big, glassy eyes.

Apparently, even in thousand-space-coin shoes, a guy can get cold feet.

"Whatever you stole must have been important," I say. "Don't you want to get it back?"

"I do," he answers, voice small.

"Then prince-up and help me!" I lean back into the house and take his sleeve, tugging him toward me. "We both want to find that *thing* you lost, and get these pirates out of here. So as much as it pains me to say . . . I'll need you to be semi-useful and join me on this mission."

Weston blinks fast, startled. An echo of his smug grin forms on his face. "You think *I'm* the semi-useful one? How would you do this without me? Were you about to jump out that window without even knowing what you were searching for?"

My cheeks flush. "Oh, just shut up for once and come with me."

"And then what were you going to do?" he asks, crawling onto the sill with me. I swing my other leg outside, nearly kicking him out the window. "Just jump into space and hope you floated into the loot?"

I dangle my legs in the air and angle myself so I won't fall into the bushes when I jump. "I'm hoping this is your segue into telling me you have a ship."

He smirks. "That semi-useful enough for you?"

Then he slides off the sill and leaps down into the dark

yard below, falling like a graceful cat. I leap after him, one leg catching in the bushes so I topple onto him and into the bush.

"Stealthy."

"Shut up."

The front door rattles open. I untangled myself from Weston's legs and grab his ankles, yanking him toward the bush.

"Someone's coming!"

Go figure we'd get caught the second we set foot outside. I should have known better than to team up with Weston. I should have known better than to let my fathers invite the royals in, and—

A light panting approaches from the front steps. Comet bounds our way, tan tail wagging excitedly behind him. The knot in my chest unravels, warm relief coursing through my veins. The dog beams and runs up to Weston, who still lies stomach-down on the ground, and licks his dirty knuckle.

Weston sits up and scratches behind Comet's head. "Comet's coming with us," he declares with a proud smile. "I'll be the brains, and he'll be the muscle. Right, little bud?"

Comet smiles and drools in response.

I stand, brushing dirt off my knees. "And what does that make me?"

"The nuisance."

"I'll take that," I agree. "It means I get things done."

A manic shriek of laughter comes from inside. A chill dances up my spine as an image of the stony-eyed pirate girl flashes through my mind. I duck so that my shadow blends with the front porch's, then angle myself away from the porch light. "Speaking of getting things done, we've got to move. Fast."

Weston scratches the side of his head. Then Comet's. "I dropped the item they want a few hours back. I'll need to check the map—"

The Queen gasps inside, loud and appalled. For a split second, I wonder if the sound alone could defeat the space pirates.

Then, by the front window, I see a shadow pass behind the curtain. The stout pirate readjusts himself on the couch, a thick silhouette. Comet pants loudly, just steps from the window, while Weston kneels beside him in open view. All the pirate has to do is turn around and we're caught.

And then what? Even if they leave with Weston, it won't stop his family from taking my home. My parents will be safe, but not for long.

I'm not sure what's happening inside, or what it means for Dad and Papa. Part of me wants to grab Weston by the sleeve and march back in, trade him over for my parents' safety. But as much as I dislike Weston, the thought of participating in a pirate takedown of the whiney little prince ties me up in knots of guilt. How could I look his parents in the eyes while I hand over their son's life in exchange for my family? Especially when—without having what they're looking for—there's no guarantee they'll leave my family unscathed?

Confusing, anxious thoughts weigh me down like anchors. And all I have to keep me afloat is my half-baked semblance of a plan.

"For now, we just have to get out of here," I say. "We can worry about directions later."

I stare into the dark, endless sky. Beyond the pirate ship's masts and the royal's parked castle is nothing but a black blanket of sky interrupted by tiny twinkling holes of light. Between each distant star there are houses like ours, villages crowded and full like ours used to be. Somewhere between here and there, Weston's loot floats aimlessly through empty space.

There's only one tangible thing in the miles of blank dark around the inn: the coil rope that binds my house to Ron's.

The idea comes together in my mind, like a supernova in reverse. "We'll start at my friend Ron's place," I say. "It will be a safe spot to regroup, stock up for the journey, and—"

Weston's lip curls up in disgust. "The *ice cream* kid?"

Comet's tail dances at the words. Ron didn't come inside the last time the royals stayed here, but we hung outside on the floating meteoroids while I vented about Weston's antics. One night Ron crawled up to my window and, standing on the sill, reached up higher than I could and clipped the bell Weston had dangled down from his room. It fell, dinging, into the bushes, and with a frantic jump, Ron soared down after it. To cover the sound, I sang an off-tune lullaby at the top of my lungs. When Weston and his dog came racing downstairs to see what the commotion was, I blinked my lashes and served a line about wanting to ensure their peaceful sleep.

Each time Ron visited after that, we'd sit on our floating rocks, O-Zone hats on, and develop plans for my revenge on Weston. We never carried any of them through, but I remember Weston watching us one day from the yard and how we'd laughed from where we floated above, untouchable.

I hadn't thought, until now, how similar that was to his whispers and giggles each time I entered the room.

"His name is Ron," I say, slow and deliberate, "and he's the best shot we've got. If we ever get into a ship and out of here, that is."

As though remembering the pirates standing literally inches behind him, Weston springs to action, gathering Comet in his arms and dashing toward his parents' ship. I follow after him, hunched in the shadow as we climb the front steps, onto the ship's patio.

"We've got a pod beneath the floorboards," he says once we're on the deck. He points at the loose boards with the toe of his shoe. "Explain to me again how the ice cream boy is of any use to us?"

I stare at the ground. "You're seriously going to make me lift these myself?"

He cuddles Comet to his vest. "My hands are full."

I let out a huff. Then I lean down and hoist the boards from the deck, revealing a compartment underneath. There, with a thin coat of dust atop its surface, is a tiny space pod built for no more than two passengers.

Two and a quarter, counting Comet.

"First of all, ice cream means provisions, and depending on how long this takes, we'll need sustenance."

Weston cringes. "Astronaut ice cream is no better than space dust."

"It's very nutritious," I snap, though I'm not the least bit sure. "The pirates will never think to check an ice cream factory, so it'll buy us time to retrace your route and start our search for . . ."

I pause, waiting for him to insert the word. But Weston just shakes his head.

It's not fair that he won't even *tell* me what he stole, especially when it's up to me to help him recover it. It makes me want to scream—but the memory of the pirate girl's shrill laugh echoes in my mind, and I know that whatever questions I have, they can wait. If we get caught now, then there's no chance of me saving my parents, *or* the inn.

"Press the button on top. It'll turn on and rise to our level," Weston says. I ball my fist and slam it down on the pod's button, glaring at Weston the whole time The pod grumbles to life and rises, with a puff of hot steam, to hover a few feet above the boards.

Weston balances Comet on his shoulder and yanks the side door open. The compartment inside is even smaller than I expected, with two cushioned seats pressed tight together in front of a protruding control board. I imagine if Ron had to come on this trip with me, how his knees would clank against his chin and jaw each time the pod bobbed up or down.

It's going to be hard to drop by Ron's place on a super-secret mission and not have him join. But maybe I can still convince him to come along—to delay the ice cream shipments his mom has planned for tomorrow and go on a *real* adventure, together, like the ones we dreamed up as kids.

Comet bumbles in and wedges his tiny, fluffy body beneath the control panel. Weston slides across the seats so he's by the wheel.

"Coming?" he asks.

I press a hand on the door and glance back at the inn. Inside, Dad and Papa are facing a cluster of space pirates on their own.

I have to believe they can hold down the fort while I'm gone. My fathers have done everything they can to protect the inn and have assured me time and time again that if space pirates ever *did* show up, they wouldn't let them hurt me. I need to trust that they have a plan for keeping each other safe, just like I have a plan to save them, too. I've never been away from my fathers before, and the thought of that is terrifying enough *without* adding space pirates into the mix. But I need to believe that they'll do whatever it takes to make it through this challenge, just like they have all the others that have ever come our way. Because even considering the alternative is impossible.

I leap into my seat, sending the pod rocking. Weston mutters, and the engine roars to life. My door snaps shut and the pod rises, bobbing and unsteady, up from the deck.

"Follow along the rope," I instruct, pointing through the windshield. "That will lead us to the ice cream factory."

He shakes his head in disbelief at the rope. "I'm not even going to ask."

The pod rises higher and higher until it's aligned with my bedroom window, right beside the rope. Then Weston reaches for the speed button, which will shoot us through space miles in a second.

As his arm lifts, finger extended, I glance back at the house. The hulky silhouette is right by the window now, a square hand holding back the curtains. Two light eyes stare up at us from below.

Weston presses the button. The pod springs to life, spiraling off so fast that space becomes nothing but a black canvas with dripping lines of white paint.

Still, I feel the pirate's eyes on us, watching as we go. They know that Weston is on the run, and as far as they're concerned, he still has whatever it is he stole from them. The knot in my chest loosens at the thought that they might leave the inn and let my fathers be now that Weston's gone. But a horrified voice in my head reminds me that if they leave the inn, it's only so they can hunt *us* down.

The race has begun.

CHAPTER FIVE

Weston's pod is faster than anything I've ever traveled in. I.e.: exponentially more expensive. Still, Ron's house is far enough away that I feel the silence between Weston and me expanding, fast and vacant as space. It leaves room for me to think about my parents, and the pirates, and the inn, and all the things pushing down on me like double gravity.

My chest throbs at the thought of my parents. I need a distraction, and fast, or else I'm going to start crying like a little kid in front of my interstellar-nemesis-turned-partner-in-crime. And that is the *last* thing I need right now.

I'm good at plans (I think), but I'm also good at talking, and talking a lot. It's a side effect of growing up in the hospitality business. Even when I would annoy customers, they'd at least think I was "cute." That's what Dad told me, at least, and I choose to believe him. So I decide to counter the silence by sharing the stormy thoughts in my head with Weston.

If I'm stuck with him on this mission, he might as well suffer with me, after all.

I pick at a loose thread on my black tights. "What do you know about the Odette Twins? Have you run into them a lot before?" The fabric yanks loose with a snap. I twist it around my pinky. "Did you run into Great Astro Bonny?"

Weston rolls his eyes. "As *if*. No one's seen her in ages. She has her lackeys do all her work for her now. It's just pirates like Mary Read's kids: pirate apprentices obsessed with living up to Astro Bonny's legacy."

I frown. "Staying back while others go on her adventures for her doesn't sound like Astro Bonny at all."

"And how do you know that? From that useless book I stole last night?" Weston lets out a condescending huff. "Your parents really give you the abridged version of homeschooling, huh?"

I want nothing more than to tug his ear again for that. But I answer with all the hostess calm my fathers taught me growing up, voice sweet and even. "Since you know so much more than me, care to share, Your Highness?"

Your Haughtiness is more like it. But I punctuate the question with a patient smile.

"Astro Bonny's directed her minions—like the Odette Twins—to capture parts of our solar system slowly. A street here or there. A village. A moon. It's gotten worse and worse as the universe expands, since so many people have moved to the central system." He shrugs. "You'd think they'd *like* that they have more people to terrorize and loot from. But Astro Bonny and all her fanboys and fangirls see the new residents as a threat to their resources. Since space pirates are, by nature, not part of the kingdom, they think they need to take over themselves to regain control of things."

It's not all new information—techno-school *has* informed me about the uptick in pirating, thank you very much. But I'd always just figured I'd misunderstood Astro Bonny's legacy—and while that's obviously true, from what Weston's saying, there's more to her and her lackeys' motivations.

While everyone picked up and left the outer system, I never thought about how crowded the central system was getting. Or that the universe expanding could leave space pirates on edge, fighting to regain control in a changing solar system.

Considering part of why I'm doing this with Weston is to save the inn, I can't help but understand the space pirate's motivations. I, too, am desperate to do anything to regain control while the universe shifts and changes around me. To ensure that I don't lose my place in it.

Thinking of the inn makes my stomach twist uncomfortably, knowing my parents are still there with the Odette Twins—who, based on Weston's story, sound like Astro Bonny's most dedicated followers. Papa grew up in the central system and spent parts of his childhood avoiding space pirates. But he's never told me anything that makes me certain he can handle *this*.

"So you've dealt with the Odette Twins before, then, right?" I ask, hating how hopeful I sound.

Weston drums his fingers against the wheel. A muscle twitches in his neck. "The guards never let pirates come close to the royal planet," he says, tight-lipped. "But I do . . . *hear* things."

I tug the thread and the tip of my finger turns bright white. "What things?"

Comet whimpers at his feet and presses his cheek to Weston's ankle. "Well, one time a guard just . . . didn't come back. His partner said he'd been totally liquidated in a space duel."

"Liquidated?" I repeat, the syllables mushy and strange on my tongue.

"Dust-ified," Weston explains. "He blew up into space particles."

The tip of my finger is purple. I unspin the thread, fast. "Like Astro Bonny did to Calico Jack."

Weston nods grimly. "There's a pirate crew that drove their ship into a star when their captives didn't tell them where they kept their treasure," he says, words speeding up. "And another that made its hostages walk the plank right above a black hole."

I sink farther into my seat so I can't see through the window. There's nothing that creeps me out more than black holes. As far as I can tell, they're the only challenge I can't develop a plan to combat. If I get sucked into one, that's it. No amount of Galaxy Jones finagling can get me out.

He falls silent. The pod is soundless as it cuts through space, and I wonder if we'd even hear the pirates if they sneaked up behind us.

I talk to fill the quiet. Though most of what I say makes everything way worse. "We had a man who came by once who told us some pirates tie their enemies to the front of the ship like figureheads."

Weston's cheeks turn green. Either from the story or his own subpar driving.

"If this is supposed to psych me up, it's not working. All it's making me want to do is vomit."

I frown. "I think Comet does that enough for the two of you."

His eyes flash sharp as a shooting star. "That was *one time*."

"It haunts me almost every day, so, in a way, it's still happening right now."

He presses a button to reduce the speed of our craft. A few stray hairs settle by my cheeks. "Don't get me started on the space-time stuff. I can't handle that right now."

The rope stretches out before us, a tiny flicker of light at its end. We're getting closer. "There are space pirates hunting us to get back something you lost in the middle of deep space. But you can't handle the concept of *time*?"

Weston waves his hand, gesturing for me to shush. Which makes me want to shout in his ear until it rings, but for the sake of Comet's supersensitive dog ears, I take the higher ground.

Even after all the miserable hours I've been subjected to Weston's presence, I can't begin to imagine what he'd want badly enough to steal from space pirates, or how a boy seemingly sheltered by his royal guard managed to get close enough to pirates to snag their loot. Or how, while being chased by said space pirates, he could be freaked out by something as mundane as the space-time continuum.

I shift in my seat. It's uncomfortable to think of how much I don't know about Weston. That outside of the time spent in my inn, he's been living a full life, beyond the boundaries of my memories and stories.

Out in the distance, a tiny light comes into view. As the pod soars closer, I can make out the shape of the ice cream factory, a tall brick building grounded on a piece of space rock. It's darker than usual, nothing but a tiny front light flickering at the entrance to alert us to its nearing presence.

"No wonder they don't have customers," Weston remarks.

In an eye's blink we're miles closer. Weston angles us toward the factory landing pad, following the length of the rope. There are already two ships parked on the pad: one, a tiny black pod even smaller than ours, and the other, a giant shipping shuttle. The shuttle consumes most of the space— which is a lot, considering this used to be a parking lot for tourists from all over the galaxy. It isn't large itself, but giant boxes are stacked on its top and roped to its sides, nearly doubling it in size.

I knew Ron's family had to fulfill orders this weekend, but had no idea the shipment would be this big. If his family is processing orders this large, business *must* be picking up.

I smile. There's still hope for our corner of the universe after all.

The pod buzzes as we approach the pad, hovering a few feet, then a few inches, then rattling to a halt on the ground. A strawberry-blond head pops out from behind the shipment shuttle. Ron appears around the boxes, hands gripping a thick coil as he binds the boxes to the side of the ship. His eyes lock on Weston and go as big as flying saucers.

"Incredible!" he gasps. His voice sounds muffled from inside our pod. "Mom, we have another guest!"

Another? I remember the tiny pod on the other side of the shipment shuttle. Not only is the factory processing giant orders—they've got foot traffic, too! I wrestle with my door and hop out onto the tarmac, bursting with energy.

Ron steps around from the other side of the shuttle and I run right toward him. Just like I saw in our video chat, he's taller than the last time I visited him—which was far too long ago, since I don't have a super-speedy pod like the spoiled prince's. I fling my arms around his midsection, cheek pressed to his collarbone, and squeeze with all my might.

"Lexi?" he gasps, windpipe constricted by my grip.

I pull back, hands grasping his elbows. "You have another guest? Besides me?"

Ron blinks like he's experiencing whiplash. It hits me next, too, like my words are boomeranging back at me. It's been *weeks* since I've seen Ron in person. I didn't give him any heads-up we were coming, and the first thing I asked was about his family's business?

My grip slackens on his arms. In my head, a guest at the factory means a guest at the inn. Which means income, which means we can stay here, together, longer, in this corner of space. But right now, with my words tasting sour on my tongue, I feel caught like a moon in orbit, circling lazily within a gravitational pull I can't break free from.

"You're the guest I'm most excited to see," he says. I open my eyes to see him smiling cautiously, light eyes framed by bright brown freckles. "Though I am a bit curious about your driver."

Weston. I almost forgot. He stumbles out of the pod, hunched and awkward with Comet tripping over his heels.

Wiggling Comet from his feet, Weston straightens up, poised, with one hand on the pod door. "I remember you, ice cream boy. You would hang outside the inn during my stay and encourage this nightmarish host"—he gestures to me—"to taunt and torment me."

Ron leans to whisper by my ear. "Lexi, if you're currently being held as a hostage in a revenge plot, blink twice."

"Unfortunately, I have to admit that I've brought him here of my own accord," I say with a weary sigh. Weston rolls his eyes. In a softer voice, I ask Ron, "Can we go upstairs and talk privately? I don't want to scare off your customer, and this story is a doozy."

Ron starts to back toward the factory, leading us toward the building. "I'm going to need the dwarf-planet-sized version of the story, not the Galaxy-sized version, though." I open my mouth to object, and he quickly adds, "I'm spending the afternoon wedged in a delivery pod, remember? As soon as Mom's customer leaves, she's going to load me in there with the rest of the boxes."

That sinking feeling I got on our way here returns, like my stomach is experiencing double gravity. I glance back at the factory's stuffed delivery pod, parked next to the one Weston and I will be leaving in as soon as we're ready for our mission.

"If you're starting to get in-person customers," I say, as

though one guest ensures others, "maybe you can convince your mom to push the deliveries back just one day?"

I wait for Ron to get that animated look, with a broad grin and eyes twinkling, like he did when we'd act out stories of guests' adventures out on my lawn.

But instead, he nibbles his lower lip and averts his gaze.

"I don't think the customers would like that. We need the money *now*, and . . ." His words fade for a moment, light and unformed like the tail of a comet. "I'm actually hoping that if we get these deliveries done early, we'll have time for Mom to bring me to this cooking class I read is happening on one of the central planets."

For some reason, *this* is when that familiar, bright look returns to his face. In a giddy, hurried voice, he explains, "This chef has developed this technique that's, like, the *opposite* of dehydration. They use microgravity to make the food as light as they can while still maintaining substance, and . . ."

He keeps talking, but his words jumble together in my mind. I shake my head slowly, as though I could snap them back into place. "You can just watch a video about it here, when you get home," I say. "Besides, nothing can be better than astronaut ice cream."

It comes out more like a question than a statement, and I wish I could swallow the words back from the O-Zoned air. Ron's lips part, a response brewing on his tongue. For the first time I'm scared of what my best friend is about to say.

Something yanks my hair, hard. I let out a yelp as my

roots burn under the grip. Having fully secured my attention, Weston releases me and offers a tight grin.

"Love the local chitchat," he says, snide, "but what Lexi's failing to mention as we stand here, out in the very open air, is that we're being hunted by space pirates."

Ron stumbles over his feet, nearly toppling flat onto the driveway. The skin between his freckles goes green. "Should I assume it's a coincidence our customer's pod has an air freshener shaped like an alien skull?"

My eyes bug. "They *what?*"

Ron's words double in speed, slurring together. "I assumed they were just, like, *alternative*, or a runaway from the pirate colony on the outskirts of central system, or that it was supposed to be ironic, or anything *but* a real space pirate!" He stares at me dubiously, finally sounding like my Ron again when he says aloud what I've been thinking all day: "We *never* get *actual* space pirates out here!"

I run around Ron and the shipment shuttle, Weston at my heels. The tiny black pod rests on the opposite side of the tarmac. Its windows are dark and tinted, but through the glass I can make out the dangling piece of scented paper by the rearview mirror.

Weston appears at my side, fists clenched to hide the way he's shaking. "It's a single-passenger pod. Which means less weight, which means it's faster than mine." He locks eyes with me. "Which means your dead weight let an Odette Twin beat us here."

I shake my head. "How did they know where we—"

The rope. It's basically a straight arrow pointing directly to our destination. How could we be so naive?

Apparently, playing pirates as a kid did not prepare me for the real deal. Not only had we walked right back into the trap, but we'd dragged Ron and his family into it too.

"Forget dead weight," I say, voice sounding a light-year away, "we're just plain-old dead."

CHAPTER SIX

Ron waves us around the back, to the employees' entrance. The thick wooden door opens to a dark stairwell, leading up to all five floors. The first three belong to the factory. The fourth is where he, his mom, and little sisters live. The fifth floor is basically an attic. Ron and I used to hide up there when his mom thought we were packaging ice cream, ducking behind the stacks of unfolded cardboard shipping boxes every time her footsteps came up the stairs.

He leads us up there now, but this time we have Weston (and his dog) following behind. Ron tiptoes up the stairs and I follow his feet, careful to avoid the squeaks and whines his old stairwell gives under pressure.

It's like remembering an old dance, following him up these stairs, doing all I can not to get caught. Each step is one I've taken before, each soft creak of the floorboards like an echo from a memory—like the time we sneaked a vat of chocolate sauce upstairs for what turned out to be a less-delicious, more-nauseating, and totally messy eating contest. Or the time I tricked my fathers into thinking Ron's mom invited me for a sleepover, when my real plan was to sneak in and keep Ron company—because I know he always gets sad the night before his birthday, never sure if his dad would just send an e-card or actually attend the party.

Ron pauses at the top of the first flight and holds up a pale hand, barely visible in the dark. A stream of yellow light pours out from the doorway to the second-floor landing. No passing shadows interrupt it and, hard as I listen, there's no echo of distant voices and footsteps.

"They must be on the third floor," Ron whispers. He glances back at me and offers a solemn nod. "Be extra quiet on the next flight, okay? Hold your breath if you have to."

"I'm not that out of shape. Or practice," I tease. Ron's looking at Weston, though, brow pinched and eyes judging. I follow his gaze. Weston is a few steps behind us, gripping Comet to his chest. The dog writhes in his grip, and Weston muffles his whimpers against his vest.

I square my jaw. "To translate Ron's politeness: you're loud."

Weston tightens his grip on Comet in response. "He's an old dog, okay?" he snaps, eyes flashing at me. "Even if he *thinks* he can climb these stairs, I know he can't. Not without hurting himself, at least." When Ron and I don't move, he adds, "It'll be a lot louder if he hurts his knee!"

"Shh!" I throw my arms up in exasperation. But knowing how to pick my battles, I usher Ron up the next flight of stairs. He slows at the last steps, hand placed gingerly on the railing. The low murmur of voices carries through the wall.

" . . .where we dehydrate the ice cream," his mom is saying. "The scoops go through this machine, and when they come out—"

"Again, miss," a boy's voice interrupts. Not just any boy— the Odette boy. "It really is just *so* interesting. I'm sure there must be another tour group arriving soon. Shouldn't we go downstairs and wait for them?"

Unless he's looked outside and seen our pod, he shouldn't know we're here yet. But he's here because he knows it was our plan to come, so it won't be long until he figures us out. Goose bumps rise on my arm like inside-out craters.

Ron holds a silent finger to his lips, then tiptoes past the door and to the next flight of stairs. I follow, lingering at the foot of the stairs as I wait for Weston. I don't trust him not to reveal us—after all, he's made it his life's work to make dramatic entrances.

Comet wiggles against his shoulder and Weston overlaps his arms to lock him in place. He pushes one shoe forward, toward the stream of light from the doorway. I stand on the first step, nodding him on. He grits his teeth and takes the step.

Comet pokes his head over his shoulder and whines. A loud, puppy-eyed, treat-begging, irresistible canine whine.

"What was that?" the pirate's voice comes. Weston scampers up the stairs, right past me and Ron. Leaving us standing in the shadows, terrified eyes locked on the closed door with our lungs tight and empty.

"These machines are old," Ron's mom says with a high

laugh. "Older than I'd like. As soon as we have the funds, we plan on replacing—"

"That didn't sound like a machine," the pirate insists. "It sounded like . . . a *dog.*"

Ron's mom laughs. "Well, there're no dogs here, so I'm embarrassed to admit, our machines really *are* that old. If you look over here, we still have one of the original . . ."

Their voices trail off. But as their shadows pass the light from below the door, one pauses, a long, dark streak through the pool of light. I press back against the wall, my shadow out of view. And keep holding my breath.

Five agonizing seconds. Then the shadow moves on.

But even if he's physically moved on, his mind probably hasn't. He knows Weston has a dog and that the dog left with us. So part of him suspects we're here.

We have to move fast.

I scramble up the steps, grabbing Ron's sleeve and pulling him with me. Forget quiet, forget squeaky floorboards. We run up to the fifth floor, where Weston waits with Comet panting happily by his ankles. Ron jiggles the trick doorknob until it finally swings open, and we duck inside.

The sea of cardboard boxes has been replaced with . . . well, maybe three to four small stacks of cardboard boxes. The maze of stacks we used to hide behind are gone, leaving square imprints on the dusty ground alongside scattered footprints.

"It's so empty," I say, voice vaguely echoing against the slanted ceiling.

Ron scratches the back of his head. "Can't buy more boxes

until we get paid for the weekend's orders. So I can't offer an ideal hiding space. And speaking of hiding," Ron says, voice going high, "mind telling me *why* you're being chased by space pirates? Space pirates who are currently with my *mom?*"

I wince. I hadn't thought that coming to Ron's with space pirates on my trail was no different than Weston coming to my house in the same situation. Whatever Ron's feeling must be like what I experienced watching my fathers in the dining room while the pirates ransacked our house.

Weston's brilliant response? "One pirate. Singular. Pictor Odette, brother to Celeste Odette."

Celeste—the stone-faced pirate who ordered her crew to ransack my house and torment my parents. I'm still reeling with guilt at the thought of Ron's mom alone with her brother, but the mention of her name sends more subzero chills up my spine than his does.

"They're Mary Read's kids. And Weston stole from them," I explain. Ron's face goes blank and wide-eyed, and I imagine a buffering symbol spinning between his eyes. "And we're finding what Weston stole so we can return it to the pirates. So they leave my inn and my fathers be. And so that Weston's family will leave, too."

I shoot Weston a meaningful glare. He holds up his hands. "If Lexi helps me, I'll convince my parents not to buy her inn. See, I'm sticking to my promise!"

Ron's eyes bug. "Someone wants to buy your inn? And by someone, I mean . . . the *royals* want to *buy* your *inn?*"

"Stop stressing your words like that," I say with a cringe.

"And stop stressing!" I cross the empty space and give his arm a squeeze. "No one's going to buy it, okay? I'm not going anywhere. We'll always be here, roped together. No matter how the universe changes. Okay?"

Ron stares down at me, lips parted. His too-big teeth clench, and for a second I think he's about to say something. But then he clamps his mouth into a tight line and nods.

"Okay, Lexi," he says. Even though he's right there, for a moment his voice sounds far-off, like he's talking through the speakers of my phone on video chat. "I'm impressed, honestly. I mean, fighting *pirates*? That's something we always talked about doing. But you're *doing* it."

"We're not fighting anyone!" Weston objects.

"You can still join us," I say, voice too soft, too hopeful. I clear my throat, and next time I speak, my words are packed with the same bravado I used when we acted out stories as kids. "It can be a new Lexi and Ron adventure! One for *real*, where we show everyone in the galaxy what us deep-space kids are made of!"

I can see it now: Ron and I, cramped in Weston's tiny pod as we race through the stars. We'll get into all kinds of trouble and cause all sorts of hijinks and, just when all hope is lost, we'll win through the most unlikely means possible: a waffle cone duel.

"I've been preparing for this moment my whole life," one of us will say, and then we'll jab the pointed tip of the cone into the pirate's gut and send them falling off the edge of their own plank.

"I wish," Ron says, crashing all my daydreams down to reality. "While you're fighting space pirates, I'll be fighting for legroom against a couple dozen deliveries."

He stares at his shoes, shifting foot to foot. I slump, hands falling weightless to my sides.

Whenever I fantasized about adventures in deep space, it was *Ron* that I pictured doing it with. *Ron* who would lie with me under the stars on my front lawn, pointing up and narrating a story about our future escapades across the galaxy. Back then, we were characters in stories modeled after the ones in my Astro Bonny photobook, and ones my guests and his customers told on their visits. Daydreaming in the safety of the outer system, comfortable together in the quiet and calm, had been enough.

But now—I realize, with a soft gulp—I'm going on a *real* adventure, just like the ones we used to hear about from visitors. I'll be traveling outside of deep space for the first time, and it won't be anything like the tales we dreamed up for each other. In those, we were always together. We were always heroes, always living to the final, happy epilogue.

Now, without Ron, I'm not sure how this story will end. Facing off with space pirates is terrifying enough, but the thought of doing it without Ron feels impossible.

Weston stalks up, holding out his phone. "Thanks for providing some white noise. It gave me enough focus to pinpoint the coordinates of about where I lost the loot." He points to the map of space. Which is basically a black rectangle with thin, white coordinates. "Over here, see? A little over halfway between

Lexi's inn and the central system. About ninety degrees below the Dog Constellation."

I follow his pointed finger and frown. "That's the Moose Constellation." Then, because I need to savor *any* moment when I'm in the right, "There *is* no Dog Constellation."

Weston just shrugs. "Well, it looks like a dog to me. If you just count the stars *around* the antlers, it looks like ears, right?"

I shake my head, ready to prove Weston wrong again. Ron ignores us both, leaning to squint at the screen. "And you said you're running from pirates, right?"

We nod in unison.

He sucks his lips against his teeth. "You're heading right into pirate territory. That's a meteorite's skip from the pirate colony." Ron points to a tiny white dot on the screen. "Great Astro Bonny's crews have basically taken over the entire planet as a pirate state. You'll be within a telescope's view of them, so you'll have to be careful."

Weston and Ron study the screen. But I'm staring at Ron. "How do you know that?"

It sounds like something I'd overhear my fathers whispering about after they think I've gone to sleep. Something my classmates from closer to the central system would speculate about before online class started, sharing a mixture of things they'd heard on the news and rumors they'd heard from older kids about pirate-sieged planets.

Not something Ron—who lives out here, secluded and safe, just like me—should know so much about.

"Mom and I passed it on our last shipment," he explains,

nonchalant. "Some of their locals ordered ice cream, but we ended up reimbursing them so we wouldn't have to land."

I tuck a loose strand of hair behind my ear. While I've been back at the inn, watching the sky with Dad, Ron's been having adventures of his own—exploring parts of the universe I barely even knew existed. We used to just exist in our tiny corner, but it's as though while the universe expanded, Ron's experience with it did, too.

I thought that we'd both agreed deep space was our entire world. That those games we played as kids were just *games*, and our focus should be our families—the inn, and the factory. The thought that Ron could be leaving that behind—growing like this universe, his world expanding beyond me—sends a jolt of panic cold as liquid nitrogen through my veins.

There's a smash from the stairwell, followed by the hammer of loud footsteps coming our way. Ron's eyes bulge and he stares at the door, stammering. Comet lets out a bark and Weston crouches to hush him. I run to the door, despite Ron's objections, and peer through the crack in the frame.

Pictor Odette, hat askew, hustles up the steps. The way he glares at the door, I swear it's like he can see me.

"We have to get out of here," I declare, rushing back to the center of the room.

"No kidding," Weston snarls. "But how are we going to do that? We're basically trapped in an attic."

"Not trapped." Ron points to the window. "It's small, but you'll fit through."

"And then what?" Weston asks, voice rising. "Jump to

our deaths? There's gravity on this stupid rock, if you're forgetting."

I run to the window and whip it open, letting in the cool air. The rope is just an arm's reach away, tied to the factory's piping. "We can use the rope to swing into the fourth-floor window. Then we'll take the stairs from there. As long as we're faster than Pictor, we'll be okay."

"And I can distract him," Ron offers. "He is a paying customer, after all. It's my duty to guide him through the factory."

A warm feeling rises in my chest. Ron grew up just like me—in a home that doubled as a workspace, raised alongside a parent or two who dedicated their lives to their work. We're nothing like Weston—we're like each other.

But I'll have to leave Ron, follow Weston out into the dark horizon. Weston, who's nothing like me. Like *us*.

Weston is already climbing out the window, Comet wedged between his chest and vest. I turn to Ron, watching as he rummages through one of the few cardboard boxes. When he straightens back up, he's holding a heavy bag of astronaut ice cream.

"Provisions," he explains. "A vital part of any space adventure."

He drops the bag into my arms, and the familiar crinkle of the pink-and-white plastic sends a rush of memories through my mind. I feel nostalgic even though I haven't left yet, faced with the impossibility of going on a *space adventure* without the only person I ever imagined doing this with.

"You think we'll run into each other out there?" I gesture

to the black expanse of sky. Right now, it seems endless. Like we could get lost it in, floating in different directions. Indefinitely.

He smiles. "I think so, Galaxy Jones."

I nod, choosing to believe it. Then, with a deep inhale, I follow Weston into the cool, dark air.

CHAPTER SEVEN

Ron holds true to his word, properly distracting Pictor while Weston and I make our way back to the pod. Other than narrowly escaping Ron's mom's attention by the second-story staircase, we make it out unnoticed. I know we don't have long, though—Pictor's sure to follow shortly after, so Weston and I don't have much time.

Thinking of Ron dealing with Pictor, or my fathers dealing with Celeste, part of me wishes I could just hand Weston over to them and call it a day. But the royals will get him back on their own eventually, and then they'll come for our inn. So I have no choice—I have to stick with Weston in this bumpy pod on our trip through deep space.

Weston positions his phone on the pod dash and types in the coordinates for our destination. There's no way of knowing exactly where he left his whatever, but at least we know we're off in the right direction. I settle into the passenger seat as we take off at high speed. The engine whirs as it picks up the pace, then goes quiet once it hits the right acceleration.

Then that quiet again. Interrupted only by Comet's farts,

which he just had to save for when we all crowded back into the pod.

I glare at Weston. "He's old," he reminds me, voice high and defensive.

I continue to stare him down. "Are you seriously not going to tell me what you stole?" He opens his mouth to reply, and I ask, louder, "I mean, how am I supposed to help you find it if I don't know what *it* is? I'm the only person in the solar system offering to help you right now, so if I were you, I'd tell me what's going on."

He jabs the cruise control button and slumps back in his seat. "You're the last person I want to talk about this with."

"I'm the one person you *need* to," I remind him. Partly because it's true. And partly because I'm nosy.

Weston shifts in his seat uncomfortably. He props his shoes up on the dashboard and slumps down so his chin is aligned with his knees. He looks like a pouty kid, and it makes me wonder why he's so adamant not to tell *me* the truth. Why would anything I think about him matter? It's weird to think about Weston thinking about what I would think about him. Because that implies Weston has thought about me.

I was sure I was nothing more than a peasant to him. But I suppose you get to know someone when you have to learn how to press all of their buttons.

"It's an amulet, okay?" He draws his hands through his hair, knuckles white against his golden waves. "I dropped an amulet in deep space, and even *with* the approximate coordinates, I have no idea how I'll ever find it."

I try to imagine what that looks like: one tiny, metallic little object floating in the ever-expanding, seemingly limitless dark of deep space. How in Mars is there any way we're *ever* going to find that in time to exchange the amulet for my fathers' safety?

The impossibility of it all chokes me with dread. I close my eyes and try to muster the picture of Astro Bonny on the cover of my book, confident and fearless and full of gusto.

But Astro Bonny's not a hero—she's exactly why we're in this position in the first place, outrunning two of her apprentices. I feel untethered, desperate for some beacon of hope that can assure me that I'm cut out for this mission. That a girl from deep space who's never left the confines of her inn can somehow, someday, find this amulet in the middle of the dark nothing and save her parents' lives before it's too late.

The panic threatens to take me under, unspooling me slowly like a spaghettified star circling a black hole. So I lean in to the one other feeling Weston's words gave me: star-hot anger.

"An *amulet?*" I cry. "You put your life at risk to steal an *amulet* from the Odette Twins?" I let out a shaky laugh. "What, did it match your fancy new cloak?"

He crosses his arms over his chest. "See? This is why I didn't want to tell you."

Looking at the pouty prince now, I can't imagine him stealing from the space pirates. As impossible as this mission seems to me, at least I know how to take care of myself, to a certain degree. My fathers have always relied on me at the inn, and back when the factory was closer I used to help Ron and his family out there, too. But Weston's parents have always kept him tucked safely from danger in his big, spacious castle, like he was a precious artifact himself.

If *I'm* not cut out for this mission, he certainly isn't, either. Yet somehow, he's the one who got us into this mess.

Despite the advice Papa gave me repeatedly growing up, I decide not to keep my thoughts to myself. "How did *you* manage to get it from the pirates, anyway?" Seeing the way his nose crinkles at my tone, I add for clarity: "Offense intended."

He rolls his eyes, painstakingly and dramatically slow. "The royal army caught one of the Odette Twins' ships while they were out on a looting mission for Astro Bonny. The crew was arrested, and the loot was secured by our kingdom."

"So your parents let you take the amulet?" I ask.

Weston shrinks a bit in his chair. "Well, not exactly . . ." Reflexively, he reaches toward Comet and runs a hand across the top of his fluffy head. "The air vents in their conference room connect directly to the ones upstairs in the small library," he explains, as if it's totally normal to have so many libraries in your house you need to title them by size. "If I time it right so the guard on the second floor is completing a round on the opposite wing, I can overhear my parents getting debriefed by the soldiers."

Eavesdropping on my fathers' conversations about adult topics—like the inn, and money, and moving, and pirates— just means sneaking through the inn at night and tilting my head toward the thin door that separates their room from the hallway. It's a lot less glamorous, but kind of the same thing

Weston is describing. Despite being crammed in a space pod with a prince, running from pirates who are chasing us across the solar system, the fact that Weston and me might have something in common still feels like the strangest thing that could have possibly happened.

"I overheard a soldier reading off a list of loot recovered from the Odette Twins' crew upon capture," he continues. "And when I heard mention of the amulet, it sounded a lot like this rare artifact I'd read about in the royal archives, and . . ."

He trails off, still intending to keep the amulet's meaning to him secret. *That's* what I should care about, but instead I blurt, "You *read?*"

Weston bristles. "What, exactly, do you think I *do* all day?"

I throw up my hands in exasperation. Thanks to the tiny pod, it results in some quickly bruised knuckles. "When you visited the inn, I never saw you *read*. You were too busy snickering at me to your dog, or inventing new ways to torment me and my fathers!"

Weston smiles fondly. I give his arm a rough shove.

"Well, I don't always have a ready target like you around," he snaps.

The skin between my eyebrows pinches. When I thought of Weston's life outside his visits, I always imagined him fully decked in a crown and robe while sitting on a high throne, Comet nestled in his lap wearing a tiny version of Weston's royal ensemble. Staff would fan him and feed him grapes while he barked out tedious orders at the guards.

But the version of himself Weston's painting now makes

me picture him dodging guards instead of bossing them around. Listening in to his parents and the soldiers for information he couldn't otherwise get, tucked in a library while the books keep him company.

It reminds me of last night—how lonely he looked, left with Comet while he parents worked inside, surrounded by nothing but the inky black backdrop of endless space.

My head feels cloudy as a dark nebula. I almost miss the rest of Weston's story as he adds, "So, that night I took this very pod and sneaked out to the moon where the loot was being stored. The guards probably wouldn't have noticed anything was gone or checked the security tapes, but the Odette Twins must have come back for their crew—or, more than likely, come back for their *loot*. And once they noticed it was gone, they must have watched the videos back, saw *I'd* taken it, and for whatever reason, wanted this specific item so badly for themselves that they were willing to follow me all the way out into the astro-boonies to recover it."

If the amulet is so special only the royals and pirates have heard about it, and they want it badly enough to chase each other across space just to be its sole owner, then they both probably only want it *because* it's one of a kind. Exclusive, only for the richest and most powerful members of the solar system.

"So, you stole from pirates because you wanted an amulet you read about in a book at home," I summarize. "Isn't that just a deadly version of shopping from a catalog?"

Weston crosses his arms and shakes his head. "You don't get it," he grumbles.

I scoff. "Well, forgive *me* for valuing my fathers' lives over your jewelry."

"We're gonna get it back, okay?" he snaps, sharper than I expected. "You'll get back to your perfect life with your perfect parents soon enough."

The night sky sparkles in the distance, a cloud of space dust lingering on the horizon, white and puffy. Already, a few hundred miles from home, the universe looks less empty.

It's like driving into a memory—the way our home used to be.

"Perfect life?" I echo. "I'm risking myself for the sake of an amulet you stole, in exchange for my literal *home*. How am I the lucky one here?"

"At least you have a home," he says. "A real home. Not some cookie-cutter castle where you eat food prepared by cooks you can't name, and are told good night by guards who're paid to say it, and spend your days wandering giant, empty grounds while all the kids your age play on the other side of the gates."

I can't help but laugh. "Are you complaining about being *rich* right now?"

Weston doesn't respond, just shrinks further into himself. The words play over in my mind, more ridiculous than at first. But then I picture Weston out on that giant lawn, guards watching from the doorway while he walks alongside Comet, listening to the distant laughter of the other kids our age. It's a more glamorous, privileged version of what I've felt recently. Watching the night sky to catch a glimpse of Ron's home. Hoping to see a guest on the horizon. Replaying old memories over and over in my mind to replace the silence in our halls. Some of the kids on the other side of the wall could even be my old neighbors, settled into their bustling new lives on a central system planet.

I shake the thoughts away. Weston and I are different. Too different. The more alone I am, the poorer my family is. The more alone Weston is, the richer and more exclusive his family is. We're polar opposites. Nothing alike.

But right now, soaring through the twinkling dark in this pod, I can't help but feel closer to Weston than before.

Probably because of the cramped space and total lack of legroom. But still.

"Was it at least an important amulet?" I ask, softer than before.

"Of course it was," he grumbles. "I wouldn't go through this for just any amulet."

I picture a golden locket hanging from Weston's neck and shining bright as a supernova. It's easy to imagine Weston hoarding a precious jewel for the sake of being rich and famous enough to manage it. But maybe it's not just jewelry, the same way Dad's gravitational lens mirror wasn't *just* a mirror. Maybe the amulet is a gold-studded new space-techno I haven't heard of, like the ones Dad would read about in my Astro Bonny book. But this must be an item so rare and mysterious that only someone as rich as Weston—or close to the royals and pirate leaders as Weston—could know about.

All the gadgets Dad bought from traveling space-techno salespeople were to make the inn better, because that's what he wanted—what mattered most. Imagining what the amulet could be—or *do*—I try to imagine what would matter that much to Weston—but come up blank. Even in all the time we've spent together, I still have no idea who he is.

The thought alone means admitting that everything I *thought* I knew about him wasn't true. Or, at least, not the whole picture.

I'm about to reply when the pod jerks suddenly to the left, then dips a couple dozen feet. My stomach rises to my throat and Weston jolts upright, grasping for the controls. The pod doesn't drop lower, but tilts to the side, so Comet falls right onto my feet and my head bonks the door.

Weston grips the wheel and switches off cruise. His hands shake under the pressure of steadying the pod. "Look!"

I rub my temple and sit up. Through the dashboard I see a meteor soar past, followed by another. We're in the middle of a meteor shower, like a sudden bout of rain on a water planet.

I grasp the edge of the dashboard so tight, my nailbeds go white. I've only ever seen meteor showers from the safety of Dad's telescope before, or on videos in tele-school. I never, ever thought I'd see one in real life.

Seeing them shooting past us now, veering closer and closer as the pod propels forward, I'm filled with a mix of terror and awe.

When I used to imagine what it would be like to steer a ship like Astro Bonny's through a shower like this, I never imagined the way my pulse would drum in my chest or a cool, anxious sweat would break out across my forehead. But

I try to muster the memory of that bravery—even if it was make-believe—to find a way, *any* way, to get through this moment.

The meteors spin closer, and though none have hit us yet, the force of its speed sends us flying off course. The pod wobbles as though tossed by a heavy wind, and it takes every ounce of fake-it-till-you-make-it bravery I have not to cower at the foot of my seat next to Comet.

Weston veers us to the left, dodging a chunky meteor. Just then another soars straight ahead. I reach out and grasp the wheel, steering us below.

"I've got this," he says, hands shifting on the wheel to push mine away.

"No, you don't," I say, through gritted teeth. "We almost got hit!"

Even saying the words out loud feels surreal, like I'm a girl in a story rather than actually, truly living this moment. And *barely* living this moment, at that. With each swerve of the wheel, the meteors feel closer and closer, as does certain, deep-space death.

"Because we were dodging a meteor!"

"You have to see the full picture!"

"The full picture is a full *storm* of meteors! No matter how many I dodge, there will be another one that—"

A hard object slams into the pod. We shoot to the right, spiraling out of orbit, up and down and over in a violent spin. Heartbeat drumming between my temples, I make a desperate grasp at the wheel to keep in place. Comet bounces at my ankles and Weston screams as we're knocked again, sent flying so fast my eyes can't adjust to what's ahead.

Another meteor soars past but doesn't hit us. Weston's grip on the wheel loosens and his face goes moon-rock pale. As though embodied by the version of myself I pretended to be as a girl, I take the wheel and guide us out of the next meteor's path.

"It's okay," I say, partly to him but mostly to myself. "We're almost out."

Something slams hard into my side of the pod. We're caught in a giant meteor's track, pushed off to the side at full speed. The wheel resists my grip, but I keep steering, pulling us back on track.

"We've got this!" I say, desperate for it to be true. "I've got this!"

I don't got this. The pod breaks free from the meteor, but I've lost control of the wheel. We spin out, whipping through space at full force. I feel Comet throw up on my feet and for the first time, I don't care. I realize in this moment that there are things worse than royal dog vomit.

As we spin, I can barely make anything out through the windshield. But the dark vastness of the sky is broken by the occasional spot of brown. It takes a few nauseating spins before I realize we're spiraling down toward a planet's surface.

"We're gonna crash!" I cry. Weston is pressed back against his chair, damp spots forming at the corner of his eyes.

I reach out and grab his hand.

"It'll be over in a second," I shout above the whirring of the pod. "It'll be over in a second. It'll be over in a second. It'll be over—"

I'm hit with the hardest, sharpest force I've felt in my life. Then everything goes black.

CHAPTER EIGHT

When I was little, Dad would read stories to me before bed. I'd cuddle up against his chest, abandoning my pillow, and close my eyes as he read. Sometimes he'd read stories about space pirates, off in distant dimensions, stealing from villages and sieging entire planets. I trembled in his arms and reached out, swatting against the pages of the book.

"It has a happy ending, Lex," he assured me with a laugh.

In those moments, I didn't care. All I wanted was the happy ending, not the nonsense in between. I just shook my head and cuddled closer. The frames of his glasses pinched my scalp.

Dad closed the book so he could tighten his grip on me. His arms were warm, their weight reassuring. He spoke against the top of my curly head.

"There are no space pirates in this part of the solar system," he assured me. "And even if there were, your papa and I would keep you safe. We'll always keep you safe." His grip around me tightened. I nuzzled closer, listened to the gentle beat of his heart. "You can be sure of that."

The dark crept up around me then, sleep beckoning. I felt warm, safe. I was far, far away from space pirates—they could never reach me there.

But that's not true anymore.

"Lexi. *Lexi!*"

Something shakes my arms. My eyelids flicker open and Prince Weston hovers over me, the whites of his eyes shimmering. A dog licks the palm of my hand.

"Wake up," he says, features coming into focus. I'm not at home, tucked in bed with Dad. I don't know where I am. But my head feels funny, and Weston's voice sounds miles away.

I want to close my eyes, go back to sleep.

"Lexi, we landed somewhere weird," Weston says. "I need you to come back to me, okay? I can't be lugging you *and* Comet around unknown territory."

Unknown territory? That snaps me awake.

I sit upright, so fast my forehead bonks his. Weston lets out a whine of pain, but I'm too busy processing his words to feel it myself. "What do you mean? Where are we?"

He points to our crashed pod, doors hanging off the side and control panel sparking. A few meteorites are scattered across the ground, but otherwise we're surrounded by nothing but dirt paths and thin forest.

As if things weren't dire enough, we just lost our one ticket to finding the amulet—to my parents' and the inn's *freedom*.

Tears threaten their way up my throat, but as I watch smoke churn from the pod, I beg myself to focus. Back at the inn, when I faced crises—such as needing to meal plan on the fly for unexpected guests, or scrambling for blankets that one time the heat went out after our local space plumber moved away—I always had to slow down, take a breath, and improvise in order to survive.

The pod may be gone, but there are still supplies inside it, like the phone and the food Ron gave us. Mustering the scrappiness my fathers taught me and the bravery I've been playing at since I left the inn, I plant my elbows in the dirt and push myself upright.

I stretch my arm out, gesturing for Weston to help me up. He's too scrambled to retort and accepts my hand. He rises and pulls me to my feet with him. My legs are loose planks beneath me, wobbly and unsure. But I press on, staggering toward our broken pod.

"That thing could blow any second!" Weston shrieks.

I ignore him and crawl past the crushed side door. The control panel is smashed, but there's no sign of Weston's phone. I lean down, pushing aside broken parts and debris. At the foot of my seat lies his phone, webbed cracks stretching across its glass screen. Still, when I tap the fractured glass, the screen lights up.

After snatching the bag of astronaut ice cream, I carry the phone to where Weston stands, pacing beside a whining Comet. The cracks prick the skin of my fingers as I click to open a new call. But before I can even type for the inn, four empty bars and the words *no service* glare at me from the top of the phone screen.

One step forward, a thousand light-years back. Those darn tears threaten their way back into my eyes at the thought of my fathers being unreachable. I've never been away from home before, other than a trip to Ron's. Dad and Papa have always been a call away, ready to circle tight to my side when I need them, just like Comet does to Weston now. And not only am I faced with the reality that I can't reach them, but they're back at the inn, with Astro Bonny's apprentices and no way to reach *me*.

My head spins, partly from the crash and partly from the terrifying weight of the situation. Staring at the phone now, our mission seems impossible. But beneath all the high-pitched, screaming panic in my head is the rational voice of the innkeepers' daughter, reminding me that the only way to lose in moments of crisis is not to try at all.

"You knew how to drive it," I say—though a bit halfheartedly, my hope waning thin. "Do you know how to fix it too, by any chance?"

I must have really hit my head hard to expect that Weston is secretly harboring the skills of a pod mechanic. He gives me an incredulous look and releases a breathless laugh. "As *if* my parents would teach me anything practical like that." He huffs, running a hand through his hair so his blond curls jut upright. "No, of course not, because if I knew too much about how to take care of myself, I'd get too independent, right? And then how would they keep me tucked safely away in the castle where they don't have to worry about me—don't have to *think* about me?"

His voice picks up volume and momentum before coming to an abrupt halt, his posture suddenly sinking as though pressed down by the weight of his outburst. His hand drops from his hair, fingers trailing over his eyes and chin before his arm falls limply to his side.

"Well, hopefully they're thinking about me now, considering we have no way out of here unless someone saves us."

My stomach churns uncomfortably—probably because the crash landing has spun up all my insides, but also because of that sad, pinched look on Weston's face. It's clear that— beneath his exasperation—he's *scared*, too.

If I traced back each step that led me here, I could easily find a way to blame him for me being caught up in this, too. But I chose to embark on this mission, and I chose to do it with him.

Weston may not be Ron, but right now he's my partner. And that as much as I want to give in to the fear that's gripping me like a fist, right now I want to be there for him, too.

"We can figure this out," I say, hoping that if my voice is steady enough, I can convince us both. "We just need to find out where we are first, and then I'm sure there will be some clear way out of this place."

Weston must be *really* panicking, because he actually listens to me, nodding and turning back to his phone to draw up the map. "Well, we're definitely close to the central system," he says, "and this planet's marked with both green *and* brown on the map, so it's probably populated by more than trees. So maybe we do have a shot in the dark, after all."

I nod along, trying to appear calmer than I am. Because not only are we on a totally foreign planet with no way off— which is *already* terrifying—but I've *never* been this close to the central system or anywhere, really, outside my neighborhood. I'm both overwhelmed by all the possibilities of terrible, dangerous things that await, and *thrilled* by the thought as well.

For the first time in my life, I have truly no idea what to expect of what comes next. I feel less like myself and more like the version of myself I pretended to be acting as in our space duels with Ron as little kids. It gives me a strange, out-of-body feeling, like I'm watching myself rather than actually living this moment. But it's empowering, too, like if I can just *pretend* to be that version of me, we actually have a chance of making it out of this alive.

"Okay, let's find out where we are, then," I declare, voice packed with mock confidence. "If what you're saying is true, then there's got to be civilization on the other side of those trees, right?"

Weston slips his phone into his back pocket and nods. "Yes, but we have to be careful, considering we're being *hunted by space pirates*." He says the last part dramatically slow, as though I could have possibly forgotten that life-threatening detail. "And Comet—Comet, c'mere, boy," he calls, trailing past me toward where Comet is determinedly marking the trees lining the clearing. "Your knees are *not* cut out for this journey."

Weston scoops Comet up into his arms and we head into

the woods, slow and cautious. This is the part in the story when I'd start to squirm deeper into my covers, turn away from the pages of Dad's book. But right now I hold my shoulders back and march forward.

I get the feeling that neither of us are very used to nature: me always having lived on a floating rock in deep space and Weston usually holed up in his castle or monitored by his guards. Our slow trek works in our favor, though; our footsteps are too faint to drown out the distant rumble of traffic and voices, and we're able to follow the noises through the woods toward the village beyond.

We weave slowly, ducking from tree to tree like we did between the safety of the shadows in Ron's stairwells and attic. Up ahead, the trees break apart to let in a long stretch of light. We edge closer cautiously, Weston murmuring soothingly to Comet as he sniffs excitedly at the array of unfamiliar smells wafting from the main street.

The trees part and the faint murmur of passing feet and distant voices trails through the quiet wood. I duck behind a large oak and peer ahead, squinting hard to make out the shapes on the distant street. We're by a small road, occupied by a series of houses and a couple shops. One has baskets of fruit and vegetables by its entrance, facing the street. It's overwhelmingly stocked with oranges, and a big, hand-painted sign over the awning reads: SAY NO TO SCURVY.

Okay, *that* is weirdly specific. But I mentally shrug it off, continuing to scan the street. A few people pass by, paces quick and heads bent down. There are homes and apartments scattered between the shops, and all the homes have one thing in common: no doors.

"That's weird," I whisper to Weston. "Space bugs can get in."

I, at least, would not want a space fly in my room.

I lean forward, ignoring Weston's groans of protest as I block his view. Off to the left, I can see farther down the street toward what looks like a town hall with a high tower stretching from the roof. But instead of a giant clock, there's a big compass, needle tickling slightly left and right to mark toward north.

I frown. Dread rises in my throat and I fight to swallow it down, frantically scanning for anything that will *not* confirm my suspicions about this town and planet.

But the storm of fear and excitement in my chest picks up speed with each additional detail.

A bank with an ATM spilling out doubloons readily like a broken coin machine.

A bookstore with the spray-painted name MARY READS across its front door.

And a clothing shop with a smashed glass window—wide and open like all the other shops and houses—with a mast draped over its old sign, reading: KERCHIEFS & CALICO.

"Astro Bonny basically *invented* the kerchief as pirate fashion. And Calico—"

"Is for the garish, colorful outfits her right-hand man, Jack, wore," Weston says. "As in *Calico Jack*, the rival pirate she exploded with that crazy laser of hers."

I nod thoughtfully, pursing my lips as I say, "So, I think we may have landed on Astro Bonny's pirate planet."

Weston uses one hand to cradle Comet to his chest and gestures broadly at the scene around us with the other. "Oh, you *think?*"

"I know it's obvious *now*," I seethe, "but I mean, what are the *odds?* Ron told us we were headed in this direction, but how likely is it that we crash-landed right onto this planet, out of all the planets in the central system?"

"Well, seems we have plenty of luck," Weston says through a tight, definitely not happy smile, "*Bad* luck, specifically."

I slump back against the trunk, my legs feeling unsteady beneath me as though my atoms were peeling apart. Everything around me looks like something I would have dreamed up as a girl if I had to imagine what an Astro Bonny–themed amusement park had to look like. But knowing what I know about her now—and being the target of her lackeys—it feels like a living nightmare.

Fear and anxiety buzz through me like the hive of angry space wasps Papa had to free from our front door last year. How in the world am I supposed to get off *this* world and back home?

Weston sets Comet down into the grass and begins to pace, his shoes tracking muddy imprints in his wake. "Of *course* we landed right in the middle of one of their colonies, and with a broken pod and no way out. If we get caught, they'll get to the amulet before we do, and . . ."

His voice trails off. All the unknowns compound in my mind, sending my imagination spinning like our pod did in the meteor shower. "Is the amulet a weapon of some sort? Something they were using for their galactic takeover?"

I hold my breath, and not just because this planet smells a little garlicky. If his parents want the inn as a stopover point while they negotiate with the next solar system for support against the pirates, taking the amulet to stop the pirates' plans would be a perfect way for Weston to prove himself to his parents. And depending on his answer, I may understand the real stakes of being stuck on this planet, and what kinds of dangerous space-techno may be hoarded here, too.

The thought sends a fresh jolt of panic through me, but I maintain my focus on Weston. Because maybe, if he finally tells me the truth, I won't just understand what we're up against. Maybe I'll finally be able to understand Weston, too. "Is that why you want it so badly? So you can derail the pirates' plans?"

Weston pokes his shoe against the dirt floor and bites his lower lip. By now, the polish has run off and there's nothing but a dull shine to the shoe's surface.

"That's not why," he says. "I wanted that amulet for . . . my own reasons. It had nothing to do with the Odette Twins, or whatever reasons the pirates have for wanting it too. They just happened to have it."

His words die off and he avoids my eyes. He doesn't want me to push it. Yet he's always pushing me—finding my buttons, picking me apart, doing whatever he can to gain the upper hand. I'm stranded on an unfamiliar planet because of him, dog vomit on my soles and debris in my hair. I deserve to know why.

But seeing the way his cheeks go pale and the blues of his eyes go dull at the mention of the amulet, I realize I can't ask. Not now. Not until he's ready.

"We can't give up yet," I say. "We knew it wouldn't be easy. We can figure this out."

"You got another plan?" he asks. "Because so far your genius problem-solving hasn't lived up to its advertising."

I know he's right—I have no idea what I'm doing. I'm way out of my depth, playing make-believe as a fearless adventurer like I did as a little kid, when I'm nothing but a girl from the astro-boonies who's desperate to get back home to the safety of her fathers' embrace.

But maybe that's enough right now. Because as scary as crashing on a foreign planet is, nothing is more terrifying than the thought of *not* making it back to my fathers. Especially right now, when they're in danger, with no one to help them but me.

It doesn't matter if I feel brave. Right now I *have* to be.

"And it's not like we can just *march* into the town square. We need some sort of disguise so we don't stand out."

"So *you* don't stand out," I correct, eyeing his puffy white shirt and golden buttons. "But, yeah, you're right."

When on a pirate planet, one must think like a pirate, I decide. I hold out my hand, palm up, fingers wiggling expectantly for Weston's phone. "I need a spyglass," I declare.

He stares blankly at me, one eyebrow cocked with a mixture of confusion and classic Weston judgey-ness. I release a dramatic huff and add slowly, as though explaining something to a child, "I'll use your camera to zoom in on the clothing shop. To confirm the coast is clear."

"You could have just said that," he grumbles, slapping the phone into my palm. "And for the record, I draw the line at wearing a calico coat. Life or death, I still have boundaries."

I roll my eyes and quickly swipe to open his camera. I try not to look too long at the zero bars at the top of the screen. The words *no service* seem like a quiet threat, driving home just how far I am from my fathers—and help. "You need to think *bigger*, Weston. The costumes are *useless* if we don't capture the pirate lingo, too."

I flick my fingertips across the screen, zooming in the camera's image. *Of course* Weston has super-high-end tech, even for his phone, so with just a few quick swipes I've got a useless microscopic view of the shop. I groan as the phone screen fills with images of dust bugs.

"Why would you even *need* to zoom in this far?" I ask, swiping slower as I adjust back out. "You royals are no different from pirates: always wanting *more, more, more*, even if the things you're hoarding are useless."

Weston bristles. "Well . . . sometimes it helps me find ticks on Comet!" he snaps defensively, snuggling the dog up to his chest for emphasis.

I roll my eyes. "Do *not* use your dog's cuteness to win this argument."

It kind of works, though. Comet's mouth opens in a big, tongue-y grin as Weston tightens his hold on him. My flash of anger fades and my attention returns to the task at hand.

I hold up the screen so all three of us can see. "It looks like there's just one cashier in there." There's a thin, sullen-looking man cowering behind the front counter. The register in front of him looks like it had been smashed open, a tray with just a small handful of gold coins exposed and ready for the taking. The store has received the same treatment, too: clothing thrown across the floor, bare hangers lining the walls.

It's been fully, utterly pillaged.

Weston frowns at the image, nibbling at his lower lip. "We can return them later so it's not, like, *stealing*," he says, and I detect the unfamiliar sound of *guilt* in his tone. "And we *need* the clothes if we're going to stop the space pirates."

He makes it sound as if we're on some noble mission to stop the Odette Twins for good, and not just that we're here to get his amulet back and to save my inn. A lump rises in my throat; saving my fathers from the space pirates that are currently occupying the inn is the most important thing right now. But part of me feels guilty thinking of all the people trapped on planets like these, who won't be safe and secure once my adventure is over.

When I was little, a bigger adventure—one that involved saving *all* of our system from the pirates—would have been the one I chose for myself. Now that the inn is my entire world, I'm safer, don't need to worry about those things—don't need to be the one to take on those adventures. It feels like a relief, in a way—and reaffirms that I *do* belong at the inn, and *just* the inn, like I always have.

But seeing the shop now, and how similar it looks to the

inn after the pirates arrived and destroyed everything, I wonder again if maybe—just maybe—I could and *should* take on a bigger adventure, after all.

A high-pitched squawking sound snaps me back to focus. Startled, I stumble back and the phone moves with me, the zoomed image shifting from the shop up to the sky, where a giant, red bird soars past the screen.

"Did you see that?" I ask. Comet responds, writhing in Weston's grip and howling at the sky, his sweet, dopey smile wiped clean from his face.

I hold the phone above my head, scanning the sky for the bird. It circles back, looping overhead around the line of shops. I angle the phone to follow it and recognize the bird from the Astro Bonny book I had as a kid.

"It's a parrot," Weston says, just as I realize it. "The pirates' pet."

The way the parrot circles steadily overhead doesn't align with Weston's pet theory, though. In the images of Astro Bonny in my book, her parrot was always fixed on her shoulder, so it wasn't clear where she ended and the bird began. Kind of like Weston and Comet right now: beside me, he has Comet bundled in his arms, one hand running over the top of his furry head as he tries to soothe the barking dog.

This parrot isn't a pet. So, what is it? I frown and zoom again, imagining I'm using the spyglass at the helm of a ship, searching for threats on the horizon.

Sure enough, just the tiniest bit of zooming reveals a key detail on the parrot: where two beady black eyes should be are red, blinking lights. They remind me of the ones on the security cameras I watched Ron's mom set up outside the astronaut ice cream factory years ago, back when his dad had first left and they still weren't used to living in that big, spacious factory without him.

"The bird is space-techno!" I cry.

"*Shh!*" Weston seethes. "It's like you and Comet are *trying* to get us caught!"

Just like the parrot I, too, am not a pet, which means I don't need to listen to Weston's commands. Even if he's kind of right. "It's a surveillance drone," I say, still loud and frantic, but a *little* quieter, given the circumstances. "They probably have a bunch of these keeping tabs on the planet while the twins are off on their ship."

The words taste sour on my tongue. Astro Bonny was always pictured *with* her parrot, going on adventures together the same way Weston and Comet do. Sure, these weren't *really* parrots. But as annoying and entitled as Weston can be, I can't picture him ever developing robo-Comets and scattering them around a planet to do work for him. If there was one thing Weston cared about other than himself, it was Comet, and even the *idea* of making Comet work for him wouldn't sit well with Weston.

It didn't align with the Astro Bonny I knew—*thought* I knew. My stomach sinks like it's tied to an anchor. With each new detail I discover about her, the fearless, independent woman I looked up to as a girl feels further and further, fading like a dream in the light of day.

Of course that Astro Bonny I thought I knew wasn't real; not even her love for her pet. Because fearless, adventurous, carefree people like that can't exist in a world like this. And I was silly to ever think they could—and that I could ever be like that, too.

"We *definitely* need to get disguises, then," Weston says. He stands, inhaling a deep breath so Comet is squeezed a bit between his inflated chest and the grip of his arms. "Okay, you're right. It's time to get in the pirate mindset. And that's not just *talking* like a pirate. It's acting like one, too." He gives me a serious look and declares, "Time to ransack that shop."

When I admired Astro Bonny as a little girl, I was way more interested in her deep-space adventurers and brazen attitude than *this* part of being a pirate. But I know Weston's right, so I rise to follow as we make a beeline across the empty street to the shop door, mindful of the parrot overhead.

We stagger inside the shop, so fast I nearly slip on a pair of trousers lying on the linoleum floor. The shop owner flinches as we enter, stepping back from the counter on instinct.

"Take what you want!" he stammers, face greenish pale. "But consider leaving the coins, if you can."

His eyes dart to the open register, with the few coins that must have been left by real shoppers who lived here before the pirates took over. Guilt churns in my stomach. With the way he's looking at me now, I wonder how I ever looked up to someone like Astro Bonny, let alone wanted to be like her.

But I'm here, on a literal *pirate planet*, away from home for the first time. In a way, I *am* like her in this moment: on a faraway adventure, so distant from the inn that I can't even get service.

It's terrifying, being away from home and away from my fathers. It's terrifying knowing that at any second, that parrot could swoop down and alert the twins to our arrival. Terrifying that we have no pod, no service, no way to fight back and return to safety.

But it's also what I always dreamed of, and in a way, this is no different than playing dress-up with Ron when we were little kids. Not having Astro Bonny's legacy to follow is scary. But it also means I get to make the rules of this adventure.

I step forward, and my legs are as unsteady and wobbly as though they were made of pegs. I'm not prepared for whatever comes next, but I throw myself into it anyway, how I pretended to while playing make-believe with Ron. "We do need to take clothes," I tell the shopkeeper, slow and hesitant, "but we're not pirates."

"*Lexi!*" Weston hisses through barred teeth.

I ignore him, adding, "We need to go undercover for a bit. Until we can get off this planet."

The man's eyes go wide. Then he lets out a big, high-pitched laugh. "Get *off* the planet?" he cackles, tears sprouting to his eyes. "You think I'd still be here if there was a way off this planet?"

Weston places Comet down and grips my elbow. "We just need to take the clothes and *go*," he reminds me in a low voice.

Weston leans down and snatches a black, pointed hat off the floor, attention fixed on gathering his costume together.

But my attention remains on the shopkeeper. "What do you mean? What happened here?"

He dabs his knuckles at the tears beading at the corner of his eyes, catching his breath before he responds. "When those Astro Bonny wannabees invaded, they took all our pods and stuck them under the decks of their ships." He gestures toward the town center on the map, where a small patch of blue holds an image of a pirate ship. "Their crew uses them to sweep other planets and pillage them for goods."

With each word, his laughter fades, replaced by a heavy, tired look. Whatever hope I was starting to gather at the thought of embarking on an adventure on this planet dims at the same rate as his expression.

"No, there's no way off anymore," he says glumly. He points behind him, toward a corkboard against the back wall. There's a giant map pinned over old flyers about sales and seasonal items. "X marks the only way off this planet, if you're desperate enough to take it."

I step toward the counter to take a closer look. It must be a map of this planet: I recognize where we are now, at the line of shops across from the woods. There are small boxes representing homes throughout the village, more shops along the edge of the town, and a patch of blue representing a lake. And in the center is a big, bold X over what looks to be a sketch of a pirate's cannon.

"They say that cannon's powerful enough to propel you to another galaxy," he says, voice a mixture of awe and terror. "I've only heard it go off once when those twins shot someone straight out of our solar system with it. Whoever it was has never returned, and no one from around here's been foolish to use the cannon since."

Goose bumps erupt across my skin, and to my right, Weston freezes halfway through tying a cravat around Comet's collar. Had the twins used the cannon to scare the villagers from trying to get off this planet? Or had they had an adversary who got in the way of their plans—someone like us, who they defeated by shooting them straight out of this galaxy?

The thought grips me with terror. I feel far from home now, but if the twins managed to shoot me out of a space-techno cannon, I'd *never* make my way back home again.

Something heavy yet soft falls over my shoulders, jolting me out of my panic. Weston's arms lower as mine raise to grasp the fabric of the pirate's cloak he's slung over me. The warm embrace of the fabric soothes my muscles, which I didn't notice were shaking until now.

I turn to shoot Weston a grateful smile, but he's ducked his head, avoiding my eyes.

"We'll find another way off this planet," he says. "But for that, we need to go now."

"Wait!" the shopkeeper calls. He ducks behind the counter, and I hear the squeak of an old floorboard being lifted. "You'll need these if you stand a chance."

He pops back into view and slides a cutlass and a sharp hook across the counter.

My chest inflates at the thought that he sees potential in *me* as someone brave and strong enough to take on the twins.

But his gaze flickers between Weston and Comet, and considering he saw them both pre-pirate-ified, it's no *wonder* he figured out he who the iconic duo was.

Sure, maybe he's just helping because he recognizes Weston is a royal, and maybe thinks we're part of some secret mission set by the King and Queen to defeat the twins from within the planet. But perhaps something I said helped him realize we were trustworthy, too. Because on his own, Weston is known as nothing more than a sheltered prince. But us together—perhaps *that* looks like a pair worth believing in.

Perhaps—even if I don't have the Astro Bonny I dreamed of as a little girl anymore—I can still have the *Galaxy Jones* I dreamed of becoming after all.

I reach forward before Weston can, snagging the cutlass and hooking it to my new sheath. With the pirate's ensemble and weapon, I feel like I did playing make-believe with Ron: bold and impossibly brave, acting out a character who was fearless and unstoppable in all the ways the real me could never be.

Except right now, this *is* the real me. The cloak is a bit too big, and the cutlass is a bit too heavy, and instead of the giant crew I imagined for myself as a little kid, I have a spoiled prince and an elderly dog by my side.

But as terrifying as it is, and as much as the costume might not fit just right yet, this *is* real right now. I need to get back to my fathers and the inn, so for today, at least, I get to be the Galaxy Jones I'd dreamed of being as a kid. Because I *need* to be, if there's any chance of surviving this planet.

CHAPTER NINE

As we leave the shop, I'm immediately grateful for our new outfits; not only because of the parrot drones circling overhead, but because a real, live pirate stands at the edge of the woods, back turned to us as he pins a sign on the tree. I grasp Weston's wrist with one hand, yanking him to a halt, and position my free hand over the hilt of the cutlass—as though I have any idea how to, let alone intention of, using it to defend us.

But the pirate doesn't notice us and hobbles on toward the bank to grab a handful of doubloons before slapping another poster up on the building's front wall. As helpful as our disguises have been so far, there's no use chancing it, so we dart back toward the woods.

I don't think anything of the signs the pirate was pinning up—figuring it's probably an invitation to a looting spree, or whatever pirates do for fun—but Weston grabs the flowy sleeve of my cloak and points to another copy of the sign plastered to a tree up ahead.

Even from a distance, I can make out a distinct sketch of

Weston's face. Each detail is perfect, from the way his tiny nose curls up in a smug pout and the shadowing on his fluffy light curls. The flyer reads: WANTED.

Beside the intricate sketch of Weston is a stick figure in a dress. Beneath, it reads: PRINCE AND PEASANT, LAST SEEN IN OUTER SOLAR SYSTEM, AND WANTED FOR LOOTING. ALERT AUTHORITIES IF SEEN.

I frown. "A stick figure? Really? I deserve a bit more credit than that."

Weston shakes my arm. "Are you serious, Lexi? It's not *credit*. It's a call for our capture!"

Panic bubbles in my stomach at the words. Sure, we have disguises. And, sure, one of the villagers helped us, which means not everyone here is pro-pirate—especially considering most of them are victims of the Odette Twins, just like us.

But we have no way off this planet. This planet where we're *wanted* for capture by evil, vicious pirates who won't hesitate to toss us straight into a black hole. And if that happens, not only will I be spaghettified, but my parents will still be trapped and could suffer the same fate, too.

That stringy little stick figure stares back at me, an unformed and invisible girl. It's a cold reminder that I'm so much *smaller* than this mission, not even worth more than a few rushed lines on a piece of paper.

But dressed like the fearless space warrior I grew up admiring, I try to believe that it means there's still more brushstrokes to come. I tighten the cloak around my shoulders and stand up a bit straighter.

Not having a proper caricature also means I'm pretty incognito—but Weston, on the other hand, was recognized even *before* the posters went up. I glance back and forth between Weston and the Wanted poster, then reach forward and tug his hat a little farther down his face, similar to how Celeste wears it. He scowls but doesn't resist.

I step back and hum thoughtfully, studying my handiwork. One small, golden-blond curlicue of hair juts out from beneath the hat by his ear. I frown.

"If anyone looks too closely, we're cannon fodder," I admit. Weston groans and shoves the hat back up his forehead dramatically.

"Great! Just *great*," he shouts. In any other circumstance I'd remind him we're in hiding, but considering how conspicuous we are even in costume, it seems like a moot point.

Comet, on the other hand, stirs immediately at the sound of Weston's distress. He putters over to Weston and rises up on his back legs—a bit wobbly from his bad knees—and strains his front paws up Weston's calves as though reaching for a hug.

Weston's tense posture deflates, and he slumps a bit as he reaches down to scratch behind Comet's ears. "I should have left you at our new inn, buddy." Before I can absolutely bristle at that wording, he adds, "I never should have dragged you into this."

The reality of the situation hits me like double-gravity, because just like I'm terrified of my fathers being held captive by the pirates, Comet is Weston's family, too. And unless we find a way out of here, *none* of us are safe.

The shopkeeper listed two ways off this planet, and considering one is an intergalactic cannon, there's really only one *feasible* option.

Feasible and realistic may not be the same thing. But I hope that if I say my next words with enough conviction, they won't sound as scary as they do in my head.

"The space pirates keep the stolen pods under their ship decks," I say, "so we have to go to the town center, break into their ship, and steal a pod."

He speaks slowly, as though baffled he has to say the next words. "You want to steal a pod from a planet we just established was a *pirate* planet?"

I point at the Wanted poster. "You're practically famous for stealing from pirates! Pod snatching should be nothing after taking prized loot from the Odette Twins."

Weston runs his hand under the sides of his hat and through his hair, fingers brushing past his temples and through his wavy blond locks. Even ruffled and disheveled with a lopsided cap, he manages to look princely and perfect. "That was different. I was in . . . a different headspace then. I wasn't even scared. I was just . . . focused. Like nothing else mattered."

I try to imagine that. Every time Weston's agreed to follow my lead, he's had a spark of fear in his eyes—not determination. It's hard to picture what Weston would look like, eyes serious and mind focused, as he sneaked onto a pirate ship and snagged a precious amulet.

When I speak again, my voice is softer. "What can you do

to get back to that headspace? Can you remember why you wanted the amulet so badly in the first place? Will that help motivate you to get it back, no matter what?"

Comet settles onto Weston's shoes, sleepily nudging his pantleg with his damp nose. Weston looks down at him, mouth a tight line. Then he offers a stiff nod.

"I'll try, Lexi."

His voice is soft and devoid of its usual bravado. The sound and his slumped, withered look send a surge of guilt through my chest. I'm not sure what the amulet is for, so I'm not sure what I'm asking of him. But right now it feels bigger than I expected.

"Thank you, Weston," I say. The words are softer and more sincere than I'm used to when it comes to him. But seeing the way his shoulders slightly rise, I feel a rush of comforting warmth spread through my chest.

I try to remember the shopkeeper's map. "Which way do you think—"

Comet wags his tail and stalks off toward the path to the right. He hobbles along slowly, tail wagging in his wake. His tiny paws make fresh prints on the road.

Weston lets out a soft laugh. "All right, Captain Comet. We're right behind you."

We fall in step behind Comet, headed toward a cluster of trees. Beyond the forest is pirate territory and probably another series of Wanted signs with Weston's face on them.

It gives me a pang to think that we're no better, coming here to steal a pod just to leave. I give Weston's shoulder a nudge.

"Does the amulet really have nothing to do with it? Your parents' plan to stop the pirates, I mean?"

Weston's cheeks suck in. He stares ahead, watching as a mother ushers a young boy through their doorless entryway. "No. And I have no idea what the pirates want with it."

It would help to know what *it* does to start brainstorming the pirates' intentions.

"The coast looks clear," Weston says, angling himself away from the trunk. "This may be our chance."

He picks up Comet. We begin our trek along the outskirts of the woods.

We pass much of the same: houses and shops alongside empty streets, filled only with the occasional speed-walking pedestrian. I find myself slowing each time a villager passes by. My eyes are wide orbs as I take in all the little things that feel so similar yet so foreign to me. Women's hair braided like sailor's knots. Men in flowing white tops wearing knee-high black boots. Even the way they walk, with a pirate-like swagger, seems *almost* familiar but just distinct enough that I know I am far, far away from home.

Drifting in the dark outskirts of space, it's just me, Dad, and Papa. Previous guests float in my mind as hazy memories, but here, walking on the edge of this town, I'm closer to strangers than I've been in ages.

I wish I could invite each one back to the inn. I would sit on the rug by the sofa as each guest settled into their seat, waiting eagerly for their stories. Dad would pass them a warm cup of tea while Papa would lug their bags upstairs. Then they'd tell me all about the far-off places they'd come from, and what they saw on their way, and all the exciting and alien and wonderful things I hadn't imagined before the words passed their lips.

Ron knew about the pirate colony because while I've been waiting at the other end of our rope, he's been off traveling with his mother. While I watched out my window, hoping for a visitor, the universe had been moving on without me.

The thought makes my stomach twist. I stop by a thin tree and press my hand against the bark as warm tears spring to my eyes.

Grass and fallen leaves crunch beneath Weston's shoes, then the sound comes abruptly to a halt. I sense his eyes on me. "What's wrong? Still got whiplash from your novice pod-parking skills?"

The words are snarky, but there's a twinge of concern in his tone. He stands a few yards away, Comet nuzzled to his chest, his face scrunched with curiosity and a bit of apprehension.

I inhale a steadying breath and blink back the tears. I can't show any weakness to Weston. Knowing him, he'll use it to back out of our deal as soon as he doesn't need me anymore. And even if he did keep our promise, he'd still find some way to dismiss how I feel because I'm just an isolated, homeschooled girl from the astro-boonies.

I offer him the sincerest smile I can muster. "Yeah, whiplash. I'll let you complete the landing next time, okay?"

The skin between his eyebrows pinches, but I maintain my grin. Pushing off from the tree, I restart my trek alongside the edge of the woods.

Something rumbles in the distance. The ground trembles beneath us and the branches shake overhead, sending leaves fluttering down and birds flapping off toward the sky. The shaking is done almost as soon as it started, but Comet doesn't stop barking. He wriggles free from Weston's grip and sprints past me into the street.

Weston's arms remain crossed, as though he were holding a dog rather than empty air. "Comet, no! Come back!"

Comet isn't fast, but the second he sets foot on the road, it's already too late. Pedestrians swerve around him, casting curious glances before hurrying along on their way. He darts back and forth beneath their feet, off in the direction of the shaking and the ruckus.

Weston is after him in a second. He leaps out from the shrubbery and into the open air. I want to cry out, but I feel breathless as the passing villagers turn and stare.

All eyes go wide with recognition. Weston rushes onward, oblivious. I stand on the outskirts, watching in horror as our cover is blown.

But the villagers don't pause. They duck their heads and double their speed, away from Weston. It's as though he carries a giant eraser in his wake. There are no doors to slam and lock, but the villagers scurry inside and vanish from view, deep in their houses and within the streets' shops. Perhaps no one wants to be the one to turn Weston in, or they're assisting us as quiet rebellion against the twins like the shopkeeper did. Or perhaps they don't want to be caught in the crossfires of whatever terrible thing the Odette Twins have in store for us.

Coast officially and eerily clear, I rush after Weston. The silence, paired with the sensation of being watched, brings those crater-y goose bumps to my arms.

Comet dashes between two buildings and Weston steps sideways to shimmy through after him. I wedge myself between the buildings and sashay my way after them. A sliver of light streams up ahead, marking the end of the narrow alley-way. Beyond that, a giant structure blocks the light from the closest star.

A dark shadow flickers in the wind. I recognize the motion as a flag. And considering where we are, probably not just any flag—a space-pirate flag, attached to a giant ship.

Ahead of me, the light reaches Weston's blond curls. Comet bursts into the street, barking at the ship. Weston follows.

"Weston, wait!"

He steps out onto the main road. Comet bumbles over the redbrick street toward the ship. Crew members surround it, lugging boxes of loot from the deck.

I sprint into the warm open air and seize the hem of Weston's shirt. With a handful of smooth fabric in my grip, I yank him back and push him back into the slender alley between the buildings. He lunges forward, ready to sprint after Comet, and I leap in front of him, one finger pressed to my lips.

"I got this," I whisper. "I'll be the one to get him. Okay? Your face is on all those posters. You're the one they really want. You have to stay here."

"They could recognize you, too." I raise an eyebrow and he

shrugs. "I mean, from seeing you in person, at the inn. Or the whimsy stick figure. Either way." He regards me with questioning eyes. "You'd risk that for Comet? He's not even your dog."

"The sick on my shoes begs to differ," I say. The corner of his mouth tilts toward a smile, though his eyes are still focused and unsure. I can't tell if he's hesitant because he wants the glory of saving Comet himself or really is that confused why I'd rescue a dog that's not my own.

I may be the one who lives on a rock in the middle of nowhere, but I swear, somehow I've been more properly socialized than he has been.

Weston looks ready to say more, but we don't have time. Comet is in the middle of the street, and the second Weston steps out of the shadows, every villager and pirate nearby will recognize his princely pout. Before he can speak, I turn around and head onto the road, shoes slapping against the bricks.

Comet stands in the center of the street, tripping passersby as he barks intently at the ship. Thankfully, it's noisy enough that the pirates haven't noticed him—*yet*. I weave through the crowd and kneel to scoop him up.

"I forgive you for puking on me—again—okay?" I whisper into his droopy brown ear. "Just please be cool right now."

Comet is warm and fuzzy in my arms. He's lighter than I expected, and I feel the faint outline of his ribs beneath his fur. His chest vibrates with low growls, though he stops barking. I position him against my shoulder and run my thumb over his spine.

There's a thump a few yards away, by the ship. Leaping

down to join the crew is none other than Celeste Odette. Pictor stands on the deck, barking orders at the crew from above. I tighten my grip on Comet, as much for his sake as for mine.

I knew the ship belonged to space pirates but didn't realize the twins were with the crew. I was sure they were back at the inn, tormenting my parents and wrecking our dining room.

My chest rises with relief, then immediately plummets down to the bottom of my gut. If they're here instead of at the inn, what does that mean for my fathers? What happened to them while we were gone, that the twins felt satisfied enough to leave?

Knowing my fathers were with the crew at the inn was horrifying—but at least then I *knew* where they were, and what was happening to them. Not knowing what had happened since I left—not knowing if things had somehow gotten *worse*, or if my parents were even still in need of rescuing—fills me with a suffocating dread that threats to swallow the light from my mind like the gravitational pull of a black hole.

I can't hear a word the twins are saying from this distance. If I want to know why they're here and not with my parents, I'll have to get closer.

I swallow, knowing what I have to do next. Weston is back in the alley, watching intently and waiting for me to return. But now that I'm already in the street, I can't turn back. I have to push forward—toward the ship, and the answers about my parents.

I take a cautious step toward the ship. "Come on, little

man," I murmur to Comet. "Nice and quiet. We don't have to be like your princely dad. It's okay to stop talking for a minute or two. I promise."

As though he understands, Comet goes quiet. He nuzzles, content, against me. I swear he's on the verge of sleep and I realize he probably wasted all his energy shouting at a ship. If I were a dog, I'd probably do the same thing, so I can't really blame him.

I cradle him to my chest as I step into the shadow of the ship. Despite all the barking and vomiting and trouble, the little dog always seems to bring with him, right now I more than understand why Weston sees him as an ideal companion. My heartbeat thrashes anxiously in my chest like a caged animal, but the gentle press of Comet's soft, warm body lulls my anxiety in a way that doesn't feel possible right now.

Steadied by my partner in crime, I continue onward.

A white statue of a pirate I don't recognize stands a few yards from the loading dock, positioned as though greeting the incoming ship. Comet nestled close, I shimmy from the ship's shadow and to the side of the statue, angled so I can see the Odette Twins and their crew but they can't see us.

Huddling out of view like this reminds me of all the times Ron and I would snoop on mysterious or interesting guests at the inn—just about a thousand times deadlier. But I try to channel those safer moments with Ron in my mind, as though they *were* the same, as if those days studying the guests have somehow prepared me for this high-stakes version of the moment. We'd study them from the kitchen of the banister, watching their mannerisms and listening to their chitchat before dashing up to my room and developing grandiose theories about their epic pasts and whatever adventures we thought they were on. Comet might not have the creative bandwidth Ron has, so I'll have to listen close and gather the clues about the pirates on my own.

The crew members haul boxes onto the ground, stacked higher than they stand. Celeste paces around the piles, hands behind her back. She holds her head high and looks a bit like Weston when he sticks his little nose in the air. But considering that she wears her hat halfway down her forehead, she's probably tilting her head up to see.

"I want jewels to my right, garments in the center," she directs, voice loud and sharp. A crew member rushes to move a box from one stack to another. "And I want the techno-loot by me at all times. Right in my line of vision. I *refuse* to have a repeat of what *you* all let happen to my amulet."

She paces as she says it, taking long strides with her shiny black boots. A man wobbling under the weight of a rectangular box asks between gasps, "You mean you want us to move the boxes each time you move?"

She gestures with her hand between her brow and the space directly in front of her. "I said *in* my line of vision. Was I not clear?"

The man staggers past her, then pauses to position the box right in front of her. She walks toward it for a moment, then spins around and resumes her pacing in the opposite direction. He readjusts his grip and rushes to follow.

Techno-loot must be pirate-speak for whatever technology and gadgets she's stolen. I wonder what kinds she has packed in that oversized box, though it sounds like she's less interested in keeping close to the new loot so much as she is reminding her crew of their mistake losing the amulet to the royal guard. Even with boxes upon boxes of techno-loot in her literal line of sight, all Celeste wants is the amulet. Which makes me even hungrier to know what in the universe it could be—or *do*.

Another crew member rushes over to help him with the box. Celeste nods in approval. "Keep unloading the ship. Pictor and I will be taking a separate pod back up to track the thieves."

The thieves—she must mean us. I didn't steal anything, but I suppose if I'm supporting Weston, I'm officially part of his cause.

A third crew member calls from the deck. "We're splitting up again?"

Celeste spins around and glares daggers his way. "What did I just say?"

The man stammers, jaw shaking. "It's just that we already split up once, when we left the others back at that inn. If we split up again—"

"You can handle yourselves," she snaps. "At least, I *hope* you can."

He stutters a response I don't hear, because I'm stuck on the fact that there are pirates back at the inn. That means my parents are okay—probably. They're being surveilled, or the inn is, at least, but if there are still pirates there, it probably means there are hostages to watch. Which means my parents are still alive and in one piece.

A surge of relief bursts through me like a shooting star. But they can't be comfortable, and the inn is still at risk. I don't have much time.

Celeste mentioned *a* separate pod. Which suggests there are probably other pods on their ship, just like the shopkeeper said. If Weston and I can sneak on and take one, we can get back up into the sky and find the amulet before the twins do.

How we'll manage that, I have no idea. But thankfully, I have a thief who is an expert at sealing from pirates on my side to help.

"All right, little guy," I whisper to Comet, "let's go find our prince and make a getaway plan."

I tiptoe to the edge of the ship's shadow. Celeste is still pacing in the opposite direction, back turned to me, as her crew members lug the box within her vision. I take the chance to sprint across the street, back toward the alley. Weston stands, grasping the corner of the left building, his fingers clasping the brick wall. Comet is quiet and happily panting against my ear, and a smug grin spreads across my lips as I head toward where Weston hovers in the shadows of the alley. I've made it, to and from the ship, without catching attention.

Take that, stick figure.

Weston watches me with wide, horrified eyes. My smile spreads at his shock. Until I'm close enough to see that it's not surprise—it's *fear*. My stomach lurches and I slowly glance over my shoulder.

From the opposite side of the street, Celeste Odette watches, features shadowed by her hat.

But they didn't recognize me well enough to sketch me properly on the Wanted poster. Maybe she thinks I'm just an odd villager, running around carrying a dog that should be walking on a leash. As bitter as I felt about that stick figure earlier, right now my anonymity and no-name-ness send a surge of warm relief through my chest.

"The innkeepers' daughter!" she shrieks, pointing a bony finger my way. The crew members whip around, a series of knives and arrows appearing in their hands. A giant canon swerves on the top of the deck, pointed my way.

Nope. She definitely recognizes me. I grip Comet with shaking arms, the blood draining from my cheeks so fast it makes me dizzy with fear.

Sure, I've got the cutlass, and the pirate-inspired outfit to match. But dressing like an Astro Bonny fangirl does *not* make me an actual pirate. These pirates recognize me for what I am: the innkeepers' daughter, completely unequipped to face off with them in a duel, even if my arms *weren't* busy snuggling an old dog.

Not for the first time today, I wonder how I ever thought that I was cut out for this adventure.

"You *idiot!*" Weston hisses. He ducks back into the alley and points frantically in the direction we came from. "We have to run!"

The crew members dash from the ship, headed my way. If we run back down the alley, we'll get cornered on the other side, and still be one pod short of what we need.

I have no idea how to face off against these pirates, but the only way we stand a chance at survival is by pushing through. And if there's one thing being the daughter of deep-space inn-keepers has taught me, it's how to survive when the odds are stacked against you.

Weston will never agree with my plan, but so long as Comet is nuzzled contentedly on my shoulder, I know he'll have to go along with it.

"Follow my lead!" I call over the incoming pounding of footsteps. Weston shakes his head, fast and steady. He remains obscured by the shadows of the alley as I turn back around to face our incoming attackers.

The crew staggers toward us, weapons drawn. One is a young boy, a cracked sword waved above his head. Another, the scraggly old man I saw at the inn, with an ax drawn, dragged behind him because it's too heavy for his veiny arms. The last is a woman, closer to Dad's age, her hair an unwashed nest and a bow and arrow drawn to her chest.

"We got this, Comet," I murmur, though I might as well have said *you got this, Lexi,* because I need the encouragement more than this elderly, dozing dog does. I'm armed with noth-ing but a cutlass I don't know how to use, a pirate costume that doesn't quite fit, and nothing else but sheer determination that I *can* get through because there truly *is* no other alternative right now.

I tuck Comet close to my chest so my arms overlap across him, shielding him from danger, then stampede forward, straight toward my assailants.

The boy swings his sword my way and I veer to the right. Thankfully, his arms are too short to reach me, and my dodge is sufficient.

Unfortunately, it sends me right into the path of the wild-haired archer, who jabs me with an arrow while she strings it to her bow. I rush past her, head bent, and sprint toward the ship.

The older man tries to swing the ax over his head but topples backward under its weight.

The Odette Twins are ahead, watching me with sharp, focused eyes. Celeste's fingers twitch toward her sword. Unlike her cronies, I know she's got real skills. As she leaps off the deck and saunters toward me, I sprint sideways toward the marble statue. I duck around it as she swipes her sword in my direction and release a soft sigh of relief as I hear it clang against the statue's stony surface.

I slink around the back of the statue. If I'm quick, I can make it past Celeste and to the deck before she's able to regroup and take another swing. Comet nestles in my chest, and I sprint forward.

And right into Celeste's path.

She's faster than I thought, and there's a chilling, dark glint in her eyes as she marches toward me, teeth grit in a hard white line. Behind her, crew members hover around her stacks of loot—either too afraid to disobey her previous commands about arranging them, or so confident in her ability to take me down that they don't feel the need to provide backup. Neither option is very comforting, and I stagger backward toward the statue as her eyes flash at me with anger.

She swings her sword in the air and I duck—but it doesn't come back down toward me, remaining upward, its tip pointing toward the man and woman pirates carved in the marble.

"No deep-space recluse like you should *dare* use my mother as her cowardly shield," she shrieks, voice full of venom. "Our mother *never* ran from danger. She served Great Astro Bonny's mission until the end, never losing sight of her cause, even when she knew it would cost Mom her life."

I follow the tip of her sword to the carving of the unfamiliar pirate—taking in for the first time how she wears an angular hat that's a little too big for her head and giant boots that stretch up her calves and over her knees—and that mischievous, yet chilling smirk etched across her stony face. Looking at the statue now, all I see are the twins: like younger, smaller versions of the marble pirate come to life.

Her name is carved in wide, chiseled strokes beneath her feet: MARY READ. I've seen photos and sketches of her before in the book I grew up reading, and if I'd seen this statue in the book, too, it would have seemed like a testament to her legacy, how close she got to being as magnificent and grand as Astro Bonny herself. But looking at her now, all I see is a shadow of Celeste and Pictor, set in marble and trapped in place.

Pieces of the Odette Twins' story finally click in place in my mind, though they paint a picture more sinister and sadder than any I could have imagined. Comet stares up, wide-eyed, too—though probably with more interest in the pigeon sitting atop one of the statue's heads rather than the statue itself.

Celeste inhales a steadying breath, dark eyes returning to

focus. When she speaks again, her voice is less shrill but just as chilling. "When we took over this planet, I had this statue made and placed on our dock as a reminder of my mother's dedication to Astro Bonny's dream for a pirate-run solar system. It's the same cause I live for today, and that *you're* getting in the way of."

She moves around the statue, following me with steady, calculated footsteps. Comet whines against my neck and I continue to step away, circling backward around the statue of her mother.

I reach for my cutlass with unsteady hands. I have no idea how to use a pirate's weapon—and listening to Celeste right now, I feel like I don't know a thing about pirates at *all*. Because the Great Astro Bonny I read about as a little kid never tried to take over planets. She was always looking for her next adventure, setting out on her own in the dark, unexplored expanses of space.

As I circle a statue of the crew member she supposedly left for dead, I also wonder where this wicked, conquering Astro Bonny is now—and why someone as bold and fearless as her would have two kids like the Odette Twins doing her dirty work on her very own planet, while she remains safely out of sight?

Confusion tugs at the corners of my mind, sending an unsettling chill up my spine. "What if you get hurt doing Astro Bonny's dirty work, too? Would your mother really want this?"

Celeste glances at the statue—quick, like a reflex—before fixing her gaze on me, lips parted but silent. If her mother died on a mission for Astro Bonny, she didn't have the chance to tell her if the cause was worth it in the end. Maybe if Celeste asked her what she wanted now, she'd have a different answer than the one she expects.

I realize I've never asked my parents what they want, either. Maybe because I never felt I *had* to; our goals and legacy have always been so closely tied to the inn that there's been no reason to ask. But as the guests have dwindled off, and our neighbors moved away, I never considered that their answer could have changed.

Or maybe I'm scared that it has, and that's why I never dared to ask.

Celeste tightens her grip on her sword, but her arms waver a bit as she lifts it above her head. "*Want this?* We *need* this," she snarls. She lurches forward and I swing the cutlass blindly, our metal blades sliding together, saving me and Comet by one lucky inch. "With the universe expanding, all *your* astroboonie neighbors have moved to the central system. And while your little prince's family is more than happy to accommodate them, that leaves us *pirates* left starving with less loot to keep us alive!"

I swing the cutlass again but miss her sword. It swipes close—*too* close—and tears the fabric of my cloak sleeve. My heartbeat hammers in my chest, and I wonder for a moment if dying by black hole would be better than being chopped to bits by Celeste Odette.

"Great Astro Bonny is the fiercest, most powerful pirate in all of our galaxy's history," Celeste goes on, voice full of reverence and awe. It sends a subzero chill down my spine, thinking of how similar she sounds to me as a little girl, admiring Astro Bonny and her legacy from afar. "Your royals should have been *terrified* to leave her and her crews to suffer! But it doesn't matter, because we're taking back this universe—we will *not* be pushed to the outskirts or left behind!"

Dancing around the statue in a game of cat and mouse (plus dog) is only going to give Celeste's crew more time to circle in and help her corner me. If I want to steal a pod and get back on track with my mission, I need to make a move, and fast. I strengthen my grip on Comet and force myself to turn away from Celeste and look toward our destination, the dock. "Time to run at light speed, little guy."

I might not have a sword, but this new piece of Celeste's story could serve as the weapon I need to get her attention off me and onto something else. So instead of running straight toward the dock, I swerve at the last moment and knock her carefully stacked boxes of techno-loot to the ground. The cardboard smashes to the floor and an assortment of metal objects clatter across the brick street.

Celeste shrieks, properly distracted, as her precious loot scatters across the ground. I rush past her toward the ladder to the deck. With Comet in one arm, I begin to climb the ropes.

A boot slams down on the top step. Pictor Odette looms over me, hat dangling off the corner of his head and mouth slanted in a haughty smirk.

"Celeste won't be pleased about that mess," he drawls. "How should you make it up to her?"

I continue crawling up, pretending as though he's not there. Pictor plants his heel right on the top of my head and pushes back.

"It was you who sent me running all over that ice cream factory, wasn't it?" he snarls. "I'm not too fond of the astro-boonies, and I'm definitely not fond of being messed with by some deep-space townie who has no business in our feud with the prince."

His heel is sharp against my scalp, pressing down harder, harder, so my one-armed grip slips on the ladder. In a way, he's right—I *don't* have any business in his feud with Weston. I am just a girl from the astro-boonies—I don't belong here, on a pirate planet I didn't even know *existed* a few hours ago, dodging knives and arrows and fighting the Odette Twins like I'm in any way an equal.

I'm nothing compared to these adventures because before now, things like this were just stories that happened to other people. And I was okay with that—with living through the stories my guests brought, as though I could be anyone and everyone from the safety of the inn.

I still don't know what to expect even here, on this foreign planet, a royal dog clutched tight to my chest as a pirate over-lord digs his heel into the top of my head. I have no idea what comes next, or how I'll possibly rise to the challenge.

But right now, I have to believe I *can*. Because even if I'm a girl from the astro-boonies who's never traveled past the outskirts of her solar system, I've never been one to give up— especially when my home is at stake.

No matter where I am, I have to believe that that's the one thing that can never change.

I move up the ladder, forcing myself to advance one step at a time. Pictor's pressure doesn't relent, and the imprint of his shoe digs deep against my skin. But I press on, because on the other side of this pain is a pod—a pod that will lead to the amulet that will lead to Weston saving the inn and my family and my home. Teeth clenched and eyes watering, I force my way up until I stand in one final, swift motion. Pictor's heel remains pressed to my head, and with my final push upright, the foot pressed to my scalp swings in the air, causing his other leg to slip out beneath him as I stand. He quickly loses his footing and slams onto his back against the deck.

"Pod!" I shout, and release Comet to the ground. He scurries across the deck, sniffing, then stops by a box labeled SNACKS.

So that didn't work. I rush over and scoop Comet into my arms, then survey the deck.

Pictor is flat on his back but rising fast. Below, Weston is cornered against a building by the alley, Celeste's sword drawn. On the deck are stacks of boxes yet to be loaded and nothing but smooth, wooden paneling.

Paneling that, in the center of the deck, moves horizontal for several slats.

Remembering what the shopkeeper told us, a surge of hope shoots through my chest. "A secret door," I murmur to Comet. Then I spring forward and kneel before the wooden slats, digging the sharp point of my cutlass where the wood puckers slightly.

Behind me, I hear Pictor groan, recovering from his fall. He'll be back on his feet any second now to charge after me and Comet. Sweat breaks out across my temples as I wedge the blade farther between the wooden slats, desperately wiggling it in the hopes it'll burst open.

Sure, I've done my fair share of handiwork around the inn. But I've never used a tool like this before, and working under the pressure of a being a hostess versus being wanted by pirates is incomparable.

With a sudden pop, the door snaps open, revealing the compartment beneath. I'm about to lean down when the clack of approaching footsteps jolts me back to focus. Behind me, Pictor is back on his feet and moving forward, a cruel smirk sliding across his features.

Sweat beads on every inch of my skin and I feel suffocated by fear. Even if I leap into the hole on the deck and find a pod right now, he'll reach me and Comet before we're able to figure out how to fly off. I feel hot and heavy, my limbs constricted and unable to move quickly, the way I need them to.

Comet squirms, caught in my grip by the hanging sleeves of my pirate coat. It's an unintentional reminder that there may be more than one reason I feel like I weigh more than a neutron star and am sweating like I'm on the surface of one, too.

Whenever a guest spilled something on furniture and we didn't have time to fix it, Dad would have me place a blanket over it. "It's an accent piece," he'd say with a shrug.

Sometimes the quick fix is the only fix you have. And right now I try to convince myself that Pictor is nothing more than a stain on a cushion: a small, unwanted menace threatening to throw everything off. My options are limited, so I go with the only plan I have.

Which is shrugging off my oversized pirate's coat and tossing it on a real pirate face-first. Pictor stumbles back, and I pretend it's because he's caught off guard by how genius my plan is, rather than how ridiculous it is. As his hands raise to grab the coat off his head, I plant my heel in his stomach and shove him backward. Blinded by the coat, he loses his balance for the second time today and falls with a heavy thud onto the deck.

I turn back to the hole on the deck, knowing I have mere seconds to figure this out. In the hole, I see cots and folded piles of blankets. It reminds me of the empty rooms in the inn, and it sends a chill up my spine to think of how seemingly normal such vicious enemies could be. But beyond the sleeping arrangements, a smooth surface flickers from the light let in by the open door.

A pod, nestled against four others, small and compact and unoccupied. And waiting for me. For us.

"You got this, boy," I say, then release Comet down to the lower deck. He lands on his feet and saunters over to the nearest blanket, nestling against its warmth. I jump down after him, pick him right back up, and head toward the nearest pod.

The light from above is blocked, sending the lower deck into darkness. I look up to see Pictor's silhouette already hovering over us.

He scoffs. "And how are you gonna get out, townie?"

I tug the pod's door open. Comet settles onto the foot mat by the passenger's seat and I climb in. Pictor laughs even harder.

"Seriously, where do you think you're going?" he cackles.

He isn't taking me seriously. Which means I need to take myself double-serious. I whip out Weston's cracked phone and look up our last coordinates. I scan the pod's console, my head spinning like a quickly rotating planet. Before today, I'd never driven a pod by myself. I can only go off of what I've seen my fathers do, and watching Weston earlier today as well.

Once again, I'm struck by how little I know what I'm doing. But terrifying and impossible as it seems, I have no way out but through.

I tap the screen and a detailed map pops up. With shaking fingers, I type the amulet's approximate coordinates, just below the Moose Constellation. Then I slam the big red button that I hope means start and not combust.

The machine whirs to life beneath us. Comet barks and I grip the wheel, beaming.

Pictor waves his arms by the entrance. "No way out, dummy."

There *is* one way out, but it might hurt. I hold my breath and press go before I have a moment to second-guess myself. The pod shoots up, smashing through the ceiling so hard and fast that I don't have the time to scream. The deck floor splinters, wooden chips flying in all directions. Pictor shouts as we're propelled upward, past the deck, past the masts, past the flags and up to the O-Zone. I quickly pause the autopilot and swerve back down, past the ship, toward the entrance of the alleyway where I left Weston. He's standing, hat knocked off to his feet and the pirate hook from the shopkeeper held weakly in front of him as Celeste holds the sharp tip of her sword to his throat.

Not today, pirate.

I zoom toward them and swing the passenger door open. "Get in!"

Weston blinks, baffled. Comet offers an encouraging bark and leaps into the passenger seat wordlessly.

"Quick," I say, pressing autopilot back on, "shut the door!"

Weston grips the handle and pulls. Just as the door shuts, Celeste wedges herself into the sliver of an opening, the point of her sword jutting into our space.

"The *amulet*, your Highness," she gasps. "The amulet, right this instance, or I'll autopilot you three into the sun!"

An empty threat, since she can't reach the control panel. The pod shoots up, Celeste still dangling out.

Weston smirks. "I'd let go if I were you."

She holds on, hat flying off as we move upward. Her inky black hair whips behind her as we rise. Below, the village begins to shrink, each second she grips the pod adding more pain to her inevitable fall. Right now, I can't help but think that the Mary Read statue should serve as a warning to the twins rather than encouragement. But as easy as it is to think the Odette Twins are naive for following Astro Bonny like their mother did—no matter the stakes, or the cost—I know all too well what it's like to want to do anything to preserve your family's legacy.

Comet leans forward and licks Celeste's hand. She shrieks and her grip slips, sending her spiraling back down to the village below.

"Lethal licks," I murmur, impressed. Then I double the speed and we rise straight through the O-Zone, out toward deep space.

CHAPTER TEN

The pod propels through a whole lot of dark nothing. It feels familiar, surrounded by cool darkness. Like staring out the living room window, watching for distant guests. Yet now, after walking among crowds of villagers and fighting pirates—real space pirates—it somehow feels emptier than before.

As the guests dwindled and space expanded, I forgot just how *full* our solar system was. It felt weird to walk amid a crowd. Yet now, surrounded by nothing but the flickers of distant stars, I feel stranger than ever. Like I somehow don't belong.

I interrupt the eerie silence with a haughty laugh. "Impressed, prince? I just saved you from a whole ship-full of space pirates!"

Weston tugs Comet to his lap. He pets him furiously, as though unsure what to do with his hands when he's not driving. "Impressed? I'm the opposite of impressed, Lexi."

I roll my eyes. "You're going to wipe his fur straight off, idiot."

He doesn't slow his petting, though his touch lightens. "I'm not being snarky."

"So, you admit you're usually snarky."

"I'm just saying I'm not being snarky now," he snaps. "That wasn't impressive. It was idiotic."

Oh, he's being serious. I'm used to Weston being either rude or elusive. Never serious.

"Idiotic?" I say. "What was *your* plan? To let them take your dog?"

His hand pauses on Comet's back. "No, but I think it's a bit ambitious to call what you just did a plan."

I scoff. "Excuse me?"

"It was the opposite of a plan," he says. "You just ran into the street without thinking—twice! And when you got caught, you just charged straight for them! Onto the deck!"

His voice rises with each word, eyes wild and manic.

"You could have died, like, seven separate times!" he says. "And so could Comet!"

I frown. "I'd never endanger Comet."

"You *did*."

I stare ahead at the blank space beyond the front window, as though intently driving. Really, the pod is on autopilot, so I'm just staring and doing a whole lot of nothing else. "It worked out, okay? What's the big deal?"

He blinks, dumbfounded. Then he clenches his jaw and turns away. A muscle in his neck goes tight, and it's a moment before he speaks. "You don't know the stakes, Lexi. The Odette Twins aren't a joke. If they'd caught you, they could have killed you. Or worse."

"Worse?"

"They could have trapped you in a tiny pod like this," he says, "set it to autopilot on a track in slow, slow circles around a burning star."

"That's still killing me."

"Yeah, but *worse.*" He groans and slumps back in his seat. "You don't get it. You've been living this comfy life on the outskirts of the solar system, away from all of this. But for me, this is a real, daily thing. I know what the space pirates do to people. It's serious enough that my parents are seeking help from a whole other solar system. It's not a fun game of cat and mouse. It's dangerous. Deadly."

It sounds like a line from a story Dad read me. Sure, it makes my spine tingle and my skin go cold. But hearing it from Weston also makes me angry.

"What do you know about *dangerous?*" I snap. "You aren't the one out fighting pirates! Your parents' soldiers are. And even when you could have stood up and helped, you hid in the alley and left me and Comet to fend for ourselves."

His cheeks go pale.

"Sure, I grew up in the astro-boonies. But I know what it means to fight. I fight every day to help my parents keep the inn alive. I've been working since before I can remember, helping with guests, living alongside our customers day and night."

My voice cracks. Because I know that's not all. Yes, I can fend for myself. But not the way I did today. I've never experienced anything like that before—not in my wildest dreams. Not even in play with Ron.

And a small part of me knows that's why I acted the way I

did. Galaxy Jones always has a plan. But today I rushed into the thick of battle because it was there. Because I could. Because I needed to *know* I could, and that I had what it takes to live in the real world.

That I'm not just some deep-space, sheltered townie like Weston and the Odette Twins think I am.

Weston brushes his hand through his hair. After a few hours with him, I already know this is his sign of stress. Or distress. Upset. "I know. I know you've worked your whole life, and I've just been some sheltered little prince. And I know I was useless back there, and let you and Comet just—"

He bites his lip, hard enough to leave an imprint on the skin. A moment passes, then he turns to me, face hard.

"But at least your parents included you in what they do. Sure, I may have only *heard* about the space pirates. But that's because my parents won't let me know what's going on. They lock the doors when they hold meetings, and I only hear things by hiding in the library or bribing the guards to let me press an ear to the oak. Okay?"

His chest rises and falls, heaving with lost breaths. My mouth hangs open and Comet sits still in his lap.

"I didn't realize you felt that way about it," I admit, low and soft. I'd always seen Weston as spoiled—and he is. When he first visited, his parents enabled him to boss me around how he pleased. But when I was with my fathers in the kitchen the other day, talking openly and planning for the next day at the inn, Weston was alone in the yard with Comet, forgotten by his parents. I'd always thought that Weston saw the fact that I worked alongside my fathers as something that made me less than him—not something he could possibly *envy*.

But my fathers always ask me what I think and take my thoughts and feelings into account. Spoiled as Weston is, it doesn't mean he gets anything he wants from his parents. There are still things even Weston can't ask for.

Hopefully, one of those things is not giving up on buying the inn.

Weston shrugs. "It's stupid. I shouldn't have said any of that. Really."

"It's not stupid." I reach across the armrest and place my hand over his. He flinches, and I'm sure he's going to pull back. But his muscles relax beneath my fingers. "Before all of this, I had no idea just how isolated we'd become. How hard my parents must work to get us simple things like food and water. Seeing Ron's shipment, and how empty the factory was . . ."

I shake my head, wavy strands of hair brushing against my cheeks.

"There's a lot I'm not a part of, too. A whole *solar system* I'm no longer a part of. And I guess that's why I didn't think twice about running into the street, or challenging the Odette Twins. I wanted to be a part of that again. Like I used to be, before the universe grew up and left me on the outside."

I pull my hand from his and twist my fingers in my lap, neck bent down. I can't look at him now—not after what I've said. Why would I *say* all that? It makes it sound like I'm ashamed of living in the outer system, or feel responsible for what happened to the inn, or like I have to prove myself to someone like

Weston. I definitely shouldn't have to prove myself to someone like Weston.

But maybe I needed to prove something to myself. Especially after seeing how Ron and the ice cream factory have changed. After hearing about new villages and planets I didn't know existed from a friend I thought was as sheltered—and proud of the outer system—as me.

Maybe it's less about proving myself, and more about not feeling alone with myself. Like I can keep up with Ron and the rest of the solar system. Like I can change fast enough that the expanding universe doesn't leave me behind.

Something glimmers in the distance. I look up through the front window and see a sparkling collection of space dust ahead. The white and gray particles catch light from a distant star, shimmering on our horizon. The map blinks, noting we're close to our designated coordinates.

And, hopefully, the missing amulet.

The pod slows down, engine whirring softly. Comet leaps from Weston's lap and nuzzles the mat by his shoes.

"Does this look familiar?"

Weston nods wordlessly. His lips are slightly parted and he has a dazed look about him, like we left his mind a few miles back.

A bit absently, he reaches forward and taps the console screen. The map transforms into a view of the stretch of space before us. He presses a button on the corner of the screen and blinking boxes appear on the image, circling all the objects floating in space before us. Labels pop up for a few the camera identifies—like a loose space rock, and a distant mini moon—but some of the smaller pieces of space dust and junk have tiny question marks floating in a small typeface above them.

My stomach flips with anxious anticipation at the thought that one of them could be the amulet. The brackets blink like cursors on the screen, the question marks floating above the unmarked objects with the same curiosity I feel lingering inside me at the thought of finally finding the mysterious space-techno.

I press the glove box open. Inside are bundles of rope. I untangle the rope and wrap one end around my waist and the other to the armrest. Weston grabs one of the others from the glove box, but hesitates.

"Come on. It's probably around here. Right?" I press a button on the dash labeled O-ZONE. A giant, translucent orb projects around the pod, like an enormous replica of the one Comet wears. "We'll find the amulet. We've come this far, after all. And we have a deal."

In response, Weston fastens the rope around his waist.

I crack the door open and dangle one foot out into the empty nothing. As soon as I stick my leg outside the pod it begins to tilt upward, lost in the lack of gravity.

"Wait," Weston calls. "About what you said—"

I propel myself into the open air, then drift, weightless, through space. Dust floats around me aimlessly and I pump my arms, swimming through the dark. The rope waves behind me, tying me back to the ship. I swim forward, scooping my arms and pumping my legs into the cool dark nothing.

Weston leaps out after me, leaving Comet in the pod. "Hey, I was talking to you!"

"And I was looking for the amulet that *you* lost." I wiggle my legs, shimmying forward. I spin around, a bit too fast. I rotate twice before I'm facing Weston again. "How did you lose it, anyway? Since it's so important to you."

His blond eyebrows furrow. "I didn't lose it. I dropped it over the edge of the ship when I was trying to use it."

He claps a hand over his mouth. Like me, he moved too fast, so it makes a smacking sound like a slap. Part of me wonders if I should adjust the O-Zone levels. The larger part is hung up on exactly what he just realized.

"What do you mean, use it?" His eyelids flutter shut, a mixture between disbelief and dread. "So it's *not* just a piece of jewelry. What does it do? Is it space-techno?" When he continues to shake his head wearily, my voice drops to a hush. "Is it *magic*?"

His eyes flash open so he can make a full show of rolling them. "Magic isn't *real*, stupid."

A cluster of space dust drifts past me. I narrow my eyes to slits. "That's exactly what a royal who discovered magic would say."

In the empty space—drifting with dust and dropped objects as blinking stars wave from billions of light-years away—it's hard to remember magic doesn't exist. But even as we float here, suspended in the hazy nothing, the universe is stretching as though waking from a nap. An endless stretch, forever evolving. In each tiny solar system, we watch our suns rise and fall before welcoming a new day and, with it, a new version of the universe. It is not our own—it is alive, like its own sort of magic.

Science, too, is magic. I think of the boxes of stolen tech the Odette Twins hoarded. Maybe the amulet had been part of that. More than jewelry and less than magic: a sort of technology that exists on the outskirts of what we understand science to be.

Weston is no tech genius. He crashed one pod and made no objections to me driving the second one. So what item could he possibly need to use—especially one of so much value?

"The most important thing right now is finding it," he says, swooshing forward. As he passes, his heel narrowly misses my cheek. "There's a lot of shimmery crap out here, but the amulet is the only thing that will blink in the pod's headlights, since it's made of metal. It's all about looking at it from the right angle."

I float after him, eyes searching the dark for a glint or shimmer. The air is cool around us, and a tingle shoots up my spine as though someone dropped an ice cube down my shirt. The Odette Twins could come looking for us any second now, so we have to be fast and hope we really did select the right spot to stop and that one of the objects identified on the screen really is the amulet.

Weston twists his arms up and down, spiraling away from me fast. I rush to keep up with him, the muscles in my arms and legs screaming with each motion. "Wait up! You're supposed to be looking, not flying!"

I whoosh through the air, a bit too fast, and go spiraling into Weston. He's knocked onto his back, staring at what I think is *up*. "Are you serious right now? I thought I saw something, and now I—"

He blinks at the sky above. I roll onto my back to follow his gaze. Lonely stars blink back at us lazily from far-off galaxies.

"It's a nice view," I admit, "but we're in a rush. And also it's the same view we've been looking at our whole lives, so—"

"It's different. I know that star pattern." Color rises above his cheekbones. "When I dropped the amulet, I was so mad, I threw my arms up. Do you see it?" he asks, voice getting a bit giddy. "The Dog Constellation."

Here he goes again with his imaginary *Dog Constellation*. Not for the first time today, I try to see the world through Weston's eyes. But circling the stars around the antlers just makes two giant, bunny-sized ears on the constellation.

Part of me wants to push it and make sure Weston knows I'm right and he's wrong—just because I can. But another part of me finds it kind of sweet that he manages to find pieces of Comet everywhere he looks.

But a much, *much* bigger part of me is just thrilled by what his imaginary constellation signified. "This means that whatever you thought you saw—"

"Could be the amulet."

Our limbs knock together as we spin back in the opposite direction and begin pushing forward. There, drifting weightlessly among the dust and dirt, is a small, glinting object. Weston rushes forward, arms and legs flailing with desperate movements. His fingers grasp the object and he drifts back to me, beaming.

"This is it! The amulet." He looks excited enough to cry. "We did it, Lexi! We did it."

I try to mirror his smile. The shimmering gold object rests in his hands, and I can't believe it's here, just like that. That after I escaped capture from space pirates, fought the Odette Twins, and hijacked a pod, this is already over.

If it's over, that means going home. Saving my parents and the inn. And I want that more than anything.

Well, more than almost anything. Because part of me is afraid to return home after this adventure. Afraid it will feel like tugging on an old sweater I've outgrown, feeling the fabric scratch painfully against my skin.

"The Odette Twins will be after us any minute now," I say. It feels performative, like I'm trying to recapture the stakes from a moment ago. "We need to find somewhere to hide until we can return to the inn. So we can come up with a plan."

Weston nods, but his focus remains on the amulet clasped in his hands. The gold reflects in his eyes, glimmering.

There's still one mystery left to solve. Finding the amulet is one thing, but I still don't understand why Weston needed it in the first place. We're too far from the inn to make it back safely now—especially with the twins hot on our trail. We'll need to find somewhere to hide until we shake them off our route. That'll give us enough time to plan for the amulet's return to the twins on our terms—terms in which our families are let off the hook.

And maybe, in that time, Weston will let me know what this jewel is truly capable of.

My chest loosens, like a balloon deflating. It relieves me to still have a purpose. Time left in the mission.

But that relief almost scares me more than the prospect of a premature ending. If I really *am* proud of being a townie, and if I really *don't* want to leave the astro-boonies, I'd have no reason to feel this way.

Right?

CHAPTER ELEVEN

When we return to the pod, I zoom out from our coordinates in search of a nearby mass we can land on for the night. We won't make it all the way back to the inn, but we can head in the right direction, away from the pirate planet. There's a foresty planet a couple hundred thousand miles from us, with a series of slow-moving moons weaving through its orbit. I tap the planet randomly and the pod whirs to life, ready to start our new journey.

I've never driven a pod before today, but the tech is easier than most of the video games Ron and I used to play together. There are only a few buttons on the touch screen that I can't figure out—like a little arrow that dances back and forth across the top of the screen, as though loading something I never set to download.

Probably the battery self-charging, I think.

Weston grips the amulet in his lap as we set off toward the new planet. With the pod on autopilot, I can stare at the item instead of the dark space ahead. It's a golden orb with ornate carvings lining the sides and a plump, red stone protruding from the center. It's thick, though, sagging at the end of a long chain, and I wonder what kind of technology rests between its shimmering sides.

Weston rolls it over in his hands. By his feet Comet perks up, perhaps sensing his Weston's anxiety. Or perhaps sensing something about the amulet itself.

I tread carefully. "Why do you think the Odette Twins wanted it?" I ask. Though I'm way more curious why *Weston* wants it.

Weston shrugs. "I don't know. Pirates want everything, right? That's what they do. Steal *everything*. You saw how much junk they had."

As he speaks, his gaze remains fixed on the amulet. I narrow my eyes and frown.

Weston definitely knows more than he's letting on. But a green planet appears in the distance and the map blinks to announce we're approaching our destination. I'll have to dig the details out of him later—after we make our first non-crash landing.

I rub my hands together and straighten up in my seat. "All right, here we go. This is our shot to make up for our last landing."

Weston leans forward, squinting at the green planet on our horizon. It expands like a balloon as we approach at hundreds of miles at a time. "In my defense, I was unconscious for our last landing."

He reaches over, grasping for the wheel with one hand while the other maintains a steady grip on the amulet. I elbow his wrist, the right side of my body shielding the controls.

I can barely contain the smirk in my voice as I say, "If you want to perform the landing, you'll have to put down the amulet."

His grip around the object tightens on reflex, knuckles glaring white. "Even holding this, I'll land it better than you."

His free hand lunges forward, toward the wheel. I swing my shoulder just in time to block him. My hands are fastened around the wheel, so the motion sends the pod wobbling.

"Not if you can't reach the wheel," I say as the pod regains its path.

His hand remains in the air, like a snake debating between retreat and lunge. "Are you seriously going to crash us out of spite?"

"I'm not going to crash us because I'm using both hands," I say. "That's the point."

Comet whimpers by Weston's feet. We can't waste any more time arguing—even if I had hoped a little push would get him to talk about what the amulet does. I inhale a steadying breath and press for landing.

The pod doesn't move faster, but it *feels* faster as we break through the green planet's atmosphere. We spiral through the planet's gray-blue sky, toward the towering treetops below. I grip the wheel, veering us so we're aimed in a clearing at the center of the wood. It's a small bubble in the center of the thick forest. "I've never seen this many trees!"

I wish we could linger here a moment, floating in the space above the planet, so I could take in the view before I forget what it looks like.

"Just because you haven't seen a forest this big before doesn't mean you have to drive right into it!" Weston shouts back over Comet's cries, the whir of machinery, and whipping wind around us.

The air feels hot as we approach, so fast the blobs of green turn into branches and then the smooth lines of leaves. My nails dig into the soft plastic of the wheel. The planet's roaring winds shake the pod so it sways back and forth, sliding to the left and the right. I twist the wheel, aiming for the clearing, but before I regain control, we're headed straight for a treetop.

The pod shakes as we make impact against the high, thin branches. The tree's wooden limbs shake under our weight, a few twiggy branches snapping and spinning down toward the earth. The pod slips down a few feet before it's caught in a firm nook, suspended in the air around falling leaves. We dangle there, sideways, catching our breaths.

Weston speaks between gasps. "Told you I would have done a better landing."

My chest heaves, my seat belt rising and falling with each inhale, exhale. "Then you should have put down that amulet for two seconds and given it a try."

He frowns and looks about ready to say something more—*finally*. But then Comet lets out a low whine, drawing Weston's attention away. His right hand remains clasped on the amulet while his left brushes the top of Comet's head.

"What is it, little guy?"

Comet just shakes his head and whines louder. "I think the

landing may have been a bit rough on him," I say, giving the amulet a pointed glare.

Weston frowns. "Of course it was. In human years, he's basically a grandpa." The words sound funny, but his tone is sharp. Worry flickers in Weston's eyes as he runs his hand over Comet's thinning fur. "He's not going to be able to climb down this tree like us. We have to get to the landing."

I reach for the wheel. "I can do it."

Weston shoots me a desperate glance. "You just proved that you can't!"

"Well, your hands are a bit full," I remind him, a little sharply, I admit. "So I'll have to figure it out."

Weston rolls the amulet between his palms. He grits his teeth, squeezes his eyes shut, and inhales a breath so deep it sounds like a huff.

Then his eyes flash open and he turns to me, serious. "Hold this, and I'll get us out of the tree."

I gape. "You'd let me hold the amulet?"

"Don't make a big deal about it," he mutters, averting his gaze. "This is all for Comet. He can't get down from here. It has nothing to do with you."

I can't help but smile. Which is weird, because I wasn't giving Weston a hard time so he'd trust me with the amulet. I was hoping to pry some information out of him, figure out what the thing *did*. Why *he* wanted it so bad.

Yet, as the metal passes from his hand to mine, still warm from his grip, a sense of pride swells in my chest. Like, somehow this is even better than knowing the truth.

Which, again, makes no sense.

"We have to be careful," Weston says, his voice more direct and less whiney—or haughty—than it usually is. "I need to shimmy to where you are, and you need to get away from the wheel, and we have to do it all without redistributing our weight and sending this pod flying toward the ground."

"Easy enough," I say with false bravado. I grip the amulet—thick but light—in my hands and shimmy to the right as Weston makes his way to the left. I slink over the armrest, one leg squirming across the passenger seat and toward Comet. Weston carefully mirrors the motion in the opposite direction, one hand on the driver's seat and the other pressed against the dashboard. With each movement, the pod rocks in the branches, sending leaves fluttering down to the earth below.

The little arrow dances across the control panel, fast and steady as my heart rate.

We're basically hovering over our new seats, limbs tangled in the center of the body and weight propped up by our arms. "I'll sit first, since this side is pointing upward," Weston says through labored breaths. His voice is soft, as though sound itself could send us rocking straight out of the tree. "Then, once there's enough weight to the left, you can sit and we shouldn't fall out."

I nod. Weston lowers himself toward the driver's seat. His ankle brushes against mine and I slip before regaining my balance. My right foot kicks the air next to Comet's head. The old dog lets out a yelp and leaps to his feet.

His tail bats my leg. I slip into my seat before Weston does into his, and the pod slips out from between the branches.

The air knocks right out of my lungs. Weston grasps at the steering wheel as it spins uncontrollably through his flailing fingers. I clutch the amulet to my chest and close my eyes as the sounds of Comet's barks fill my ears.

I'm sure we're about to trash another pod when we swerve back upright, then slowly settle against the ground below. I open my eyes to see Weston, hands steady on the wheel and beads of sweat forming on his temples.

"You did it," I say, breathless. I'm shocked not only that he did, but that I'm so proud of him for it. Against my will, the corner of my lips spread high on my cheeks.

Despite his heavy breaths, Weston puffs out his chest. "I told you I could do it."

I roll my eyes and dangle the amulet between us. "Yeah, but you had to let go of this for long enough to manage it."

Weston snatches at the amulet. I pull back before his hands touch the metal. His eyes go wide. "What are you doing?"

"I'm not stealing it from you, dummy," I say, forcing a laugh. "But I am wondering why you're so anxious to get it back."

As though you don't trust me with it anymore, I think. Or that . . . "It's almost as if you plan on using it anyway. Even though our deal requires you to exchange it with the pirates for my parents' safety—and the safety of the inn."

Weston opens his mouth to object. His hand is still suspended, fingers itching toward the amulet. A knot forms in my chest, replacing the warm feeling I got when he trusted me with the jewel. "It's hard for me to trust you won't use it when I don't even know what it *does*."

His hand falls onto the armrest between us and he sighs. Comet whimpers at my feet, interrupted only by a soft growl. Weston reaches down and scoops the dog up into his arms, cradling him against his chest.

"Let's get Comet some fresh air," he says, chin pressed against the dog's furry back. "Then I'll tell you, okay?"

I nod quickly, feeling like I'm on the edge of something big. My stomach fills with that tingly, whooshing feeling it got just before the pod dived into the atmosphere, breaking through at hundreds of miles per hour. We pop our doors open and step out into the chilled air, the grayish sky darkening to black above us.

As Weston takes Comet over to the base of a tree to relieve himself, I lean back into the pod and blast the heat on high so warm air flows out by the open doors. As I turn the temperature module as far as it will go, I see the little arrow continue to dance across the screen, even as the pod is parked and the engine is off. Other than the heat, the rest of the dash is dark.

I run my finger over the arrow, but it continues to dance from left to right, unresponsive to my touch. I touch a few buttons, hoping to figure out what it is. Nothing comes up, and the sound of Weston's shoes against fallen leaves approaches. I climb out of the pod and sit with my back against its side, by the open door and push of warm air.

Comet settles into the driver seat and seems to immediately doze off. Weston sits beside me, back to the chair and

Comet. Weston's blond waves rustle from the whoosh of the air vents. He looks pale, the skin sunken beneath his eyelids.

"I owe it to you to tell the truth," he says, voice quiet and splintered, like the creak of an old door. "You and your parents are in this mess because of a stupid mistake I made. You've come this far to help me fix it, and . . ."

He picks at a strand of grass by his ankle, plucking the blade from the dark earth. A chilled breeze sweeps through the clearing, raising goose bumps to life on my left arm. The right is almost sweating from the hot air blowing from the pod.

Weston shifts where he's seated, squirming closer to the pod and to Comet. I feel the amulet weigh heavily in my pocket.

"I owe you a lot, I suppose," he says. I squint, wondering if I'm dreaming this. "I've been a bit of a nightmare to you since we first met. But it wasn't that I thought you deserved it— though sometimes you did."

He smirks a bit. I want to roll my eyes, but part of me is relieved to see that smile return.

"I was just . . ." He wraps his arms around his legs, drawing his knees close to his chest. "*Jealous*, honestly."

I blink. "Jealous of who?"

He rolls his eyes. "*You*, obviously."

I full-on pinch myself then, because there's no way this *isn't* a dream. "*Me?*"

"That's what I just said. Will you listen?" He groans, lowering his head as though he can keep the words from coming out. "I was jealous that you were running this inn with your parents. Not because I was jealous of your shoddy little deep-space motel." I frown, but don't interrupt. "But because you worked alongside your parents, like it was your business, too."

I think back to Weston's first visit. He tormented me at every chance he got—and he had plenty, since I was running around the inn making sure he and the other guests were cared for. Unlike the spoiled little prince, I've been working my whole life, since I was little. I'd always figured he thought that made him better than me. Apparently, he thought the opposite.

"Meanwhile, mine have always shut me out," he says, like he did earlier today. "Never let me get involved with anything, as though I have nothing to contribute. As though I'd just make it worse."

"But that's obviously not true," I say. "You did all of this with me. Retrieved the amulet, escaped the Odette Twins—"

"But you did most of the brave stuff." He rips a clump of grass from the ground, dirt sinking beneath his nails. "Even though you've never left your little rock before, you were better at this than *me*—the one who's been all over the solar system, and beyond, too."

I shiver against the cool night air. That sounded as much like an insult as it did a compliment, but considering Weston's new to niceness, I let him off the hook. He rocks back and forth, arms wrapped around himself like a one-person embrace, and the knot returns to my chest again, tighter than before. I'm on the verge of the truth, but it feels like I might be dragging it out of him—like a spool of yarn come undone.

Sweat forms on the back of my neck, beneath my thick

waves of hair as they're blown by the warm gush of air. I reach into my pocket and withdraw the amulet. Instead of dangling it before him like a treat before Comet, I drop it right into his lap.

"You don't have to tell me," I say, the knot immediately returning, but my newfound rush of guilt receding. "I trust you."

Weston rolls the amulet over in his hands. It's like a key to unlocking a door out of this conversation, out of committing to the truth. He twists the chain around his wrist but shakes his head.

"I trust you too," he says, voice quieter than I've ever heard it, as though the words are unfamiliar on his tongue. "That's why I want to tell you the truth."

He presses the pad of his thumb against the amulet's red bulb. The jewel pops open like a locket, revealing a series of wires and buttons inside, like a tiny, intricate computer.

My stomach swoops with a mixture of curiosity and unease. I've never seen anything quite like it before, but it reminds me of the strange space-techno Dad would look at in mail catalogs—or, once we stopped getting those catalogs in deep space, in my Astro Bonny photobook. The way its tiny parts whir and click as it stirs open make it seem almost alive.

"It's a device," he explains. "A space-time device. It can be used once to slow the passage of time within the diameter you enter into it." His eyes flash up, meeting mine for the first time. They're glassy and white against the dark of the woods. "Once programmed, it stops things from changing. For as long as you want."

I stare, wide-eyed, at the tiny device in his palm. My gaze traces every detail visible in the milky moonlight, trying to comprehend how anything he's saying can be true. I knew rare and strange space-techno like this existed, but reading about them in stories about Astro Bonny was totally different from being faced with the impossible reality of it up close.

The tiny device in Weston's palm holds more universe-bending power than I thought was possible. The realization sends a thrill, accompanied by a rush of cold terror, up my spine. There are endless ways it could be used—and used by the wrong person, something like that could literally bend space-time and warp everything I know and love in unrecognizable ways.

The thought makes me feel dizzy with worry and fear. My pulse flutters and all I can do is gawk and stare, my body unable to keep up with the way my mind races.

I have no idea what the pirates would want with something like this, but I'm faced for the first time with the possibility that saving my parents in the short term may not keep them safe in the long term. That as safe as deep space seems, if things like this exist—and if the Odette Twins take advantage of it—then anything is possible.

I wonder what something like this could be used for, what it's truly capable of. Thinking of the twins using it fills me with suffocating dread—but Weston wanted it too, which means it could be used for something not so sinister in the right hands.

Could something like this keep the universe from expanding? Could it slow its expansion long enough for my and Ron's families to find a way to remain in our corner of the solar system?

I shake my head, imagining the thoughts rattling in my mind and toppling out my ears. That's not what matters. Even if the amulet *could* do that, we need to exchange it with the Odette Twins for the inn and my family's safety. We need to bring it back to the inn, unused.

It terrifies me to think what the Odette Twins may do with it. But they're not here for me to ask, and Weston is. Why would a prince like him, who has the galaxy at his fingertips, need a device like this?

"You wanted this for yourself?" I bump my shoulder against his. "The last thing you need is to slow down your growth. A little maturity could do you well."

When that doesn't elicit so much as an eye roll, I know this is more serious than I thought. Weston's skin looks greenish under the light of the planet's many moons, and his chin quivers before he speaks.

"It's Comet," he says, fast as though afraid he won't get the words out. "It's for Comet."

The puppy dozes behind his head, slim body rising and falling with heavy breaths. His tail dangles over the edge of the seat by Weston's neck.

"Comet's old. Very old." Weston stares intently ahead, out into the dark wood, avoiding my eyes. "The vet said he doesn't have much longer—and that was months ago. He's losing weight, and hair, and can't walk or run like he used to."

I remember how frail Comet felt in my arms, how his

fur parted to expose patches of scalp. How Weston insisted on carrying him through the ice cream factory and has barely let go of him for a moment since. I knew Comet was old, but I didn't know he was dying. The O-Zone-headed puppy has been by Weston's side since his first visit to the inn. He's like a mascot—a part of Weston in my mind.

Knowing Weston's better half is dying, I wish I'd been a bit gentler with him when stealing the pod. That I hadn't teased Weston so much for the way he doted on him.

"This amulet could slow Comet's decline," Weston explains. "It could buy us a bit more time. And when I found out the Odette Twins had it, I didn't think of anything else. I didn't care what would happen. Because in my mind, in that moment, there was nothing worse than losing Comet. No one else trusts me like he does, or gets me like he does. He's my best . . ."

Weston squirms, shoulders rising to his ears, irked by his own sincerity. I don't push, though. I know what he was going to say. I understand it too. While Weston snagged a super-science device from space pirates to save his best friend, I made my and Ron's parents agree to rope the inn to the ice cream factory, so we wouldn't lose each other as the universe grew.

I, too, would do anything to prevent being swept away by change.

Weston doesn't say anything more, and I doubt that any prodding will make him. I reach out, brushing my fingertip over the smooth metal of the device. It's cool beneath my touch, even in the frigid nighttime air.

I wonder if it really could slow down the expansion of the

universe, even just in my corner of the solar system. If it could buy enough time to come up with a way to make the outer system what it used to be. To make it our home, forever.

"It doesn't matter," Weston says, as though responding to a silent thought. "Whatever it *could* have been used for, right now it's our key to getting those pirates out of your inn and saving our parents. Nothing more."

I shift in my spot on the ground, away from a hard twig digging into the base of my spine. Returning the amulet to the Odette Twins will save our parents, and my inn. But what will it mean for all those people we passed on the pirate colony planet?

"What do you think the Odette Twins want with it?" I ask.

He shrugs. "Something evil, obviously."

I swallow. "It's too bad we have to give it back."

He leans back, Comet's tail pressed to his collar. The dog sleeps soundly while a wet shimmer lines his human's eyes. "Yeah. Too bad."

I press my head against the sloped side of the pod and gaze up at the moon-filled, starry sky. The woods shake and rustle with each violent gust of wind, though I'm warm beside the pulsing air vents. The twinkling stars overheard blur together in my vision, smudging together into long rays of light.

Somewhere overhead, Ron and his mother fly through space in a pod stacked with boxes of crispy ice cream. He could be flying past me now, out on his deliveries, neither of us aware of when our paths aligned or when they veered apart.

The dark blanket of endless sky above is stretching like

dough, thinner and thinner with each inhale, exhale, each tick-tock second that passes. Weston holds in his hand a key—a key to slowing it down, just enough that I have time to think, to breathe, to decide what move to make next.

Just enough time to buy more rope, to tighten the knots that tie me and Ron together. That keep the inn alive and ours. That keep things as they are, as they always have been.

Weston slumps beside me, cheek against the driver's seat, Comet's tail now draped over his curly head. I fight sleep, eyelids weighted by gravity while my mind begs for one last glance at the night sky, once last chance to catch a glimpse of Ron. Of home.

They sag shut just as the amulet whirs to sleep, too, folding closed on itself as it rests in Weston's palm.

CHAPTER TWELVE

roll over a bit in my sleep, soft cushion pressed against my cheek. I sink into its gentle embrace, certain it's my pillow.

That is, until my neck slides against stiff metal and I remember I'm leaning against the side of a pod in the middle of a foreign wood.

I blink hazily, drool crusted at the corner of my lip. When did I end up lying against the driver's seat? When I dozed off, Weston was hogging the spot by Comet. I straighten up, wipe my chin, and blink as my eyes adjust to the dark around me. The heat still blares steadily from the pod's air vents, but Comet is no longer dozing on the seat cushion. And Weston is nowhere to be found.

I jolt to my feet. The clearing is empty other than me and the pod. It's so dark I don't even have my own shadow as company. My pulse rises in my throat, pounding like a drumbeat. I slip into the driver's seat, searching for a note, a sign of where they may have gone. Maybe he's just giving Comet a walk. Maybe I'm overreacting, or still in a bad dream, or . . . .

The tiny arrow continues to dance across the dash screen.

It seems brighter than ever, neon light pulsing in the dark. I squint, vision hazy against the stark contrast of dark and light.

Right now, the only things moving in this black clearing are me and this arrow. I know what I'm doing, but I still have no idea what the arrow means, or what it's signaling.

Signal. The word snags in my mind like a loose thread on a nail. We stole the pod from the Odette Twins and for all we know, it's still connected to them and their tech somehow. What if this arrow were a signal of something they were downloading onto the pod, like a crashing virus, or surveillance camera? Or a tracker?

Terror floods my body as realization dawns on me. My stomach feels like an avocado pit in my gut, heavy with horror. I spring out of the pod, muscles moving on pure adrenaline. I frantically circle the clearing, squinting into the night for a sign of Weston or Comet. Wherever they are, they have the amulet. Which means they're in danger, and that my one chance at saving my family is too.

My head pounds, pulse thumping between my temples as I spin around the clearing, searching for any sign of where Weston and Comet went. I want to hit myself, thinking of how we lay dozily with the amulet right out in the open, as though we were safe. *None* of us are safe—least of all my parents, who are trapped by the Odette Twins' cronies right now.

I remember Dad, jumping as Celeste swung her sword. Papa, exchanging a glance with the Queen in hope of finding a plan, a way out of being the pirates' hostages.

Something catches in my throat. I swallow, but the sob stays there, trembling its way up to the surface.

The silence is broken by a rustle of leaves behind me to the left. I spin around and sprint in the direction of the sound with no plan and a whole lot of adrenaline. I leap over a patch of thorny shrubs, unsure if I'll run straight into a trap, or Celeste Odette's sword. Whatever is on the other side of these woods, I'll have to face it—for my fathers' sake. For their *lives*.

I pause, listen, hear another rustle, and continue forward. Twigs crack beneath my shoes and I dodge the thick trunks that loom like chunky shadows in the dark. I can barely make out shapes, and move based on sound and feel alone.

A snarled bush catches on my tights and I tumble into the dark, arms flailing in front of me. The fabric by my shin tears and a sharp branch scrapes the skin beneath. I trip onto the rocky earth, hard dirt pressing imprints into the soft skin of my arms. I catch myself, nose just inches from smacking the ground, and gasp for breath.

Kicking myself free from the bush, I move to rise. Eyes adjusting steadily, I can now make out a single form a few feet forward: a head, turned toward me.

"Weston?"

I push up off the ground, wipe dirt from my arms. The cool night air whispers against my exposed knee and shin as I stagger forward, Weston's golden locks are barely visible in the moons' light. He's cradling Comet in one arm, who is slumped tiredly in the crook of Weston's elbow.

My eyes scan the clearing, wide and desperate. But there's

no sign of any pirates. Weston is safe, unharmed.

My heartbeat slows, but a squirmy, nauseous feeling settles in my stomach. If we're not in danger, why is Weston out here, alone? Why did he leave me back at the pod?

The moonlight captures the edge of the amulet: open, whirring, and ready for use in Weston's hand.

My lips part. I imagine my jaw hanging, all the way to the center of this grassy planet. "You were going to use the amulet."

He steps forward, eyes wide and shimmering. He's shaking his head, but doesn't explain himself. Doesn't defend himself. Doesn't say a thing.

"You were going to use it after all we did to get it back. To exchange it for my fathers' safety. Their *survival.*"

I left them behind there, with the pirates, trusting that Weston would help me save them. All this time, without realizing it, I'd been trusting Weston with my parents' lives. I thought if I was here, ushering our mission along, nothing could go wrong. Nothing could veer off track. But I'd never been on this mission alone. And because of that, I'd left their fates in his hands.

"Lexi," he says, slow and cautious. "Listen, I—"

"I thought you were in danger. I thought something had happened to you, and the Odette Twins had found us, and—" My voice sounds too loud, the only thing in these empty woods. I clench my jaw, mostly to keep from crying. "I came running to save you."

And because I, too, need the amulet. For the exchange, for my parents. As he holds Comet in his arms, I wonder which of us is the selfish one.

"Why didn't you wake me up?" I ask. "We could have figured something out together. A way to save my family *and* Comet. To save both our families. We still—"

But we can't. Because I'm the one covered in dirt and scratches while Weston stands, yards away, the amulet in his hands. He hadn't thought to wake me up, or ask for my help, or make a new plan together, because we're not friends. Weston was *never* my friend—not like Ron is. We're nothing alike, and one little adventure doesn't change that.

From the first time we met, I've been nothing more than a pawn to Weston. Someone to tease and torment back at the inn. And now someone he'd bribe so he could get what he wanted and run away before he had to fulfill his end of the deal.

"You used me," I realize. "You promised to help me find this so the twins wouldn't hurt my family. You promised we'd save my parents and you'd give us back the inn. But what you really wanted was the amulet you lost." I shake my head, hair sticking at my tearstained cheeks. "That's all you wanted this whole time."

I wipe my cheeks feverishly, wishing he couldn't see. I don't want him to know how badly I need this. How afraid I am for my parents, my home. I've already trusted him too much. Opened up to him as though we were friends.

But he's a prince and I've always been a hostess, waiting on his every need. Even when I didn't realize I was being commanded.

He hasn't changed. He's just gotten cleverer about getting me to do what he wants.

Weston takes another step forward. I mirror it, in the opposite direction.

"This wasn't some master plan of mine," he says, voice shaking. His cheeks are white in the moonlight. His lower lip trembles as he speaks, and his eyes are wide and frantic— either from guilt or—I think, heart clenching painfully at the thought—frustration at being caught. "It was just what we were talking about, before we fell asleep. It got me thinking about why I stole the amulet. And once I started thinking about it, I couldn't help but . . ."

His voice trails off. But, again, I can guess where his words are leading. He couldn't help but take it, like he did the first time from the Odette Twins. He couldn't help but want to use it, despite the consequences, despite what stealing it might mean.

I wish that when he'd felt that, he'd woken me up so we could have developed a plan, some way we could save my parents *and* save Comet. I wish he'd asked for my help, like we really were friends, and I feel stupider than ever for thinking it.

I shake my head and back up. I stumble against loose rocks and twigs but don't lose balance as I stagger backward. "I need to go," I say. Not to him, or the woods, but to myself. "I need to go to my parents. I need to help them. I've . . ."

Wasted too much time. Left them in danger. And for nothing. Just to come back empty-handed. Helpless, not a hero.

Weston shouts as I turn and sprint off, back through the woods toward the pod. Branches scrape my skin and leaves catch in my hair, but I don't stop running. I spot the clearing up ahead, feel the inviting warmth from the pod. I break through the trees, promising myself I can steer it on my own. I'll call for backup the second I have clearer service, and the royals can come fetch Weston. By then, he'll have used the amulet, but it will be up to the royals and their guard to deal with the Odette Twins. *Not* my fathers, who are innocent in all of this.

I leap into the driver's seat. Then something grasps my ankle.

I kick, shaking off whatever bit of bramble I've carried from the woods. But the tight grip on my leg doesn't loosen. I look down and find not a bramble, but a rope lassoed around my heel. I let out a shriek just as its owner gives a hard yank and I'm dragged out from the seat and onto the earth with a thud.

I topple to the ground and am dragged across the clearing. Terror clogs my throat, and I can't find the air to scream. I dig my fingers into the dirt, but it barely slows the pull of the rope and all I get is a whole lot of gunk beneath my nails. I roll over, kicking and flailing desperately, and see the Odette Twins emerge from the dark of the woods.

Celeste stands, tall and smirking, while Pictor grips the rope. Their ship looms overhead, blocking the light from one of the planet's many moons.

"You didn't turn off the tracker," Celeste says with a laugh.

The little arrow dances in my mind. Realization washes over me like an uneasy sweat.

"You thought you could outrun us, and you didn't even know how to turn off the tracker."

Pictor laughs loud and hard, like a hydrogen-filled hyena. He gives the rope a tug and I slide toward them like a fish on a line.

Celeste's face goes serious. "Now, before I shoot you into a supernova: where is the amulet?"

I prop myself up on my elbows and push to stand. Pictor yanks the rope so I topple back over. "I don't have it. It's . . ."

I stare past the twins, out into the dark woods. The trees are still, silent. Weston is out there, hiding. Leaving me for the twins as a distraction, a sacrifice, while he runs off with the amulet.

It's out there, with Prince Weston, I think.

Yet I say, "I don't know where it is."

The twins exchange an amused glance. Pictor tightens his grip on the rope.

"Is that your final answer?" Celeste drawls.

"All I want is to go home," I say, voice rising and frantic. I wonder if Weston is just beyond the trees. If he can hear me. If Comet is squirming in his arms, wanting to run to my side. "I just want to go back to my parents and forget any of this happened. I don't care about the amulet. You can find it and you can take it, okay? I just want to go home."

Pictor flicks his fist by his eye as though wiping a giant tear. "I just want to go home!" he mimics in a singsong voice. "I just wanna go home!"

Celeste throws back her head and laughs. Her hat is pushed so far on her forehead, it doesn't budge with the motion. "This solar system is basically ours now. This planet is ours, these moons are ours—your *inn* is ours." She smiles, lips curling like a bow on her cheeks. "So, in a way, if you're with us, you are home."

She steps forward, boot crunching a twig beneath her heel. Pictor tugs the rope so I'm pulled forward, the distance between the three of us closing.

"Now," she says, voice icy and low, "I asked if that was your final answer."

Her eyes are cool and steely, pupils dark as the galaxy above. My throat feels tight, as though the rope were tied around my neck rather than my ankle. This is my last chance to escape. To trade Weston's safety for mine, like he traded my parents' safety for the amulet.

But I grit my teeth and shake my head.

Maybe I do it for Comet, so the evil twins don't get their gloved hands on him. Maybe I do it for Weston, because as mad as I may be, I also understand his motivations—more than I'd like. Or maybe I do it for me, to clear my conscience before I leave this chapter behind once and for all.

Whatever the reason, it's done. The pirate ship lowers overhead, its looming shadow spreading until it swallows the clearing. A wood-and-rope ladder flies over its side, clanking against the edge of the boat as it swings down to us.

I scramble to my feet, tripping over the loose rope, and I grab onto the ladder. I climb as her blade follows my movements, my head tilted up to the edge of the ship. Crew members lean over, peering down at me with greedy smiles, their laughter carrying through the night.

I have no idea how I'm going to get out of this, but it's too late to change my answer now. And for whatever reason, I'm not sure I want to.

CHAPTER THIRTEEN

I slowly wake from a deep sleep, drowsiness threatening to tug me back under like a sonic wave. My eyelids feel heavy, and I'm dreading opening them. Because as soon as I do, I'll have to face the reality of my situation *and* deal with it.

Right now—temples throbbing and muscles whining in protest as I roll onto my back—my capture feels inevitable. How did I ever trick myself into believing that Galaxy Jones stood a chance on this adventure?

I open my eyes, blinking against the light filtering in from one small, square window at the corner of the room. Blearily, I take in my surroundings, blinking over and over again because the more I see, the more I feel like I must still be asleep.

I expected to wake up in a dank cell, space roaches scuttering over my ankles. Or in a tight coffin that's already been thrown overboard, spinning helplessly through space. Or even inside the cannon back on the pirate planet, forced to listen to Celeste and Pictor count down before the fuse blows and I'm shot a hundred galaxies away.

Instead, I'm surrounded by images from *The Great Space Pirate Astro Bonny Unofficial Photobiography*.

There's a photo collage on the wall, depicting everything from her triumphant pose on the front cover to the pencil sketches scribbled by travelers lucky enough to spot her out in space. There's a quilt made of newspaper clippings thrown over the bed I'm lying in, featuring headlines ranging from Astro Bonny's renegade days to her current sinister takeover. And in the center of the room by the closet is a large glass box with her iconic cutlass on display inside.

The confusion morphs to awe and quickly fades to panic. The threat of Astro Bonny and her apprentices has driven this entire adventure so far, but I didn't think I was close to *actually* meeting her—let alone that I could be held in *her* capture. Even when I imagined going on adventures like her as a little kid, I never, *ever* wanted to cross paths with the pirate herself.

Though right now—surrounded by articles about her famous duels with rival pirates and scrimmages with the royal guard—I wonder where she *has* been this entire time. Because in everything I used to read about her, Astro Bonny always led her own missions. She didn't assign kids like Celeste and Pictor to run them for her.

Once again, I'm reminded I never understood her legacy at all.

The door swings open so abruptly, it smacks against the wall, knocking a framed photo of Astro Bonny askew. I let out a shriek so high it'd probably make Comet's ears hurt. But I feel the smallest, tiniest, micro-sized bit of relief when I realize it's just Celeste in the doorway and not the Great Astro Bonny herself.

But again, I wonder where Astro Bonny *is*. If she wants this amulet for her plans so badly, why hasn't she shown up yet?

"Like my decorations?" Celeste asks, almost giddy. "It's much more terrifying than a regular old prison cell, isn't it?"

She gestures to the quilt at my ankles. The words *liquefied* and *spaghettified* jump out at me.

I swallow. Fear claws its way up my throat, but at the same time, there's something eerily familiar about this room. I was never *this* obsessed with Astro Bonny's legacy, but most of the things here were in the book I grew up reading, or in stories I hear about her on the news. But while I grew out of my Astro Bonny obsession when she turned into a villainous planet conqueror, Celeste's obsession only grew and grew.

Even after it cost her mother, Mary Read, her life.

"The only thing scary about this room is how pathetically obsessed you are with Astro Bonny." I say it as quick and snarky as I can, as if I'm bickering with Weston rather than facing off with an armed space pirate. But I don't have much to fight with right now, and our shared obsession with Astro Bonny is all I've got. "Why should I be afraid of *you* when you're threatening me with facts about a woman who isn't even *here?*"

Celeste steps into the room, fingers curling into fists by her sides. I'm not sure if I should see her reaction as a victory or as foreshadowing for my imminent death. But I try not to think at all, talking fast so the worries can't catch up to me.

"You'll never be her," I say. "*No one* can ever be her. And chasing her shadow is what got your mother *killed*. Is that really what you want for you and Pictor, too?"

Guilt swarms my body at the words. But Celeste's expression doesn't fall. In fact, that chilling, stony smirk slides easily across her face.

"That's *rich* coming from you," she snarls. She paces toward me and I beg my muscles to stay put, even though I want nothing more than to yank up that quilt and hide as far from her cutting gaze as I can. "The little deep-space townie," she drawls mockingly, "so desperate to get back home to her daddies and stay trapped on her safe little rock till the day she dies."

She slams her palm on the glass display box. I jump, muscles finally betraying me.

"At least my mother did something *great*," she cries, acid leaking in her voice. "Astro Bonny was so impressed by her contributions to the cause, she gifted her with her iconic cutlass."

Celeste's fingers drum against the glass, and suddenly I can't look anywhere but at the sharp-tipped sword behind it. All she has to do is break that glass and swing the weapon, and she could slice me to pieces. If our last duel proved anything, I'm scrappy but without skill. Fueled by nothing but desperation. And now, without even Weston and Comet by my side, facing Celeste feels downright impossible.

The longer I look at the cutlass, the more uneasy I feel. Which makes sense, considering Astro Bonny used it to behead much more fearsome space travelers than me. But also because it just *doesn't make sense* that she could give away her precious cutlass.

"That doesn't sound like something Astro Bonny would do," I say. Celeste raises an eyebrow, and it vanishes fully beneath her low-brimmed hat. "Giving away her most prized possession, I mean."

Celeste shakes her head. "Of *course* it makes sense. Mary Read was her most dedicated follower, and she gave this to her the last time they saw each other—before Mom died valiantly in a battle against the royal guard."

She puffs her chest out at the last words, but it doesn't hide the way her voice wavers, choked at the end. A surge of pity runs through my chest, alongside a deep, now too familiar fear that I, too, may not get to see my parents again.

"It just . . . it doesn't sound like the Astro Bonny I grew up reading about," I say. "She worked alongside others, sure—but she was a *pirate*. She took and *pillaged* and did whatever *she* wanted, with or without the help of anyone else."

It's another reminder that I'm nothing like Astro Bonny— that I never was, and never could be. Because as much as I wanted to think I could be brave and valiant and fearless on my own, right now I feel completely and utterly *lost* without the comfort of having Weston and Comet by my side.

Thinking of Weston and Comet forms a lump in my throat, the image of Weston and the amulet shooting through my mind like a star. But that love he has for Comet—it reminds me of the way Astro Bonny treasured her parrot. And how impossible it seemed that she would ever make drones that looked like him work for her.

Weston loved Comet as family. Weston would never make

even a Comet *drone* do dirty work for him. And maybe Astro Bonny never loved anything at all, including her parrot. But I feel unsettled, watching the image of Astro Bonny falling apart like a jigsaw puzzle scattering.

"Astro Bonny's legacy was about being *free* and *untamed*, not about conquering and dictating," I go on. "Why would she ever want to take over planets and be tied down by them? Why would she willingly give up the thrill of the unknowns in this world by making everything she touched no better than an Astro Bonny theme park?"

I swing my legs over the edge of the bed, ignoring the way they wobble beneath me. Because Celeste is right: I *can't* know what it's like to be great like her mom was, and I *am* just a girl from the astro-boonies. But because of the inn, I've *met* great people, and listened to their stories. I lived off tales of their adventures, rushed through the chores set by my parents so I could sit with guests at dinner and collect their stories the same way Astro Bonny collected her loot.

Because I'm just an innkeeper, I know people. And right now, Celeste's version of Astro Bonny isn't adding up.

"Whatever version of Astro Bonny you're following now isn't even the one who was *great* in the first place," I say. "I get it; I used to admire her too. But she's *changed*, and for the worse. And if you keep following her down this path, she's just going to ruin you, too."

I stand straighter, feeling like I've just said something brilliant and compelling. But Celeste just throws back her head and laughs like a hyena. "Says the girl who ties her entire identity to a dingy, empty, failing inn the entire galaxy has *forgotten* about!"

Her words hit me like a slap. Because as much as she's nothing like the Great Astro Bonny I read about as a little girl, I'm nothing like the innkeeper I was back then, too. The people I met stopped coming, taking their stories and adventures with them. Even my neighbors left—Ron, too, in his own way, both as the factory drifted farther away before we roped it, and now that he's off doing deliveries in parts of the universe I've never seen.

I'm not a larger-than-life traveler like Astro Bonny, but I'm also not really an innkeeper anymore, either. Right now I feel like a cluster of unformed space particles, made of pieces floating aimlessly without taking shape.

Yet seeing Celeste standing along beside her mother's cutlass, I wonder if fighting too hard to be one thing is just as scary.

"I didn't capture you for the entertainment, townie," she continues. "You're part of my plan to get the amulet back."

The mention of the amulet sends a cool sweat across the back of my neck. That image of Weston in the woods flashes through my mind again, and I wonder how long it took for him to notice I was gone. If he was scared or worried for me.

The thought fills me with a mix of guilt and hope.

"I saw all your space-techno loot back on your planet," I say. "All sorts of weapons and devices. What could Astro Bonny possibly want with the amulet?"

Celeste knocks her knuckles on the low ceiling above, and I hear the scuffle of footsteps overhead on the deck. Whatever she has planned for me is happening *now*, and there's nothing I can do to stop it. My legs give out and I fall back onto the bed. Muscles petrified from fear, I squirm against the quilt, feeling smaller than this mission, smaller than all the epic headlines about Astro Bonny's escapes that are woven into the fabric around me.

"Acquiring the amulet is the final piece to Astro Bonny's plans," Celeste says as the scurry of footsteps draws nearer, "and the final task she assigned to our mother before she passed. That amulet is the *key* to our ultimate takeover, and fulfilling Astro Bonny's legacy as our mother planned. And either we fulfill that legacy today, or you die the pointless, forgetful death you deserve."

The door bursts open and a pair of broad-shouldered pirates squeeze their way through the doorframe, their fiery, bloodshot eyes fixed on me. "To the deck!" Celeste calls, and they grasp my arms like tiny toothpicks in their grip, lifting me clean off the quilted bed.

Fear clogs my throat, and there's no way I can talk my way out of this. I'm not brave enough to think straight in the face of danger. Not strong enough to fight back against these pirates twice my size. I'm just a sheltered little townie who wants her dad to hug her and her papa to promise she's safe. I'm nothing like Astro Bonny, as she was or as she is now.

They yank me up the narrow stairs toward the deck, and I'm gripped with a vise-like certainty that I'm about to die. And I wish, not for the first time since being captured, that I hadn't run away from Weston before hearing him out.

CHAPTER FOURTEEN

I stand, tied to the ship's thick, wooden mast. Billowing sails flutter overhead, a rough wind whipping through the O-Zone projection as we travel through space. The scratchy rope paints red blotches on the bare skin of my arms and elbows, but I wriggle nonetheless, imagining that if I manage *just* the right position, I'll slip free and make my escape.

The ropes are the least of my problems, though. The deck is flooded with crew members, eyeing me from the forecastle and sitting on the stairs as they swig from dark bottles and toss the caps at my feet. Even if I somehow managed to free myself from the ropes, I'd have a whole crew of space pirates to get past before I'd make it to safety. Even then, I have no pod with which to make my escape.

Celeste and Pictor emerge from the bottom deck, shoulders back and heads high. They stand upright and firm, everything sharp, dark lines except their perfectly slanted smirks. Celeste's sword dangles lazily from her hand, though I know her pale white fingers could tighten around the handle in an instant and the blade would be right by my neck once again.

I lean back against the pole, imagining that I can become one with the wood until I'm nothing but a carving of a scared little girl.

Because right now, that last part is exactly what I am.

The twins saunter toward me, maintaining a few feet between us when they finally stop, heels clanking against the wooden floor. A hush sweeps over the crew and they watch with attentive eyes. It's the same look Dad wears when we watch scary movies: queasy, but intrigued.

Celeste swings her arm. The sword sways back and forth, sharp tip scraping the floor. "There she is. The key to reclaiming our amulet."

I squirm against the ropes. The tough fabric burns my skin. There's a hungry look in the pirates' eyes that makes me feel like the appetizer before a big meal. I am far from having a plan, so I at least need to stall until I get my thoughts together to make one.

"Why do you want it, anyway?" I ask, my tone a bit mocking. "Back on the grassy planet, you were bragging about how you basically own the entire solar system. So why do you need an ugly, tacky little jewel?"

Her nose crinkles and her face goes dark. Regardless of what they plan to do with the amulet, I know Celeste doesn't want a townie like me critiquing her loot.

Pictor, on the other hand, is laughing. "Did the little prince really not tell you what it was?"

"He did," I say, fast. Too fast. As if the tables have already turned on me, and now I'm the defensive one. As if the flimsy fabric that ties Weston and I together—that I thought was friendship—is now my sore spot. "But that's what makes even less sense. Why do you need to slow time down, when you're trying to speed up your takeover of this solar system?"

I stare pointedly at Celeste. Her ego's more likely to make her spill than Pictor's giggly amusement ever will.

Sure enough, her stony expression has only hardened. Celeste saunters toward me, closing the distance between us. A few crew members let out *oohs* and *ahs*, and one spits his drink down his front. She raises her sword so the tip pinches the soft skin beneath my chin. I want to tilt my head up but know she'll just keep raising the blade until it's right through my throat.

When she speaks, her voice is low and slow, as if she'd swallowed the amulet and it was stuck in her vocal cords. "We're going to slow time down so much that by the time we switch back, it'll be like we conquered the universe in a *day*," she declares. "No, an hour! A *second!*"

Her sword rises with each exclamation. It pierces my skin, sharp like a needle prickle, and I can't help but let out a yelp.

"We're going to stretch time until we snatch up every corner of this solar system," she says, eyes glimmering, "then live out the rest of our days as your leaders! In the name of Astro Bonny."

The crew leaps to their feet and shout out cheers over the sounds of the whipping sails and toppling bottles. Pictor throws his head back and lets out a cry of victory, as though they already had the amulet.

Speaking of which. I shimmy up a bit, relieving my skin

from the press of her blade. My voice is tight and quiet as I say, "There's nothing you can do to me that will get you that amulet back. You're wasting your time here."

I let out a grateful sigh when Celeste's shoulders relax and her sword lowers from my throat. She releases a gentle laugh. "No, no—*you're* what's going to get it back for us. For once in your small, townie, outer-system boonies life, you're going to do something useful."

I suck in my cheeks. "There's nothing I can do to get it back that you can't."

If I could, I wouldn't be here. I'd be home, at the inn, with my parents. Like I was supposed to be if things have gone to plan.

If things had gone to *my* plan, that is. I'm starting to realize the agreement Weston and I made probably wasn't a part of *his* plan all along.

Celeste turns to her crew, spinning on her heel so her coat swings at her knees. They stand at attention, snapping into focus. A lump rises in my throat as I realize the torture is about to begin.

But there's nothing I can tell her about the location of the amulet that she doesn't already know. It's somewhere on that planet, with Weston. And, if he's already used it, it'll be useless now, too.

What could torturing me possibly accomplish? I have no hidden truths to spill.

"Untie the captive and bind her wrists," Celeste commands. "Then . . ."

Her voice trails off and she gestures theatrically to her brother. With dramatic flair, he shouts, *"Take her to the plaaaaaaaaaaaaaank!"*

Within a fraction of a second the crew is on me, swarming my pole and closing in like a heavy shadow. My eyes nearly bug out of my head and I start to sputter. Forget torture—killing me definitely won't do anything! It won't help them get the amulet back at all! I know this for a fact, and that it's quite a compelling case for my survival, but my tongue feels heavy and foreign in my mouth, and I can't seem to form the syllables I need. All I can think about are the sweaty palms fastening my arms to my sides, and the heavy heels pressing my feet into place, and the meaty arms tearing the rope from my middle as I'm released from the pole. I stagger forward as though in zero gravity, and within an instant my arms are twisted behind my back and my wrists are roughly pressed together. Rope—even tighter than before—binds my hands behind my back.

Someone gives my shoulder blade a shove and I stagger forward. The crew members part so as I regain my balance, I'm standing right before the twins.

"Go on," Celeste mocks, pointing her sword toward the edge of the boat.

Pictor wiggles his thick brow. "To the plank."

"To the plank!" the crew members chant, and Celeste jabs her blade at my back—hard enough to draw blood—and I scamper forward, toward the plank.

Fear rises in my throat and a sweat breaks out across my

forehead as if I were walking on the surface of a burning star. I wish I could crawl back under the deck and curl up in that Astro Bonny quilt until I dream that I'm home again, reading stories about pirates from the safety of Dad's arms. Anywhere rather than *here*, facing off with them myself, a nameless victim in the pages of a bedtime story about someone else's great adventure.

I cross the deck and arrive at the tiny set of stairs leading to the plank. It's a wooden, wobbly thing, bouncing along as the ship soars through space. I plant my heel on the first step, then turn back toward the twins. They stand behind me like a wall, blocking my way to safety.

"I don't understand," I say. My mouth remains open, as though waiting for something a bit cleverer, but really, that's all I've got.

Pictor nods to the plank. "Go on, then. Take a look."

This could be a trap, and a flimsy one at that. What cat is so curious they really are killed by a phrase as simple as "take a look?" Yet their giddy smirks suggest there really is something more, and I might as well know my full situation before I solidify my nonexistent escape plan. So I take the last steps until I'm standing at the edge of the plank, high enough to peer over the side of the boat.

The plank juts out into empty space. But when I look down, far below the ship, I see an orangey orb of light spinning in the distance. The light swirls and stretches, like liquid pouring down a drain. The blurry rays circle a coal-black core positioned dead center in the dancing lights. The orange, glowing streaks vanish as they reach the center, sudden and thorough as though they'd never been there in the first place.

I feel weightless, as though I could drift up from the edge of this plank and float off into deep space. It's like staring into a nightmare, like remembering the feeling right before I woke up shouting for Papa with fistfuls of blanket in my grip. My throat is tight, as though a fist were clamped around it. My eyes are watery, my skin hot, searing hot like the surface of a star.

I want to move, want to scream, but all I do is stare. Because I've never seen one this close, and I can't believe it's real.

That I'm about to walk a plank into a black hole.

Pictor rubs his hands together. "I've *always* wanted to toss someone into a black hole. Just like Astro Bonny!" He steps closer. The muscles in my knees twitch with fear. "And here we are doing it just for her! A sort of ribbon-cutting ceremony for the amulet's return."

Celeste jabs her sword into my back. A damp sweat trickles down my temple, and my voice is shaking as I ask, "How will sending me into a black hole get you the amulet?"

Celeste quickly explains, "You're disposable enough that it doesn't matter if you fall in or not. But hopefully the prince won't let things get that far."

My stomach falls. I imagine it dropping straight out of my body and being sucked up by the black hole, followed shortly by the rest of me. "What does Weston have to do with this?"

The twins exchange a glance, excited to share their master plan. "He still has a pod," Pictor says. "And just like we were able to track you, we made sure he was able to track us."

"The ships are connected by our technology," Celeste explains. "If we allow it, that is. And in this case, we did! Even the audio."

I stare, eyes wide as moons. "He's listening? Right now?"

Her lower lip puffs out. "If he's in the pod, yes. And we have no doubt that he is."

Pictor plants his hands on his hips, juts out his chest. "Because we're certain he'll come running to save his little friend!"

Celeste smiles, full and chilling. "*And* hand over the amulet in exchange for your life."

They stare at me expectantly, proud grins strapped on their faces. My heartbeat quickens like a pod on hyperspeed.

They took me instead of searching the woods for Weston, probably because roughing up an outer-system townie would cause a lot less backlash than roughing up the prince himself. I'm a bartering tool to save them some time and trouble while providing a bit of plank-walking amusement.

But. *But.*

My voice is hushed, syllables splintered. "You're saying my life depends on *Weston?*"

Something rough and coarse escapes my lips. A laugh. It opens the gateway for several more and within seconds, I'm laughing hard enough that my stomach aches.

"You think *Weston* is going to give up his precious amulet for my sake?" I ask. "Weston never worked with me. The whole time, he was using me! Working *against* me. The amulet is useless by now—he's already used it for his own reasons, and you'll never be getting it back. And if he's in a pod right now, he's on his way home with the sound turned down so he doesn't have to be bothered by my voice any longer."

I shake my head, a few soft, higher laughs escaping my lips. "He was never my friend. Which means you've been fooled just as I have."

Celeste and Pictor exchange a glance I can't read. The black hole swarms below me, hungry and waiting. I have to act fast.

"Making me walk the plank won't fix anything," I insist. "The amulet is gone. You've already lost."

The twins' eyes remain locked. Then Pictor turns to me and shrugs. "You can walk the plank anyway. We'll see what happens."

Celeste nods. "*We've* got nothing to lose."

I stare, gawking. She raises her sword.

"That means *go.*"

I step forward, the plank unsteady beneath my feet. It's hard to walk straight and balanced with my arms bound behind me. I raise my left foot cautiously, feeling myself tilt as I rely on one foot. I plant it down, one step ahead, and begin my trek forward. My limbs quake unsteadily with fear, and every muscle in my body begs me to turn and run back to safety. But Celeste's blade remains pressed to the small of my back, forcing me forward.

The plank wobbles beneath my weight. I stand toward the edge, the black hole spinning below me. I close my eyes, blocking out the crew's laughter, Pictor's hoots of joy, Celeste's incessant monologue. If I focus hard enough, I'm back home, at the inn. I'm staring lazily out my window, watching the rope that ties my home to Ron's bob back and forth, moved by the tension of an ever-expanding universe. I'm in the kitchen with Papa, flour caked on my hands and every flat surface, the smell of fresh cookies tickling my nose. I'm by the telescope with Dad, hear the clink of his spectacles against the eyepiece as he edges for a closer and closer look.

I'm crammed in a pod, Weston at the wheel and Comet dozing at my feet. And despite myself, I'm laughing, warm and bubbly and light, as though that was home, too.

My toe dips. I open my eyes and see nothing ahead but the hazy glow of the O-Zone projection and the dark blanket of space beyond. Glancing down, I see the tip of my shoe aligned with the swarming black hole, its arms of light gesturing me forward.

"Guess you'll have to jump after all," Celeste drones. "Oh, what a waste."

I bite my lip. Down there, I'll be peeled apart, molecule by molecule. I'll be melted like butter on a hot piece of bread until there's not a shred of me left.

I'm about to be torn from existence. All because I let myself be conned by a thieving guest.

My foot dangles over empty space. Then a rough crash rocks the boat.

I topple to the right, barely capturing my balance before I'm thrown off the plank. I spin around to see Celeste gripping the side of the ship, her other hand clasped around her sword as it dangles dangerously over the black hole below. I follow

Pictor's gaze to the smoking pod that's wedged in the center of the deck, cracked wooden boards and splintery pieces poking up around it.

And then, one sound: a bark.

Comet's bark.

I walk forward so I'm at the center of the plank, squinting through the smoke and debris as the pod door swings open. A scratched, dented black shoe, with just a sliver of remaining polish, plants a heel onto the broken floorboards.

There, stepping out onto the Odette Twins' deck, is Prince Weston.

CHAPTER FIFTEEN

Celeste beams. Her sword remains angled at me as she turns to face Weston. "You came after all, little prince!"

Weston stands in front of the pod door, gaze fixed on Celeste. His eyes are unrecognizable, hard and stony as they bore into the armed twin. Comet rests on the driver's seat behind him, droopy eyes attentively watching the scene, though he makes no moves to follow his human onto the deck.

I try to catch Weston's gaze—to figure out what brought him here and decipher his plan—but his eyes remained fixed on Celeste. The amulet is nowhere to be seen and his hands hang, empty and tense, by his sides.

Pictor stretches a hand into the open air. His fingers wiggle greedily. "Come on, then. I'm sure you heard it all. Pass the amulet over and we'll let the townie go."

Perfect chance for Weston to make eye contact and give me just the kind of look that lets me in on his whole plan. But his focus remains fixed on Celeste.

"Lower your sword, will you?" he says, voice sharp and scathing. "We're trying to make a civilized exchange here."

Celeste chuckles softly. "Oh, so sorry, Your Highness," she drawls. "I forgot my manners!"

Pictor grins slyly. "And that you still think it's *you* who rules this universe," he scoffs.

Celeste's arm lowers, angling the sword away from me. But she keeps it in her hand and sways it back and forth, reminding us she can strike at any moment.

"Now," she says, tone turning dark. "The amulet."

"Not before we set ground rules."

Pictor rolls his eyes and puts on his best singsong voice. "We *promise* not to send your friend into the black hole. With all our hearts, we *promise*, Your Majesty!" His fingers wiggle again, faster than before so his knuckles audibly crack. "Now: amulet, pretty please!"

Weston doesn't budge—barely blinks. For the first time, I see a bit of the Queen in him. "I'm not lifting a finger until you've let her off that plank."

My mind spins as though filled with loose puzzle pieces. As the twins consider, I scramble to figure out Weston's plan.

The amulet is broken. He probably used it as soon as I left. So perhaps he'll start to hand it over and, just as they realize it's in use, we'll take off with it and come up with a new plan.

But even that doesn't make sense. There's too much risk with confronting the twins, and if Weston already used the amulet, there's no reason for him to come back for me.

I was sure Weston had some master plan, but it's looking more and more like the Odette Twins were right: that threatening me with a black hole was enough leverage to get the amulet back from Weston. But after all that's happened, it doesn't make sense.

He could have saved Comet. Why is he here, saving *me?*

I look past Weston, at the old dog trembling in the front seat. I thought Weston had betrayed me when he went to use the amulet. He stole it to save Comet, and had he not dropped it in deep space, and had the Odette Twins not tracked him to the inn, he would have used it days ago. But once my family— and his life—were at stake, I'd made him promise to turn it over in exchange for my parents' safety.

In a way, I'd done the same thing he tried to do. If he was selfish, I was just as bad. But at least he'd been a good enough friend not to give up on me. I, on the other hand, had lost all faith in him. I hadn't given him a chance, and yet he'd come all this way to face the twins. To come to my rescue.

Celeste flicks the sword, a gesture for me to step forward. I ease my way across the plank, one careful step at a time. The black hole feels like a giant, dark eye watching behind me, its gaze boring into my back. It's not until I'm descending the small steps that relief floods my chest. I inhale a deep breath, as though finding the O-Zone projection's oxygen for the first time.

Pictor steps forward, arm outstretched. Weston ignores him, attention still on Celeste. "Before I turn it over, I need one more promise."

She huffs. "I can still toss her into that hole, you know."

Weston scowls. "Your remaining crew members will evac-uate the inn," he declares. "They'll leave the Jones family alone, and they won't be bothered by you or your crew again."

The twins exchange a glance. Then they shrug in unison.

"Of course," Celeste says. "I wouldn't want to torture any of my crew by making them remain in the boonies."

Pictor cackles. Then his face goes hard. "Amulet, now."

Celeste clamps her free hand around my elbow. Her fingers pinch my muscles as she marches me forward, toward Weston for the exchange. My hands remain tied behind my back, the rope scraping the sore indents in my skin.

Weston reaches into his back pocket and withdraws the amulet. It's closed. Unused. The jewel catches light from a distant star and blinks gently in its glow. He doesn't look at it, but I notice his hand tremble as he prepares to hand it over.

The next words tumble off my tongue so fast, it's like they've been poised there all along. "Don't do it."

Part of me wants to gulp the words back. Part of me wishes I'd said them sooner.

My chin trembles. "Just . . . save Comet."

Weston finally turns to look at me. I recognize a flicker of fear in his eyes, emotion welling behind the walls he's built around him.

"This isn't the way," he says. "Comet would agree. This isn't the way."

He holds the amulet out to Celeste. She releases my arm and snatches the loot from his grip.

After that, things happen in a flash.

The crew begins to cheer and crowd around us. Celeste tosses the amulet over her head and Pictor, with choreographed ease, captures it in his outstretched palm. She draws her sword and lunges for us. Weston yanks me to his side and pushes us both into the pod. The door slams behind us and, even though we're a tangled mess of limbs (both human and puppy), Weston turns the pod on and hits drive. We soar up from the deck, past the masts, through the O-Zone projection, and away from the ship. Our hurried retreat doesn't matter, though. When I look back, I see the twins huddled together, attention fixed solely on the amulet in Pictor's hands. But even though we're no longer being chased, Weston puts the pod into high speed, and we shoot up into the sky. I've barely had a moment to catch my breath by the time we're back to soaring through deep space, far away from the Odette Twins and far away from the amulet.

CHAPTER SIXTEEN

I straighten up in my seat, feet settling onto the mat below. Even after just a few minutes on the plank, I'm craving solid ground. I stomp my heels a bit, but nothing wobbles beneath me. The floor will not open up, no black hole will consume me.

I'm safe. That seems surreal enough, but knowing it's due to the most spoiled prince in the galaxy making a personal sacrifice really pushes my mind over the edge. My thoughts zigzag and squiggle, and all I can do is keep lifting and replanting my heels against the carpet to remind myself I'm okay.

The tracker is off on the dashboard, and Weston has entered the coordinates for the inn. We're zooming forward, thousands of miles at a time, back to home. To my parents, who should be safe now. Whom the Odette Twins will leave alone, because Weston gave up the amulet for good.

The solar system is dark around us. A few stars blink hazily in the distance. A distant, lonely spacecraft zooms in and out of vision on the horizon. The quiet is thick like a fog. It feels surreal that—for the first time in days—the Odette Twins aren't chasing us. I squeeze my eyes shut and conjure an image of them in my mind, hunched over the amulet and indifferent to our abrupt departure. There's no reason for them to chase us anymore, but my spine still tingles with the sensation that we're being watched.

Comet rests idly on the armrest between the driver and passenger chairs. I draw him into my lap, arms pretzeled around his skinny frame. Leaning down, I press my nose against the fuzzy top of his head and inhale his familiar scent.

There's so many things I want to ask Weston: why he came back for me, whether he thinks our battle is really over, if he believes our parents will be safe. But with Comet's frail body wrapped between my arms and his tiny paws pressed gently against my thighs, I can't bring myself to ask. Not yet.

"You should have used it," I say. My voice is as unsteady as the ship's plank. "Comet deserves saving more than me. More than anyone."

I close my eyes and inhale the musty smell of the old dog's fur. My arms tighten around him and I hope it's an apology he can understand.

"That's . . ." I lick my chapped lips. "That's what I should have said when I saw you in the woods."

All I could think about were Dad and Papa—*my* family. But in doing so, I'd forced Weston to give up his. I never thought Weston had that in him—perhaps that's part of why I acted how I did, not expecting any consequences. But really, I was just so selfish I didn't even see the *real* Weston in front of me. I wasn't friend enough to give him a chance to explain.

Weston shakes his head. His gaze remains fixed forward,

to the empty space before us. His muscles are tense, like his body's a big clenched fist. But the hard look in his eyes he wore with the twins is fading, and his chin wobbles a bit as he speaks.

"I meant what I said back there. That Comet wouldn't have wanted this." His eyes flicker to the dog in my arms. I loosen my grip, but he makes no move to take him from me. "The amulet won't make him younger. It won't stop the pain in his ankles and knees when we walk too far. It won't make the hair he's lost grow back, or increase his appetite, or improve his hearing. All it would do is drag out his suffering."

A speckle of meteors appears on the horizon, obscuring the distant stars and sole craft ahead from view. Weston sits up, eyes squinting with concentration.

"When I first stole the amulet, I didn't think *once* about how Comet would feel. I only thought about how lonely I'd be without him. How I'd have no one there to talk to when my parents were frustrating. When I felt shut out of my own life. I wouldn't have anyone who took me seriously."

The first meteor zooms toward us. Weston steers up and to the right, smoothly veering us from its path. There are more on the horizon, the gaps between them smaller, narrower. I sit upright, focus flickering between Weston and the swarm of space rocks ahead.

Weston sucks in his cheeks. Perhaps in fear of what's approaching our pod, or perhaps because of what he's about to say. "When I saw you in the woods, looking at me like that . . ."

I cringe, remembering how I turned from him and ran, even as he shouted my name. Even as Comet rested, tired and weak, in his arms. I almost wish one of the meteors would strike me then, knocking my head in just the right way that the memory pops out of my ear and floats off into deep space.

"I was a jerk back there," I admit. "I was a jerk, and I was wrong, and—"

We narrowly swerve from the next meteor and the pod tilts. My head bumps against the side door and Comet squirms in my grip. "Stop reminding me what an idiot you are!" Weston snaps, straightening out the pod. "It's going to make what I'm about to say next even harder."

His face is all scrunched up, brows knit together and nose pinched. My eyes widen. "Wait, are you about to say something nice?"

"Not if you keep interrupting."

"This is the one time I *don't* deserve your praise, and you're about to say something nice to me." I huff dramatically. "Not when I waited on you, hand and foot, during your first visit to the inn. Not when I agreed to help you fight the Odette Twins, or when I rescued you and Comet back on that pirate planet—"

"In the woods, you reminded me that Comet's not the only person who's taken me seriously!"

He shouts the words, loud and fast, perhaps to drown out the meteor zooming by. But really, it just sounds like he's throwing them up to get them out of his system.

"You looked *disappointed* in me. Like you expected better. Which means you expected *something*. And no one else has ever expected *anything* from me before. No one's taken me seriously enough, or listened to me enough, or gotten to know me well enough to be let down."

We enter the thick of the meteor shower. It's like entering a memory from the day before, but this time, Weston weaves us between the meteors with ease. I grip the dashboard as we duck under one just in time to veer past another. The motion is dizzying, and I wonder if I'm imagining his words. If my head is spinning so fast that I'm getting them out of order and he's saying something else entirely.

But he goes on. "When I got Comet as a puppy, I knew I'd outlive him. It's inevitable. But I didn't think I could *survive* without him. I'm still not totally sure what I'll do when that day comes, or who I'll be without him. But at least now I know I *can* be someone without him. All that's happened over the past few days . . . I did that with Comet. But I did it with you, too."

The words make my chest throb. Sentimentality from Weston is *always* unexpected, but after he put so much on the line to save me, I feel more warmth at his admission than I do shock. I've spent years living passively through other people's stories, so it feels surreal that *I* could have a significant impact on someone. It fills my chest with a surge of affection for my nemesis-turned-friend, alongside a sort of gratitude as well.

Weston blinks fast, eyes watering. A meteor looms just feet ahead, but his hands don't move fast enough. I reach over, Comet smooshed against my midsection as I grasp the steers and twist us from the meteor's path.

Instead of saying thanks, Weston swats my hands away and takes the controls back. "I'm done talking about this now," he declares with finality, "because if I keep going on, you're going to make me crash."

This time, I swat him. "How is *you* going on about your feelings *my* fault? Just because they're *about* me doesn't mean they're *because* of me."

"If you want the credit for anything I just said, you have to take the blame, too."

"That makes *no* sense," I snap, "and veer right—*right!*"

He swerves left instead, putting us right in the path of the meteor. I press the accelerator and we double left, out of the rock's way. It smacks the side of our pod, spinning us like a top. The view outside the window is a streaky stream of light as we dance on our axis.

Our spinning slows until we come to a halt just outside of the shower. It zooms on in front of us, like an image on a giant movie screen. My stomach lurches and I swallow hard to keep from getting sick. I'm about ready to empty the contents of my stomach into my lap, but poor Comet is still dozing there, half-alert, so I push it down for his sake.

As I focus on my breathing, Weston turns toward me, eyes focused on my hands. I follow his gaze and notice the dark, red creases glaring from my skin. Deep, angry rope burns.

"I'm glad you're okay, Lexi," he says. His voice is softer, more serious than I expected. I pull down my sleeves, hiding my wrists. "We're going to get back to the inn once this storm passes. The pirates will leave your family alone; so will me and my parents. You'll go back to how things were before you got wrapped up in this mess."

He smiles weakly. Then, straightening up in his seat to leverage every inch of his princely posture, he declares, in a voice not quite steady, and not quite certain, but dripping with finality all the less: "Our deal is done."

I gawk. My jaw hangs as though dropping from my head and all the way down through space, back to that black hole. The last place I expected Weston's mushy monologue to end was *goodbye,* even though that's what this whole thing has been about. Us helping each other out so we'd get out of each other's hair for good. I could go back to the inn, royal free, and he'd resume his travels with his parents to finish their plan to stop the Odette Twins' ever-expanding empire.

I was never the one who would stop the twins. In fact, I only made things worse by forcing Weston into a situation where he had to hand over the amulet in exchange for my life. Yet I'd started to feel like I was a part of it. Even when I'd never wanted a thing to do with it in the first place.

Weston will move on with his parents, a bit more confident than before. He'll see he can have worth, speak up a bit more when he wants to be involved. When Comet's day comes, he'll be heartbroken but steady, knowing he can survive and carry on being the person Comet knew he could be.

But what about me? I'll go home to the inn, rescue my parents. But how does that leave me any different from where I was before?

It's a silly thought, because the whole point was that I didn't *want* anything to change. But since leaving home, I'd stolen two pirate pods, visited the ice cream factory for the first time in ages, explored two unfamiliar planets, survived two meteor showers, and fought a crew of space pirates.

How can I go home and move on, knowing the Odette Twins are still out there? Knowing they're hurting people like they hurt me? Hurting people *because* of me?

It's for someone else to worry about, I tell myself. Someone like the Queen, or the members of the royal army. I'm the innkeepers' daughter—it's who I am, who I'll always be. I know how to be the girl who loves deep space, who loves to listen to her guests, who's best friends with the boy from the ice cream factory. Despite making it through my adventures the past few days, I don't know a thing about fighting pirates. I can't say for sure it's what I'm good at, or who I am. Not the way I can about innkeeping and living in deep space.

But a small voice in my mind, quiet as the flicker of a distant planet, wonders who I could become if I was brave enough to try.

I want to say something, but Weston is distracted. He messes with the control panel, using the front camera to zoom in on the empty space ahead. An image of a nearby craft amplifies on the screen, pixel by pixel. Weston presses the button repeatedly, the image inflating before us.

There's no reason for the Odette Twins to come after us. They got the amulet—in a way, they've already *won*. But the image of the craft still causes a sense of uneasiness to settle on my shoulders, tingling all the way down my spine.

"You don't think it's another pirate ship, do you?" He mumbles it in a way that makes me feel like he's not sure if

I should answer. As if I'm already no longer a part of this adventure.

I make a show of sticking my head forward, so my nose almost bops the screen. A small craft soars through space ahead of us, seemingly on the same track as our pod. It's a bit oddly shaped, with a brown, square extension on its side.

Weston presses the zoom button about ten more times.

I frown. "You're gonna break it."

He squints at the image and presses the button in a fast-paced rhythm. "If we're attacked and crash again, then everything will break anyway."

The image bloats on the screen, until we're staring at a small scrape on the side of the craft instead of a full image of it. I swat his arm. "It's too close to see *anything*."

"Says the girl who just smashed her face against the screen."

"Because you're hogging the view."

"First the view is too big, then you're not getting enough of it—"

I huff and sit up so fast, our foreheads almost bump. "Just zoom out, will you?" He rubs his temple as though our heads had hit. Dramatic as always. "What are you going to do without me, you particular little prince?"

I mean the words to come out teasing, but my tone is a bit too soft. As though I expect an answer. Weston's dramatic scowl falters, lips parting. I blink and quickly turn back to the screen.

The craft, zoomed out, is a medium-sized ship with a few cardboard boxes strapped to its sides. "It's not a pirate ship," I say with certainty. "It's *Ron*."

CHAPTER SEVENTEEN

I excitedly press the pod's horn, which, instead of making sound, beams a star-bright light through the space ahead of us, alerting the ship ahead to our presence. I'm smashing the button as hard and fast as Weston did the zoom, but if he's complaining, I don't hear it. I'm too focused on the surge of joy and relief that comes with watching Ron's ship grow on the horizon as the space closes between us.

His ship flashes a light in return, acknowledging our approach. We come up on his ship fast, a signal that they've stopped moving to meet us. I lean back, making room for Weston to pull us into park by their ship. He does so word-lessly, which is unusual for him. Part of me wants to ask what he's thinking, but after all he's already said, I'm pretty sure it'd just be something about how he wants to drop me home and get on with his life.

We've already said goodbye, after all.

The pod parks next to Ron's ship. I push on the O-Zone projector and rope myself to the inside of the pod. By the time we slow to a stop, I'm already climbing out.

Ron leaps out of his ship to greet me. His long limbs pump through the empty air as he swims from his O-Zone projection and into mine. His mom calls something out to him that I can't hear, and he turns slightly and offers a nod before heading back toward me.

I can't help but beam at the sight of him, though I still can't believe he's here. Part of me wonders if he's part of the O-Zone projection, and I'm imagining it all. "What are the odds that in this giant solar system, we'd run into each other out here?"

Ron grins, his freckles pinching along the bridge of his nose. "We've always had a knack for sticking together, no matter how big this place gets."

The space closes between us as we float toward each other. His long arms wrap around me and I give his midsection a squeeze tight enough to pop his head off his neck. "Do I look shorter?" he asks. "I feel like being crammed in that pod is making me shorter."

I laugh. "Lower the pod's gravity and you'll gain that height back soon enough. With interest."

Pressed against his shoulder, I see his mom waiting in the front seat, shoe tapping against the foot mat.

"Let me guess," I say, drawing back. "She said you can't stop for long."

Ron smiles sadly. "I hate how well you can read that."

I shrug. It's like reading the same script over and over again until we've memorized the lines.

"You're heading home, though," I say, hopeful. "I am too.

We finished our mission. I saved the inn." I smile. "We'll both be home again, together."

The words drip with promise. Promise that going home is what I'm meant to do. That running into Ron on my way is a sign.

"We're heading back to the ice cream factory," he says. I nod along to each syllable eagerly. His smile doesn't reach his eyes. "We have to stock up for some more deliveries."

I stare blankly. "More deliveries? As in you'll be leaving again?"

He throws his arms up weakly. "I'm becoming one with the pod."

My feet squirm beneath me as though seeking solid ground. "I'm surprised that after tasting the ice cream, none of the customers are making the trip to see how it's made. It tastes best fresh, straight from the factory!"

"There's nothing *fresh* about astronaut ice cream," Ron says with a scratchy laugh. "And no one wants to make the trip all the way to the outer system."

I frown. "But they expect *you* to."

He runs a hand through his reddish hair, sending a few strands jutting upright as though he'd pressed his finger in a socket. "I love the factory, but now I spend all my time crammed in a pod with Mom. We didn't even make it to the cooking class because we just got more orders and have to go back home."

There's defeat in his voice, devoid of the warmth I'd expect for the words *back home*. I want to call it out, to push back, to twist things somehow to make his face light up like a star at the mention of home. But it wouldn't be fair, considering the weight as heavy and dense as a neutron star that's been pressed against my chest since Weston declared our adventure together was over.

Tight lines mark Ron's speckled forehead. "No one wants to come see us. They want us to come to them, over and over again." His eyes meet mine, wide and desperate, as though I may have some secret answer. Or perhaps because he's scared that I won't. "I don't know how much longer we can keep it up, and—"

"Don't say that!"

I jump at the volume of my own voice, the loudest thing out here in this empty pocket of the universe. Ron flinches and I press my fingertips to my lips. But the next words arrive nonetheless.

"You can't say that. Not after all I just did to save the inn."

He shakes his head. "Lex, this has nothing to do with—"

"But it *does*. It has *everything* to do with it." I wave back at the pod, where Weston sits, cramped, with Comet dozing in his lap. "Everything I did was for the outer system! To save my parents, and the inn, from the Odette Twins and the royal family. It was all so we could keep going on as we always have." I grab his hands, gripping until his fingers turn white in mine. "*Together.*"

Ron stares at our hands, head bent and jaw loose and trembling. He blinks fast and swallows hard. "What you did was amazing. *All* of it. I can't wait to hear about your adventures, like the stories we used to tell each other but this time, for *real*. Still, it doesn't change . . ."

His mom watches from their ship, her foot tapping even faster than before. It's like a stopwatch doubling in speed, rushing through the little time we have left.

I need her foot to slow. I need Ron's hands, slipping out from mine, to slow. I need everything to slow down long enough that I can come up with a new plan, a way to fix this, to keep us together, to make this trip worth it. To make everything worth it. To keep the rope between our homes from snapping for good.

"My adventure's not over," I say. His hands still slip from mine, peeled from my grip. I don't resist, knowing that if all goes to plan, we'll be back together again, soon. "I have a way to save the factory, and the inn, for good. And in doing so I'll save the system from pirates, too!"

Ron's brow pinches with doubt. I barrel on.

"So you won't have to keep making these trips, and everything doesn't keep drifting farther and farther away from us," I say. "So we can take back *control*."

"Ron!" his mom calls from their ship. "We have to go!"

He shakes his head. "I don't understand—"

"Leave it to Galaxy Jones! I'll fix all of this. For good." I smile tightly so he doesn't see how my chin trembles, doesn't hear my voice shake. "For us. Okay?"

"Ron, honey!" his mom cries. "It's time!"

He sucks in his cheeks, eyes darting from mine. But he nods. "Okay, Lex. Okay."

He's about to turn away, head back to his ship. I don't want to watch him go again—not yet. So I turn first, spinning a bit too fast in the O-Zone projection. I push toward the pod from there, moving in sweeping, confident motions through the awkward gravity. The door is still open as I left it and I climb inside.

Weston shifts sluggishly, as though stirred from a nap. "You done?"

"Far from it," I say. "And neither are you."

I slam the on button and the engine stirs to life. He straightens up in his seat, hands grasping the armrests.

"I know you said our deal is done, but so long as the Odette Twins have the amulet, our *work* isn't done. Our adventure isn't over."

The words taste strange and unfamiliar on my tongue. This close to safety—to returning home and continuing on as I always have at the inn, with my fathers—it goes against all my instincts to declare our adventure should continue, that somehow me, Weston, and Comet will be the ones to face off with the Odette Twins. But if I go home now, home *won't* be the same as it always was—as it should be. Even if Weston convinces his parents not to buy the inn, Ron may leave the outer system.

Right now I'm running on nothing but stubborn determination and blind faith that after all we've accomplished on this trip, my story can only end with victory. I imagine that when I return to the inn, I'll be like one of our customers, sitting by the hearth and telling my fathers about my great travels and adventures—beginning, middle, *and* triumphant end.

I tap the map, erasing the coordinates for the inn. I zoom and select the pirate planet. Weston's eyes bug out of his head.

"No, no, no!" He grabs at my wrist but I shake him off, smacking the go button. The pod spins around, back toward the direction from where we came. "It's over, Lexi! It's up to my parents now. Your job is to just go back home, and—"

"And sit there as the universe is taken over?" I shout over the whirring engine. "To sit there as it keeps expanding until there's nothing and no one left in the outer system? I don't think so."

We shoot off, back along our previous trail. Ron's craft vanishes in the distance and I force myself not to look back. Not to zoom in for a glimpse of his ship until it's really, truly out of view.

"We can't turn our backs on all those people," I say. And it's true—as safe as I feel here, nestled in the pod, there's a pit in my stomach as I think of the amulet in the hands of the Odette Twins and of what it will do to all those people on all those distant planets.

The world is so much bigger than I knew before this adventure.

"And even if using the amulet on Comet is wrong, we can still use it for good." The dog nuzzles against my ankle, as though nodding to my words. Prolonging Comet's life would only bring both him and Weston pain. But using the amulet on the outer system could save Ron's family. It could save mine.

It could save our friendship. Preserve it for good, before the deliveries become too much. Before his mother moves the factory. Before my parents sell the inn to Weston's parents, or the next available buyer.

"No, we're going to get back the amulet," I declare. "And we're going to use it for something good—something that can actually *help* someone. We'll use it to slow the expansion of the outer system, and once it's used, it'll be of no use to the pirates. They can never come for it again."

Saying it now, it sounds like the perfect end to our story. What I'd want to tell my fathers when I return home, what I'll tell all our future guests for years to come as we exchange stories of our adventures over dinner. If we *don't* use the amulet, the pirates will keep coming back for it. The only way to end this is to use it. And if using it on Comet would just hurt him, then using it to save the outer system is the best solution.

I nod to myself, properly convinced and hoping Weston is too. Because I need to believe this is possible. I *need* to believe this is true.

The alternative—losing to the pirates, losing my home—is too heavy to even consider.

"Call for backup," I say, tapping the console. "We should have service by now, right? We'll face off with the pirates, take the amulet, and the royal guard can make sure they can't fight back when I use it before they can."

"Lexi, this sounds impossible," Weston grumbles, though he doesn't hesitate to reach for the touchscreen, eager to call backup.

"So does everything else we've accomplished so far," I

remind him—and, honestly, *me*. "And so does a time-warping amulet. But—"

Suddenly, the pod propels backward—which would be hard to tell in empty space if the sensation of flying in the wrong direction didn't make my stomach lurch. Weston falls back, too, fingers slipping from the touchscreen.

I grasp the dashboard with one hand to steady myself, fighting back nausea as I turn to glare at Weston. "If you disagree with the plan, you could *say* so instead of driving in the opposite direction like a maniac!"

Weston slams at the controls and wiggles the wheel frantically. "I didn't press reverse! It's just doing this!"

Comet plants his front paws on his knees and cranes his neck toward the side window. His nose points forward on alert, and then he lets out a low series of barks.

Worst-case scenarios spin through my mind. Were we being sucked into the very black hole I'd just been saved from? Was there a planet with an extra-strong gravitational pull reeling us in, with no plans of letting go?

Seeing Ron had filled me with a bout of nostalgia for home, but that feeling also propelled me right back into this adventure. Right now, with a hard pang to my chest, I can't help but wonder if I missed my one shot at getting home.

Part of me wants to duck under my chair and hide from whatever Comet's barking at. But the new, fearless Galaxy Jones I'd decided to be—as unfamiliar and unformed as she is—reminds me that while the mission chose me at the beginning of this adventure, *I* chose to keep going. My chin trembles as I turn toward the window, but despite the nagging fear, I don't let myself turn away.

I immediately spot the one other visible object in the empty space behind our pod. It's a tiny rocket, about half the size of our pod, with a giant horseshoe magnet strapped to the front. Exhaust steams out of the bottom of the rocket in uneven puffs of fire and smoke, as though the vehicle is struggling to remain afloat. A tiny, ragged black flag sticks up from the rocket's pointed tip, an alien skull with crossed bones painted on it white.

I don't bother hiding my fear when I speak, voice high and shrill in a way I barely recognize. "I know why *we* wanted to find the pirates, but why did *they* want to find us?"

Weston spins around so fast, his forehead nearly knocks mine. He follows me and Comet's gaze toward the ship in the distance. "What kind of retro, dingy pod is *that?*"

I elbow him back into his seat. "We're being magnetized by space pirates and you're concerned that their *pod is out of style?*" I shriek.

He shoots me a wide-eyed, incredulous glance. "You were the one who saw all their pods under the ship deck before. Does that look like anything they use?"

Explanations soar through my mind—because the pirates *must* have taken every last pod off the planet they conquered to make sure the residents couldn't escape. Even goofy little rockets like this. But that doesn't explain why they'd actually use it, when they had dozens of newer pods at their disposal.

The magnetic pull increases and we swing back so fast

that whatever theories had begun forming in my mind scatter like a handful of dropped marbles. I grasp at the dashboard to keep from lurching forward, and Weston cups one arm around Comet while the other continues to frantically slam against the control panel. Within seconds, a violent *thud* sends all three of us slamming backward and forward with the intensity of breaking through an atmosphere.

My mind spins from the whiplash, any coherent thoughts I have begging me to pull it together because whoever this is, their flag is a clear sign they are *not* an ally. But just as I'm coming to and getting my bearings again, there's a violent knock on the driver's side of the pod.

"Open up, little prince! I'm commandeering your pod—and all fighting back will do is get you a sharp hook to the throat!"

Pressed against the side of the pod, an O-Zone bubble floating around her blond head, is none other than Great Astro Bonny.

CHAPTER EIGHTEEN

stare, gawking. Because the woman pressed against the side of the pod is somehow, inexplicably, the same one who was on all the news clipping sewn onto Celeste's quilt. The same one who was featured on the pages of the photobook I kept under my bed (until Weston rudely stole it). The same woman I dressed up as when I was a little kid, imagining that I too could go on epic adventures throughout all of space.

She has that iconic, flyaway blond hair that's held back by her signature checkered handkerchief. Her clothes are worse for wear, but the same as I've seen in the photobook: an oversized cloak, like the one I wore back on the pirate planet, draped over a white, puffy shirt and high-waisted trousers. Her eyes are fierce slits, irises bright and smoldering as the surface of a star. And her posture is wide and proud and fearless as she grips onto the side of the pod, her body outlined by the pitch-black of space.

I'm dreaming, I think. I was sucked into the black hole and I'm dreaming that Weston came back, that I saw Ron, and that Astro Bonny chased me down to the corners of space. I'm not really seeing this right now; it's just the noodle effect taking over as my brain is tugged into pink, squiggly pieces of string.

I'm jolted back to harsh reality when she knocks one fist on the glass again, waving a sharp hook in the other. "I don't have all light-year, kid!"

Weston shoots me a desperate glance. But I'm sure I look just as shocked, because *how* did Astro Bonny find us, and *why* did Astro Bonny find us, and *what* could she possibly be doing in a retro little rocket, commandeering our pod in deep space?

And also, my brain unhelpfully circles back to I *can't believe I'm in the presence of the real, live Astro Bonny.*

It was always possible I'd cross paths with her on this mission. I knew that, rationally. But seeing her now—even though her cheeks are flushed with angry red patches and her fists are smudging against the glass as she knocks and bangs—feels like seeing a photo come to life. Like the imaginary duels I acted out with Ron when we were little somehow transformed from fantasy to reality before my very eyes.

She smashes the hook against the glass window of the pod, the tiniest crack forming on its surface. "Open up now, you amoeba-brained space rats, or I'll break the window and rip you both to shreds next! Yours isn't the only pod I can take, so let me in or die resisting!"

Comet's barking transforms to whimpering. "He's got a point," I say.

Weston groans and reaches for the door handle with a shaky hand.

Astro Bonny bursts in, shoving her way through the door

with no regard for how her knees knock directly into Weston's stomach or how the swing of her arms sends Comet leaping into the safety of my lap. This pod is barely built for two humans and a dog, let alone the larger-than-life Astro Bonny. But she moves easily, as though unfazed by the way our elbows and knees bump together and shoulders squeeze as she wedges her way into the driver's seat. I imagine that beneath her ratted cloak and knee-high boots, her skin is made of granite.

My mind spins faster than a vortex. I am breathing the same air as *the* Astro Bonny. I am equal parts terrified and thrilled, both emotions so strong they keep me paralyzed in my seat, staring at her with an open-mouthed, dumbfounded expression.

She's probably used to that look; she doesn't so much as glance at me or Weston as she adjusts the controls for her height and starts the pod up again.

"This thing's as cramped as that other piece of trash I was flying, but I'll take it," she says, mostly to herself. I still hang off every word, noting the coarse drone of her voice, the way her thick blond eyebrows furrow below her kerchief. "Type in the coordinates for that planet Mary Read's brats are running under my name, will you?"

Weston frantically retypes the coordinates on the electronic map with trembling hands. I turn to look at Astro Bonny—best as I can, considering I'm smooshed tight between Weston and the passenger door. Something about her words snag in my mind, and while there're a thousand other thoughts competing in my brain—like, *How are you going to survive this, Galaxy?* And, *Why didn't you call for help when you could, Galaxy?*—the innkeeper in me can't help but try to find the story our pod's latest guest has hiding in her words.

She's a crass pirate, sure—but would she really talk like that about the twins if she cared for Mary Read as much as Celeste said? And why does she sound so bitter about the planet being run under her name, when that's apparently part of her grand plan to take over the solar system?

All of this—combined with the fact that *the* Astro Bonny needed to steal *our* pod just to get back to her planet—leaves me feeling more confused than ever.

The pod whirs and spins around before shooting back in the direction we originally came from, toward the pirate planet. Thankfully, the meteor shower has cleared. But my heartbeat hammers just as fast as if the meteors were still swarming around us, and even Comet's warm weight in my lap doesn't provide enough comfort to slow my breathing.

So far, I've gotten through this adventure by dipping into the bravery I played at as a little girl, mimicking the very space pirate who's cramped in our pod right now. But it's as though she's sucked up all the oxygen in our space, and I can't find the words to question her or her motives, even though a voice in my head screams that our lives depend on it.

"Have you seen the place?" Astro Bonny scream-asks, hunched over the dashboard as though leaning forward will propel the pod faster. "Last travelers I hitchhiked with said they'd heard about *parrot drones* circling the planet."

Astro Bonny, hitchhiking? I remember the cover of my photobook: how she stood tall and proud at the helm of her ship. Weston and I exchange a glance which, this close in the pod, nearly sends our noses bumping together.

"*Parrot* drones!" she screams, making Comet whimper and snuggle deeper into my lap. "As if Mr. Echo were a lowly *crew member*. No, worse—a *ship prisoner*, forced to do hard labor in exchange for his survival! How could Mary Read sink so low as to do that to *my* Mr. Echo?"

Despite my numbing fear, I feel a warm, bubbly *giddiness* rising in my chest at her words. If room permitted, I could jump in my seat right now, because I was *right*: Astro Bonny would *never* make drones that looked like her pet parrot, and something was seriously, seriously wrong with all of this.

The warm rush of victory quickly fades.

Oh, Mars. Something is seriously wrong.

I swing right back to fear, yet somehow Weston finds it in him to ask, "You named your parrot Mr. Echo? Are you *serious?*"

I shoot him a glare as sharp as her hook, because if he keeps talking like that, he may *actually* get a hook to the head. But Astro Bonny just rolls her eyes. "Says the kid who named his dog *Comet*," she snaps back easily, a soft reminder that I'm somehow the only no-name, non-celebrity in this pod.

"Hey!" Weston cries, clasping his hands over Comet's saggy ears protectively as though he could have understood the insult.

I close my eyes and inhale a steadying breath, trying to

run through the pieces of this strange, terrifying puzzle in my mind. Back when I listened to guests tell their stories by the warm hearth of the inn's fireplace, they always shared the beginning, middle, and end in clear detail. This feels like listening to a dozen guests telling bits and pieces of a story out of order, hoping that I can rearrange and piece them together.

But I know I can do it—that all the stories and tales of deep-space adventures I've listened to and dreamed about over the years have led me to this. So I drown out Weston and Astro Bonny's bickering—drown out my amazement that I'm even in the same pod as *Astro Bonny*—and trace back through what she said.

Astro Bonny does *not* approve of the parrot drones. She referred to the planet as being Mary Read's, not as her own.

No one I've met, on the planet or the ship, has mentioned actually *seeing* Astro Bonny. And apparently, she's been hitchhiking through space, making her way back to the planet with whatever spacecraft she can find.

And if she left the pirate planet and she didn't have a pod, there was only one way she was so deep in space.

"The *cannon!*" I shout, so loud Comet jumps out of my lap and into Weston's.

Weston curls back, wincing in pain. "*Right by my ear,* Lexi—"

But I'm feeling too much to add *guilt* to the mix. "Astro Bonny," I say, too shocked by a trillion other things to register the fact that I'm addressing my childhood idol who—if I'm right—may not be *as* evil as I'd been led to believe these past few years. "Before she died, did Mary Read shoot you out of an intergalactic space cannon?"

"Lexi, that's insane," Weston snaps at the same time Astro Bonny replies, "She sure did!"

Even though I'm the one who guessed it, I stare at her with the same dumbfounded awe as Weston as she explains, "Bet she thought I'd be finding my way back till the end of the universe! But I hooked myself to every shooting star, commandeered every saucer and every rocket, and even nosedived through a wormhole to get back here!"

Her journey sounds impossibly epic—and it *is*, because *everything* about Astro Bonny is outside the confines of normal, of reality. But thinking about it, I'm surprised that it sounds similar to the story I'll get to tell my fathers when I get home—so long as I *do* get home—about my own impossible, epic journey through space.

"As if *anything* would stop me from getting back to my galaxy and stopping that leech's spawn from stealing my legacy," she snarls. "How *dare* that second-class, deck-scrubbing wannabe use *my* name to assist in her half-baked takeover plan? As if I have any interest in owning planets." Her upper lip curls in disgust. "Who wants to live on a *rock*, let alone *own* a rock, when you could live on an ever-moving, never-stationary *ship*?"

And *this* is the Astro Bonny I knew growing up, the one that's felt so far and distant as Celeste and Pictor shared stories about a mighty pirate who sounded nothing like the one I'd admired as a little girl. She's still a sinister pirate—still someone who would put a hook through your throat for telling her no, and would steal your pod without notice as if you had nowhere better to be—but she's not a conqueror of worlds, *not* someone who has her followers collect her planets like prizes while she hides away in the shadows.

This is the Astro Bonny I dreamed of being as a girl. But the way she talks about traveling, about never settling down—and hearing her say it now, after I'd just decided to get the amulet to save deep space and make sure I never had to leave the inn—is like a nitrogen-cold reminder that I am nothing like her either way.

Weston presses his fingertips to his temple. "Wait, so before she died, Mary Read shot you out of the galaxy? And her kids are continuing this whole pirate takeover because Mary Read said that's what *you* wanted?"

Astro Bonny spins the controllers, narrowly missing a lonely piece of floating space rock. "That's literally what I just said. Learn to listen, kid."

Ignoring her, Weston turns to me. I'm shocked to see a smile forming on his lips. "My parents!" he scream-whispers. "This is intel even my *parents* don't know! This changes *everything!*" He runs a hand down Comet's fluffy spine in that same, familiar way he does when he's overwhelmed. "*I* can change everything. They'll *need* this from me."

Comet leans up and gives Weston's chin a gentle lick. I settle on giving him a big, encouraging smile.

"They should have *always* listened to you, whether or not

you had anything to prove they should," I say. "But I'm glad that now, they'll *have* to see that."

The pod lurches back as we double in speed, and I'm quickly reminded that I'm in a pod with Astro Bonny and that this is *not* the moment for an emotional revelation. We move so fast I swear I feel the skin of my cheeks rippling. In the distance, a hazy brown dot of a planet comes into focus.

"Time for my greatest looting of all time," Astro Bonny announces, voice grandiose and brimming with dramatic flair. "I'm about to steal back my *legacy*."

Before I can react, we break through the atmosphere of the pirate planet, soaring straight through the tips of the treetops and toward the town square. As the pod slows I spot the twins' ship docked up ahead, returned from their spot by the black hole where they'd planned to turn me to space noodles.

This is where we'd planned on heading anyway—but *after* calling backup. *After* assuring we could safely secure the amulet and use it for the good of deep space. But instead, I'm returning with Astro Bonny, a wronged pirate dead set on revenge. As exciting as it was to have my theories about Astro Bonny confirmed, having her here makes my quest to steal the amulet all the more complicated, and borderline *impossible*.

Celeste was right: I'm just an innkeeper's daughter. I'm a girl from the astro-boonies who has no business playing at greatness and going on epic quests for rare space-techno.

But right now—if I play my cards right—maybe I can still be that girl from deep space, working at the inn forever like I'm supposed to. And maybe I can do that *because* today, I'm going to have my great, brave moment. The moment where Galaxy Jones makes history, just like Astro Bonny did.

The pod slows to land, and I have no idea what to do next. But with Weston and Comet by my side, and the real, *true* Astro Bonny from my childhood finally restored, I know that I have to try.

CHAPTER NINETEEN

Astro Bonny lands the pod right on the center of the Odette Twins' ship deck. Which is in typical, fearless Astro Bonny fashion—but doesn't leave much time for me to figure out what *our* next move is. In my mind we'd landed back in the center of the village and Astro Bonny had stormed out of the pod and made a dramatic entrance onto the twins' ship, leaving time for Weston and me to call for backup.

Instead, she swings her hook so it points less than an inch from my throat and declares, "You two are my temporary crew, until I get my old one back."

Weston gapes. "Shouldn't you take me hostage or something instead? I'm literally a prince."

I jab my elbow into his ribs. "*Why* would you ask that?"

"I'd rather know what I'm up against!" he seethes between clenched teeth.

Astro Bonny rolls her eyes, then brandishes her hook again, causing us both to jump. "Maybe another day, prince. I don't have time to mess with the royals right now, so you're more use to me as an extra set of hands than anything else. Now: off we go."

The hook swings between my neck and Weston's, and we don't even have to exchange a glance before falling into synchronized step, leaping out of the pod and onto the ship deck, Comet at our heels.

Marching onto the Odette Twins' deck with Astro Bonny gives me a tingly, out-of-body feeling. When I was here earlier, captive in Celeste's Astro Bonny shrine belowdeck, I'd felt myself shrinking under the weight of her epic legacy. Celeste's snide remarks about me being a townie and nothing more than the innkeepers' daughter had almost drowned out everything I'd learned about myself on this adventure—everything I'd accomplished, as brave and brilliant as any of the headlines sewn on her quilt. But now, with Astro Bonny by my side with a (at least semi-shared) mission to stop the twins, Celeste's words fade from my head.

I stand tall as I march onto the deck, immediately searching for sight of Celeste, hungry to see the way her face falls when she realizes Galaxy Jones—the sheltered girl from the astro-boonies—had been right about Astro Bonny all along. But thinking of Celeste also reminds me that I'm here on a mission separate from Astro Bonny's, too: to secure the amulet and use it to save deep space.

My head spins fast as it did while navigating our last meteor shower. The two wants compete in my head like pirates in a duel: irreconcilable, one needing to defeat the other to survive.

Suddenly my skin feels too tight for my body. An anxious sweat breaks across my body and all the bravado I felt stepping out of the pod with Astro Bonny melts into a murky, dark puddle.

It doesn't help that this is when I spot a crowd of the Odette Twins' crew members surrounding us and our pod, weapons drawn. Most of them have almost bored expressions on their dirt-crusted, unshaven faces, probably expecting to find lost travelers who landed on their deck in error. But one pirate's eye (singular, given the tacky eyepatch) widens with recognition.

"Plank!" the man shrieks, eye on me. "Plank! Girl! Plank!"

Another pirate knocks his shoulder against Eyepatch, pushing him out of the way with one hand and stroking his two-foot bush of a beard with the other. His eyes look over my head at the tall, wild-haired woman behind me.

"The Great Astro Bonny!" he cries out, eliciting a series of gasps from the crew around him. There's no shock or horror in his voice, though—just awe and exhilaration. I'm reminded that the Odette Twins and their crew were duped by Mary Read, and likely didn't know Astro Bonny had been cannoned out of our galaxy years ago.

As impressed as they are to see Astro Bonny, she's equally unimpressed. She shoves past me and Weston, stepping to the front of our three-person, one-dog crew. "Where are Mary Read's spawn?" she snarls, stomping her weatherworn boots on the deck. "I'd like to have a word with them—with my mouth or with my hook, I haven't decided yet."

The crowd parts like a jacket being unzipped down the

middle, Celeste and Pictor rushing forward in the crew's wake. Celeste clutches the amulet in her hand, her dark eyes wider than I've ever seen. Pictor stumbles after her, mouth hanging open like his jaw came loose.

"The Great Astro Bonny herself!" Celeste shrieks, at least three pitches higher than her usual tone. She stammers for a good ten seconds, lips quivering with half-started words before she cries, "Mother told us you'd come see us one day—once we'd truly, fully fulfilled your orders. I didn't think that day would come so soon."

Pictor gives her shoulder a push and shoots her an encouraging glance. Celeste cups her hands, holding the amulet in her palms like an offering.

It's almost close enough to grab. I envision myself leaping forward and snatching it from Celeste's open palms before Astro Bonny can reach it. I'd grab Weston by the elbow and we'd make a mad dash to the pod, soaring off in the sky while Comet barks and yelps triumphantly from our laps.

I teeter forward, toward the amulet. But my foolhardy plan crumbles when Astro Bonny lets out a hard laugh. "You think I'd order you to find me *that* bit of space junk? What am I even supposed to *do* with that?"

Celeste's fingers curl up around the amulet and she recoils. Pictor scratches the side of his head, tilting his hat so it's even more lopsided than usual. "Um," he drawls, his tone tentative and uncertain as if he'd just been called on by a teacher in techno-school. "To slow down time so we can take over the solar system uncontested?"

Astro Bonny scoffs, the sound so loud and harsh I feel it vibrate in my chest. "So, what, I can run this solar system like it's my job? As if I'm some tight-laced, stuffy diplomat like this kid?"

She gestures back to Weston, swinging the hook alarmingly close to his face. I grasp his elbow and yank him back just in time for the hook to swing safely past his upturned nose.

"As *if,*" Astro Bonny snorts, and Weston lets out an offended huff.

Celeste and Pictor gawk at Astro Bonny. I watch with disappointment as Celeste's fingers wrap tighter around the amulet and she draws it securely to her chest.

"What have you cretins done to Astro Bonny?" Celeste shrieks, piercing eyes turning to me and Weston for the first time.

Even with Astro Bonny stationed in front of us, a glare from Celeste still manages to shake me to my core. I tighten my grip on Weston's arms, fingernails digging into his skin. He must be equally terrified, because, for once, he doesn't complain.

"Is this a robot meant to fool us?" Pictor asks, voice filled with a strange sort of thrilled terror. "Did you spin her 'round a planet's ring until her brain became space goo? Or! Or"—he sways on his heels, body vibrating with anxious energy—"have you used some strange, sinister space-techno to brainwash her?"

I blink against the slew of questions. I've known from the start that something about their version of Astro Bonny—the one shared with them by their power-hungry mother—was wrong, and I have no doubt the pirate standing between us now is the one, true Astro Bonny. Her behavior isn't what's strange—what's strange is that the Odette Twins think there's any way *I'm* responsible for it. As if *I'm* capable of overpowering Astro Bonny, of twisting her mind and warping her into *my* plans. It feels impossible that the twins would ever consider that, let alone voice such a ridiculous theory out loud.

But at the same time, I *have* bested them over and over again, on a mixture of grit and guts that only a deep-space townie like me could manage. And I *did* find a precious piece of space loot with Weston, and then ran into the Great Astro Bonny herself. None of Pictor's theories are true, but they're not so downright *impossible* as I would have believed at the start of this journey.

The thought that *Galaxy Jones* could have influenced *Astro Bonny* isn't totally absurd—which makes me wonder if I, too, am becoming a great space adventurer just like her. But being a great adventurer means having a clear mission, and as my eyes flit from Celeste's gaze to the amulet clutched to her chest, I feel more confused than ever.

"*Me*, brainwashed?" Astro Bonny shrieks. "*You* two are the ones who were brainwashed—by that legacy-looting mother of yours."

She moves forward, her back to me and Weston, and continues her lecture to the twins and their crew. I lean as though caught in her gravitational pull, but Weston snags my wrist and tugs me back.

"This is our chance," he whispers, low and frantic.

I scan the scene. Astro Bonny stands between us and the twins, so we'd have to get past her first. Then we'd have to somehow get the amulet out of Celeste's hands, without her or Pictor getting the best of us. And then there's the issue of the entire crew surrounding them in a semicircle. And even if we survived all of *that*, we'd still have to get back to the pod and run off before any of them caught up to us.

"How?" I ask, dubious. "We need a way to distract them from the amulet—some way to, I don't know, get Celeste to drop it, or put it down, so we can grab it and go safely."

"What?" Weston gapes, shaking his head fast so his blond curls dance around his ears. "No way—*forget* the amulet! We just need to get you back to your inn and let my parents take care of this."

Panic snakes it way up my throat. I was fine calling for backup, so they'd support our mission as if they were *our* crew members. But if we make a run for the pod and leave now, we'll never get the amulet. I won't end my epic story with my grand, heroic finale, making a name for Galaxy Jones as the hero of deep space. And if I don't save deep space, then the universe will keep expanding, and I'll lose everything that's ever been worth fighting for in my life. I'll lose my *home*.

The two competing thoughts—Galaxy Jones as the epic hero of deep space, and Galaxy Jones as a lifelong, never-changing innkeeper—continue to battle in my mind in that same, confusing way I can't work my way out of. So I turn my focus to Weston instead.

I smack his arm and he recoils with a soft hiss. "Do you hear yourself?"

He rubs his upper arm. " . . . Yes?"

"No, really! This whole thing was about wishing your parents took you more seriously. About wanting *anyone* to take you seriously. Well, right now, I am!"

I grip his shoulders in my hands and force him to look at me, dead-on. He squirms a bit and glances quickly at his shoes, then meets my steady gaze.

"Prince Weston," I say, all authoritative, "I take you more seriously than I will ever take Astro Bonny and the Odette Twins combined. I believe you can do anything your parents can do—"

"Even though we're unarmed and have no backup but an elderly dog—"

"And there's no *inn* for me to go back to if I don't get the amulet and slow down the outer system universe expansion." I inhale deeply, a bit out of breath from that last part.

My grip tightens on his shoulders and he straightens up on reflex. Even when he's doubting himself, Weston wants others to take him seriously. To see him as someone important, someone capable.

Throughout our adventure, Weston crashed the pod—more than once. He hid in an alley while Comet and I faced the Odette Twins and their crew. He left me asleep in a clearing while he sneaked off to break our deal.

But he did all he could to navigate us where we needed to go and kept us alive through two meteor showers. He opened up about things he never shared with anyone else, even when it was awkward or embarrassing. And more than anything, he gave up the thing he wanted when he realized it wasn't what Comet needed. And he made up for it by facing the Odette Twins and rescuing me.

Even if the odds are against us, I know we can get through—because despite all that's happened and everything that's changed, Weston hasn't given up. And he's gotten better as a person, as a prince. As a friend.

Weston's chin quivers. His shoulders tremble beneath my palms. But then he clenches his fists by his sides, as though willing himself to tighten up, to be brave. But it's the steadfast look in his eyes that sends a comforting warmth through my chest. "Okay. If you think I can do it, I'll pretend I can do it. For you, and for Comet, and for my parents and everyone else who lives in our solar system." He exhales slowly from pressed lips. "I can do this."

I give his shoulders one last squeeze, then let go. "*We* can do this. And we're about to. Right now."

I turn back to the scene before us, determined to find a weak point we can leverage to secure the amulet. I figured out the truth about Astro Bonny before even the pirates did—and that was because of my ability to listen, to piece together parts of a story just like I'd learned from my life as an innkeeper. Right now I need to do the same: study the details until I find the path forward where this story ends with me and Weston as heroes.

Astro Bonny is circling past the twins, and the crew parts

again to make room for her as she heads toward the center of the ship. Celeste's porcelain skin has gone red as a ruby as she shouts, "Seize her! She's an imposter!"

But the crew doesn't make a move to follow Celeste's order. Astro Bonny doesn't look back at her as she snaps, "Back down, brat, or I'll toss you in the very cannon your mother did me!" The crew circles around her like a herd of animals following a shepherd, and she stalks toward the foot of the crow's nest. "Forego Mary Read's treachery and *maybe*—if you prove useful enough—I will let you help me clean up the very mess *you've* made, and in my name, no less!"

Astro Bonny begins her ascent up the rickety ladder leading to the crow's nest. Crew members circle at the bottom of the mast, arms extended so their long, flowy sleeves dangle from their arms like cushions ready to catch her should she fall. Celeste makes an aborted move to follow, Pictor pacing frantically behind her.

The amulet, I note, is still in Celeste's hands—rejected by Astro Bonny and forgotten by the crew.

"No, you don't understand!" Celeste shouts, her voice partially drowned out by the whip of the sails in the wind overhead. "Mom said *this* was your plan to protect pirates!" She clamps the amulet in her hand and waves her fist over her head. "You've been gone for years—you don't know how bad it's gotten! The central system is *flooded* with all these deep-space transplants, so there's hardly any loot to spare! The skies were *stuffed* with all their pods and ships until *we* took over planets and cleared them up, so *our* ships can get through. If we don't use the amulet—if we don't take over . . . then . . . then we'll . . ."

Her voice trails off, words dying on her tongue as Astro Bonny and the crew don't spare her a second glance. The choked, desperate sound of her voice is like a stab to my chest. I don't want to feel bad for Celeste—especially not now, when I need to find a way to get the amulet from her. But that pleading, hopeless tone feels familiar in a way that echoes in my chest.

I try to focus on that feeling rather than the fact that I'm sharing it with Celeste. Because while she's desperate to use the amulet for the pirates to take over, I'm going to use it not just for me, but for everyone in deep space. I need to be the one to take the amulet, to use it so no one else will. So I can ensure it's used for good, the way a true hero would at the end of their epic adventure.

I straighten my shoulders, imagining all the doubt and uncertainty rolling off my body with the motion. Then I cross the deck, no longer hesitantly checking each floorboard as I approach. My steps are loud and creaky, and the twins spot me immediately. I don't have a sword or even a waffle cone. When it comes to facing Celeste and Pictor, all I have is the tiny bit of their story I've collected over the past few days.

I need to believe that this—that *I*—will be enough.

"What now, townie?" Celeste snaps, half-annoyed, half-tired. "We've freed you and your family. Can't you see we're busy?"

Pictor joins her side. "Go back to your quaint little inn so we can forget about you."

"Or, if you insist on staying," Celeste says, "we're still more than happy to toss you into a black hole!"

As she saunters toward me, teeth bared and shoulders back, the idea of jumping in the pod and escaping while we still can sounds just a *bit* enticing. But I can't leave—not without the amulet. I faced off with Celeste once before, and I know I can do it again for the sake of this final mission.

The floorboards creak to my right. Weston steps forward, Comet smooshed between the crook of his elbow and his left shoulder. He straightens up and moves to my side and we stand, shoulders touching, like a human wall. "You'll do nothing of the sort—and that's an order from your *prince!*"

The twins exchange a glance. With one hand Celeste unsheathes her sword. In the other, she dangles the amulet by the side of her head. "You're running out of time to run, townie."

I point up at her, arm stiff and muscles clenched. In my mind I pretend my arm is my sword. "I know you thought this is what Astro Bonny wanted, but your mother lied to you," I start, trying to keep my voice calm, even as my mind spins like a moon in orbit. "But just because she never had the chance to abort this mission doesn't mean you can't. You could do something new, *be* someone new, outside of her *or* Astro Bonny. Wouldn't your mom have wanted that for you?"

Celeste's grip tightens on the amulet, knuckles screaming white. "Don't speak of our mother, townie! You have no idea what she would have wanted."

She continues forward, amulet in hand. I imagine that

she's bringing it to me rather than getting ready for the attack. After all, the closer she is, the closer I am to the amulet.

Weston goes pale as she approaches, but he doesn't interrupt as I go on. "That's probably true," I admit. A triumphant smirk twitches at the corner of Celeste's mouth, and I quickly add, "But what do *you* want? Because none of *this* is about you."

I gesture to the ship, to the planet beyond. To the crew, hovering at the base of the crow's nest. To Astro Bonny, positioned high above us all and surveying the twins' handiwork with exasperated eyes. And, finally, to the amulet.

"You've copied everything about Astro Bonny, from your ill-fitting costumes to the hideous alien skull mascot. You've taken her name and her legacy and worn them like an oversized hat you'll never grow into. Because that's what your *mother* wanted for herself."

Pictor readjusts his hat, fidgeting at the words. But Celeste's focus remains fixed on me as she steadily closes the distant between us.

"Mary Read wanted to surpass Astro Bonny's legacy by taking over the solar system, and it cost her her life," I go on, voice gaining momentum despite the way my heartbeat hammers frantically in my chest. "Astro Bonny said she'll put you in the cannon if you don't give up this mission. But just because your mother was willing to die for this mission doesn't mean *you* also have to."

Celeste's sword extends and she jabs its tip toward my chin. Weston grasps my elbow and yanks us back, which only seems to amuse her more.

"And how are either of you any different?" she scoffs. "A little prince pretending he's a leader like his mummy and poppy, when he can't even successfully steal a trinket"—she wiggles the amulet mockingly—"without the help of a no-name townie. And you"—her sharp eyes turn to me—"a lackey so vacant of original thought she'd do anything to save a failing business her loser parents keep holding on to." She tilts her head to the side and smiles. "Does that sound right?"

"No," I shout at the same time Weston mutters, "Kind of."

"Excuse me?" My eyes flicker between him and the smirking twins. "I thought you were on my side, buddy."

"*Our* side," he corrects, puffing his chest. "And of course I am. But she can be evil and still have a point."

"No, she can't. That's the literal definition of *evil*."

"But we're not perfect, either." He shrugs. "And it's almost exactly what you said to me a moment ago. That I've been so caught up in trying to be the Queen and King that I never tried anything myself."

My head spins. All the while, Celeste is inching closer.

"That's not what I said."

He frowns. "It's literally what you said."

The blade swipes the air before us again, snapping us back into focus. Celeste glares as though aggravated the attention was off her for so long. "As entertaining as your two-brain-celled bickering is, we're going to have to speed this up—"

"So that we can slow everything else down," Pictor jokes, his arm sweeping toward the empty village streets.

My eyes fix on the amulet. I'm getting too caught up in

the noise to focus on what matters. This isn't about talking the Odette Twins out of following Mary Read's plans. That's Astro Bonny's job now. For me, this is only about retrieving the amulet and using it for good—for the outer system. My home.

Now I just need to figure out a way to get past her sword and snag the amulet. And I won't get any closer if I keep arguing with Weston.

"Astro Bonny!" Celeste calls, the point of her blade directed to my throat, "what would you like me to do with the little townie and the wee prince?"

Above, Astro Bonny stands in the crow's nest, barking orders to the nearest crew members. A few of them have climbed halfway up the crow's nest with grappling hooks, while others dangle from the ladder beneath her, echoing her orders back to the crew members on deck. She continues on without missing a beat or sparing a glance at Celeste.

"What do you think, Astro Bonny?" she calls again. "Just as it was for my mother before me, your word is my command."

A crew member rushes across the deck, something tucked beneath her thick right bicep. She passes the object to the crew member lowest on the ladder, and the object trails upward until it reaches Astro Bonny. She clutches it in her hand and waves it overhead, light from a distant sun catching on the shiny metal blade of her cutlass.

"Reunited at last!" she cries, swinging it madly above her head. I gulp; as glad as I am that Astro Bonny isn't after the amulet, being in proximity to her still makes me feel like the odds of succeeding are stacked against us.

Celeste sucks in her cheeks. Pictor goes tense behind her, hat slipping off the side of his small head. "She can't hear us from up there," Celeste explains. "The winds."

"She doesn't *care* to hear," I argue. "She doesn't care about *any* of this. She doesn't *want* the amulet, doesn't *want* to rule the solar system. She doesn't even want us!" I say, gesturing between me and Weston.

"It's true," Weston pipes up. "She even said she'll be too busy cleaning up your mess to hold me for royal ransom."

Celeste rolls her eyes,. "Then why are you still here?"

My gaze deceivingly flickers to the techno-loot in her hands. A haunting smile spreads across Celeste's face.

"What could *you* possibly want with the amulet, little townie?" Her grip on it loosens, and just as I consider sprinting toward, she begins to spin it on her finger tauntingly. "What could a little nobody like you need with something as grand as this?"

Little nobody. Maybe that was me before the last few days, left behind and forgotten as the world went on without me. But now I'm on posters all over this town, wanted by the most sinister pirates in the universe. And after this, I won't just be a hero to our solar system—I'll be a hero to deep space, where it really matters.

"I'm *not* a nobody," I snap, hating how desperate my voice sounds. "Not to my parents, or our guests! *That's* what I'm fighting for, and why if either of us should use the amulet, it's *me*."

I fall silent, watching as Celeste's grin broadens. It doesn't

make sense. I'm winning this argument. We may be outnum-
bered, but Astro Bonny and the crew are ignoring her, proving
her mother's warped mission isn't worth fighting for.

So why is Celeste *smiling* like she's won?

The blade of her sword taps my chin, guiding my head
upright so I'm looking right into her eyes as she gets close. When
she lowers the sword, I remain still, eyes locked with hers.

"Oh, little townie," she drawls. "You're exactly like me, aren't
you?"

Her eyes shimmer, caught between glee and fear. As though
she's eager to catch me off guard but afraid what that would
mean for her.

This comment, I realize, is her final blow. And it's one that
could take us both down.

My chin quivers, skin brushing against the cool metal
of her weapon. How could we be the same, when she's *taking* people's homes, while at the inn, I'm *providing* a home to
them? When she wants to slow time to make the solar system
her own, and I want to slow time to save my family?

There's no universe in which those motivations are the
same. Once the amulet is mine, I'll be the one to use it right.
Not like Weston, and not like the twins. I'll be the one to make
things different.

My hands tremble by my sides. Comet whines somewhere
to my left and Weston is a blur in my peripheral vision, pale
and shaky. Pictor hangs back behind Celeste, Astro Bonny and
the crew inattentive figures in the distance.

It's just me. Just her.

And the amulet.

The amulet.

I tilt my head toward her. "Maybe you're right," I say. "Maybe we are alike."

Then I stomp on her foot with all my might. She lets out a shocked howl and I snatch the amulet from her hands and scamper backward. Celeste lunges for me, sword drawn. Comet sparks to life and dashes, barking at her feet. He opens his droopy, tired mouth and chomps down on her ankle. She shrieks and falls flat on her bottom, so hard her hat pops off her head and flutters onto the deck.

Before she has a moment to recover, Weston pins her to the boards, snatching her sword and holding it to her throat.

"Make one move," Weston shouts, eyes boring into Pictor and the crew, "and your sister—"

Pictor throws his hands up in defeat, relieving Weston from finishing a threat we both know he couldn't live up to. "I won't. I swear. I won't."

Celeste squirms under Weston's grip, twisting her neck to glare at her brother. "You coward! Astro Bonny—"

Pictor gestures up to the crow's nest. "Doesn't even *want* this! I'm not about to let this goon chop your head off."

Weston's nose crinkles at Pictor's take on events, but doesn't loosen his grip on Celeste. She watches her brother, eyebrows pinched and stern but eyes watery and wide.

"Pictor," she says, voice hard but quiet, "the *amulet*."

He shrugs, the slant of his shoulders paralleling the tilt of his hat. "She doesn't care. Why should we, if it means *this?*

We've already lost our mother over this fight. I don't want to lose you, too."

The amulet is slippery in my grip. I stand back, yards from Weston and the twins and a growling Comet, on the outskirts of the scene. After all that's happened, it still feels surreal to be on a foreign planet, surrounded by pirates and a prince and a royal puppy. To have landed in a pod and be recognized immediately as though I existed beyond the walls of the inn. As though I, Galaxy Jones, could be the hero of my own story. Could do something real.

I close my eyes. The wind whips hard and I imagine it's what an ocean would sound like, if I'd ever seen one.

Next time I see Ron, I'll ask him what the ocean is like. He's probably seen one before, on his deliveries. He's probably seen things I've never heard of, never imagined. Maybe Dad and Papa have, too, long before they opened the inn. Or even back when the universe was smaller, condensed. When there were adventures at the turn of each corner.

Before I tethered us to the outer system with a single, tired rope.

My fingers stretch by my side, flexing toward the amulet. The scene behind me fades until I'm the only person in the solar system, alone with the jewel.

I'll leap into the pod and head back home at full speed. I'll flip it open and watch it stir to life. I'll slow the pace of time so nothing else slips away from me ever again. So all the things I know, all the things I grew up with, never have to change.

Including me.

I wait for the rush of relief and warmth that comes at the thought of staying in deep space, of returning to the inn and never leaving. But standing here now—with my childhood hero, my nemesis-turned-friend, and a team of fear-worthy pirates—the thought makes a planet-sized lump rise in my throat.

Using the amulet to stop the expansion of deep space would be my legacy: something as grand and epic as anything Astro Bonny has done. But when I return to the inn, this will be my one story. One I tell every guest by the hearth, over and over again for years and years until it sounds more like pages read from a book than a real, live memory.

Behind me, I hear Celeste stammering. "This is all Mom ever wanted," I hear her say over the winds. "What she lost her life fighting for! It's our job to maintain her legacy. It's our *destiny.*"

My back is to the scene. There's a beat of silence, then Pictor speaks, so quiet I can barely hear it over the winds: "If it was our destiny, it couldn't hurt you like this, Celeste."

Pictor is right—the twins need to find a new destiny, outside of Mary Read's failed attempt at overshadowing Astro Bonny. Just like Astro Bonny is going to take on a new mission by paving a fresh path forward for pirates in our ever-changing solar system—but one that *doesn't* involve conquering planets.

But this *is* my destiny. Deep space is my destiny. Being an innkeeper is my destiny. After all, it's the skills from years as a hostess that helped me see through Mary Read's lies. That made me scrappy and determined and unflappable under pressure. The entire reason I *have* reached the end of this epic quest is *because* I'm an innkeeper.

The amulet slips through my fingers, clatters to the floor. I wipe my clammy palms on the edge of my shirt and bend over to pick it up. My shoe knocks the amulet and it spins farther, rolling from me. I scamper after it, the only person on this side of the ship, but still terrified as it slips from my grip and slides away, far from my grasp.

I wish my hands would stop sweating. I wish it wasn't so hard to breathe, as though there was no protective O-Zone swirling around the planet. I wish I had a rope I could tether to the amulet to keep it attached to me at all times. To ensure it couldn't roll away.

The amulet rests several feet from me, glinting in the light from the distant suns. I'll use it so the pirates never have the chance to. So I can prove I'm as brave and unstoppable as the Astro Bonny I grew up admiring and be our solar system's hero. I'll use it so my fathers won't sell the inn, and so Ron never leaves. So *I* never leave, and so nothing and no one ever changes and things can stay exactly as they are now. As they should be—as they need to be—forever.

I approach the amulet, my shadow leaking onto its smooth surface. I hover over it, watching as it lies on the deck. My fingertips twitch by my side. But it's my leg that moves, rising so it's angled above the amulet.

Then, with sharp precision, my heel comes down hard on the shimmering surface.

Its golden shell cracks, its insides shattering beneath the

weight of my shoe. I stomp again and again, the pieces scatter-ing, useless, across the deck. Someone shouts behind me but all I hear are the cracks and clinks of the loose gold and metal as they spin across the wood, as they smack beneath my shoe.

The amulet is a thousand pieces at my heels. Each splin-tered piece glares up at me, and my reflection stares back in uneven, jagged pieces. I see me as a little girl, skipping across meteorites while playing make-believe with Ron. Inside the inn, answering a doorbell that won't stop ringing as guests pile their coats into my tiny arms. I taste the crunchy, stale sweet-ness of astronaut ice cream and smell the warm aromas from Papa's kitchen. I watch myself, hunched beside Dad at the tele-scope, squinting at the distant planets I never dreamed I'd visit.

I blink, and my real, present-day reflection comes into focus. My cheeks are distorted and my eyes are too big or too small depending on the size and shape of the shard—but it's *me*. The new Lexi, the one who traveled the solar system with its prince and his pup in pursuit of a not-magical amulet stolen by space pirates. The one who slipped into her new, adventur-ous skin as though she'd been waiting for it all along.

I've always been this Lexi, I realize. Before our little corner of the universe was enough. But since then, I'd outgrown it without realizing. And I'd crammed my family and Ron's in that shrunken space in our past, as though we could shrink back down to fit in its embrace.

A hand grasps my elbow and spins me around. I turn to face Celeste, jaw hard.

But it's Weston. Celeste's sword dangles from his other

hand and his eyes are wide and anxious. His thumb jabs into the crook of my elbow and his eyebrows pinch together so the skin above his nose creases into a worried wrinkle.

"Lexi," he says, voice low, "I thought—"

"I did too. But I was wrong."

His grip tightens, and I realize I'm trembling. My body is shaking like the flag above as it wiggles in the wind. Smashing that amulet—losing my last chance to save the inn—goes against everything I thought I was, thought I *should* do, for my entire life. Even as the knot in my chest loosens—the one that's been growing with each inch our universe expands—I feel a hard sob rising in my throat.

My eyes water but I swallow it back. When my eyes meet Weston's, I smile. "Now no one can use it. As it should be."

My fathers, Ron, everyone else in deep space—I can't know for sure if they would have wanted me to slow down time. Doing something as grand and extraordinary as slowing time would have made me as legendary as Astro Bonny, as I dreamed of being as a little girl. But no matter how much I insisted it was the right way to use the amulet, it would have just been for *me*. To preserve my version of deep space, or uplift some childhood vision of what being an epic space explorer should look like.

I'm not sure who I am without either of those things. But for the first time, I'm not afraid to find out.

Weston's chin wobbles. The sword slips from his fingers and clatters to the deck. With a bang of impact, he wraps me in a tight hug.

"We did it, Lexi," he says, voice muffled by my shoulder. "We both gave the amulet up."

I squirm in his grip, trying to see over his shoulder. "I love the uncharacteristic bout of sentiment, Weston, but the pirates—"

He pulls back, clearing my view of the pirates. Pictor hunches over Celeste, neither of them making a move toward us or the sword. Her face is streaked with hot tears, and Pictor looks as pale as the clouds overhead. They look up when we turn to them, their faces hard but lacking the threatening edge from minutes before.

"We don't need the amulet to take over," Celeste barks. Her voice is louder, overcompensating for the way it wavers against her tears. "We'll continue as we did before. Bit by bit, just like our mother wanted."

Pictor glances down as she says it. Her wet eyes flicker with determination, and I wonder how long she'll stubbornly hang on to her mother's failed legacy.

Weston shrugs. "Fine with me. My parents will find a way to take you down for good." He clears his throat. "That is, my parents *and* I."

Comet waddles over and nudges the sword's handle toward us. I bend down, lift it up, and hold it loosely but defensively before us. "We'll be going now," I say, "though I doubt it'll be the last time we see each other."

Celeste rolls her eyes as Weston, Comet, and I back our way to the pod.

All we did was slow the Odette Twins down. There's no

way to know for sure if they'll give up on Mary Read's vision for the pirates, or what Astro Bonny will do once she gets her crews back in order. We couldn't save this entire planet, just the three of us. But soon, Weston and his family will free all the villagers. They'll stop the pirate takeover for good. Probably with the help of our neighboring solar system.

Probably with the help of their new inn.

Weston leaps right into the pod and turns it on, engine whirring to life. I pause before stepping in, turning to take one last glance up at the crow's nest. Astro Bonny looms above the crew, arms waving with each command she shouts. It still feels surreal to be this close to her, like stepping into a page from my book. But after facing off with the Odette Twins and destroying the amulet, the awe and reverence I held for her feels subdued, and my mind is more willing to believe that this is real.

Because for the first time, I feel like I'm just as much a part of this universe as larger-than-life Astro Bonny. Like this world is just as much mine to take as it is hers.

As though sensing my gaze, Astro Bonny looks my way. I still jump a bit—she *was* my idol for nearly half my life, after all—but my nerves fade when the smallest, crooked smile slips across her weathered cheeks. Within a single blink, she's turned away, attention shifted back to her crew. But a pool of warmth remains in my chest, and I find myself smiling, feeling a bit weightless as I turn back to the pod's open door.

That's when I notice a stack of the twins' loot to the right of the pod. Placed absently on top of a barrel of loot is an uneven stack of paper. The Wanted posters stare up at me from the pile, my eye-less, curly-haired caricature rustling in the wind. In one sweeping motion, I grasp a handful of the flyers. A few scatter in the breeze—all but one, which I fold and tuck in my pocket. It'll be my first decoration in my new room, wherever that is. It can replace my Astro Bonny memorabilia, a reminder of how I made a legacy for myself on my own deep-space adventure. A memory of the day I broke the amulet.

The day I let go.

CHAPTER TWENTY

For the first time in what feels like light-years, I see the inn on the horizon. The miles close between us until it's all I can see through the front window. It floats on our slab of space rock, quiet and lonely. The rope strains across the solar system, off toward a factory too far away to see. Weston's ship is still docked on the front yard, empty and restful. There's no sign of the pirates, and relief rushes through my chest as I remember my parents have been safe since Weston first exchanged the amulet when I was on the plank. As we land, I see a warm, yellow glow emitting from the living room windows and know I'm home.

The inn still feels like home, even now that—in smashing the amulet—I let a large part of it go. It will *always* feel like home, no matter how far we move, no matter how much time passes at its quick, natural pace. I'll just have to live with that: with the space expanding between me and the inn, even as a part of me can never really, fully let it go.

There will be Lexi before and after we left the outer system, and I will live with both. I will learn to hold on to the inn without letting it stop me from moving on.

I leap out and rush to the front door. I wrestle with the knob, then start pounding on the wooden surface.

"Dad! Papa!" I shout. "It's me! Not pirates!"

"That's exactly what a pirate would say," Weston grumbles as he and Comet catch up.

My fathers don't seem to care, because the door swings open so fast I nearly topple onto the welcome mat. Dad and Papa stand, crammed in the doorway, eyes wide and desperate. Seeing it's really me, Dad breaks into an enormous grin and relief sweeps across Papa's face.

Dad yanks me to him and into a tight embrace. The air leaves my lungs as though the O-Zone projection was switched off outside. But I don't mind. I close my eyes and lean into his embrace, letting the oxygen escape my lips as his warm, sturdy arms tighten around me. "Lexi! Lexi, honey, thank Mars you're safe!"

Papa stands beside us, one hand on Dad's back and the other on mine. His thumb runs over my shoulder and he gives it a squeeze. "Galaxy Jones, I don't know what you've done or where you've been, but you have taken twelve years off my life. Seriously."

"I know you're serious because you used my full name," I say, voice muffled by Dad's sweater. "So that's redundant."

Papa huffs but tightens his grip on me, arms folding over me and Dad so we're tangled up in a giant, crushing hug.

It feels both like a thousand years and a thousand years too soon when my fathers release me from their suffocating embrace. Past them, the Queen rises from the sectional, her gown falling unwrinkled around her. Her hands remain folded by her midsection and her posture is perfectly straight, but there's a waver in her voice that betrays her. "Weston, we didn't know when to expect you back."

I turn from my fathers to offer Weston a reassuring nod. Simultaneously, Comet leans up to boop his wet little nose against Weston's calf. I imagine we're both silently reminding him of all he did while he was gone—of all the things he has for his parents to be proud of, because Comet and I are proud of him too.

The King moves forward as though about to reach for Weston like my fathers did me. But he and the Queen hover back, stiff and awkward, as though their bodies are unfamiliar with how to handle the wave of emotions.

Weston straightens up and puffs out his chest, lips parting as he sucks in a steadying breath. I beam, eager to hear him list all the grand things he did and how pivotal he will be to helping his parents and the royal guard stop the space pirates once and for all.

But instead, he closes his mouth again and jolts forward, tossing his arms around his parents so they're wrapped up in an awkward, clanky version of the bear hugs my fathers just gave me.

Despite the way their gold-crusted clothing clanks together in off-tune chimes, or how their elbows and arms move like parts of an unoiled machine, I feel a rush of deep warmth run through my chest at the sight. Comet dances at the King's and

Queen's shiny heels, his small tail flapping faster than a pod windshield wiper.

The King clears his throat after a beat. "Our hosts in the neighboring system have been quite kind to delay our visit," he says, voice unsteady with emotion, "but we really must get going."

Weston gives his parents one last squeeze before pulling back. All three of them immediately begin brushing their hands down their fronts, smoothing out where their shirts and her gown wrinkled during the hug. It makes me want to roll my eyes, but somehow I just find myself smiling more.

"You're right," Weston says. "And I have a lot to fill you in on about the Odette Twins and Astro Bonny along the way."

The Queen and King exchange a glance. Weston's gaze flickers to his shoes, but he inhales a steadying breath and turns to his parents again.

"Astro Bonny's plans are not what you think they are," he says, "and now that she's returned from her intergalactic space travels—"

The Queen's eyes go wide. "Her *what?*"

"—it's unclear what her plans are, or whether the Odette Twins will carry on with their original mission or follow Astro Bonny now that she's back."

He speaks in a rush, cheeks flushing as he finally pauses for breath. But his parents make no move to interrupt him again, mouths gaping as they stare at him with confused awe.

"Let's get going, then," he says. "You're gonna want to hear this."

His parents look dubious but don't object.

As Weston's parents begin their goodbyes to mine, he lifts his gold-trimmed cloak from the coat hanger. He holds it for a moment, as though debating pulling it on, before tossing it at me so hard and fast my vision goes black and I nearly topple over.

I tear it from atop my head, feeling my hair stand in static-y strands around me. "Seriously, Weston? After all we—"

"Keep it," he says. "As a reminder of how much fun you had being incessantly annoyed by me. And Comet." He leans down to scoop up the dog, cradling him to his chest. Comet looks tired from the trip, but there's still a mischievous flicker in the dog's dark eyes.

I clip the cloak at my neck and smooth it over my shoulders. The fabric is thick and heavy and smells a bit too much of sweet cologne. But I make no move to remove it. "I'll see you again," I say. "I'm sure of it."

Somehow, Weston has always orbited his way back to me. Even if I'm not at the inn, I'm sure we'll find each other again somewhere in space—just like I happened upon Ron on our travels. I'm even more certain now, knowing that I won't be fixed like a statue at the inn and that Weston won't let his parents keep him tucked away in the castle anymore, either.

My chest feels hollow at the thought of them leaving, as if part of my heart were being carved out by one of Ron's ice cream scoopers. But I need to trust that we'll see each other again—and that as long as we hold true to the new parts of ourselves that we gained on this journey together, the distance will feel narrower, as if we never really left each other at all.

I scratch behind Comet's ear and think, for a moment, of holding them both in one last tight embrace. But I remain still and smile as I watch them go, out the door and across the lawn, toward the royal ship.

"We'll be in touch," Papa is saying to the Queen as I rejoin them. Weston's parents murmur thanks and farewells before following after him and Comet. We wave from the doorway until their ship whirs to life. Then, before the engine whooshes dirt into the house, Dad shuts the door.

I'm still staring at its wooden surface as I ask, "You'll be in touch about selling the inn. Right?"

Dad stammers. "Lexi, we were never seriously considering—"

"Well, you should."

Dad and Papa stare, dumbfounded. Papa clears his throat and speaks in a low, serious voice. "I know the past few days have been stressful, Galaxy. I don't know what happened to you and the prince, but I promise the inn is safe. Those pirates are too far to reach us, and even if they did, your dad and I would never let anything happen to you."

"But a lot *has* happened to me," I say. "And I *made* a lot happen, too! All because I left the inn. It was scary, and there were times I hated it, but . . ."

There's too much to say. Too many things to explain, stories to tell. And I want to take the time to tell them all. To show my parents what I did and all I faced. Everything I overcame and accomplished. But there's something I have to do first.

"I'll show you," I say, then slip past them and toward the stairs. They hesitate for a moment before following me up the flight, toward my room.

I take the steps two a time to make sure I'm a bit ahead of them. I lead us into my room and right up to my window. When I yank it open, the cool night air whooshes in.

Below, the lawn is empty, Weston and his family already gone. My chest twists a bit as I wonder how long it'll be before I see him and Comet again. But I take a steadying breath and snuggle deeper into my cloak like a promise.

As my fathers slip through the doorway, my hands find the rope that ties my home to Ron's. It's hard and scratchy against my palms. I close my eyes and focus on the feeling of the rope between my fingers. It sways in empty space, rustling beneath my touch. I can almost feel it straining in my hands. Can almost feel the universe as it stretches out before me like an ever-expanding puddle.

"Lexi, what are you doing?" Dad rushes up behind me, clamps a hand on my shoulder. "You need to talk to us—"

"And I will. I promise. But first . . ."

I open my eyes and find the knot at the root of my window. I dig my nail, then my fingertip, then my fingers within its tight bow. Part of me is still terrified that doing this will sever my final ties to Ron, and to the happy, warm life we had here in deep space. But even when I was far from the inn and the security of this rope, I'd felt Ron with me on my adventure. I'd channeled the bravado we had while playing pirates as kids, and embodied the things about being the kids of deep-space business owners that helped me complete my mission in ways only I could.

Because of Ron, even when he wasn't there. The same way I plan on holding true to this new Lexi that I discovered through Weston, even long after he and Comet have left.

I wiggle the knot undone and, slowly, it slips apart. The rope unravels and floats, untethered, in the empty space.

The end within our O-Zone flops to the ground, down in the lawn. Beyond the O-Zone it lingers, weightless in the empty black. Then, as though releasing a sigh, it slithers off. Down the driveway, through the yard, and off the edge of our lawn. It dangles in space, suspended in zero-gravity. I watch as it sways and wonder if it'll linger there forever or drift off, out of view, by the time I wake in the morning.

"Lexi, hon," Dad says, scratching the back of his head. "That was hard enough to rope the first time. I'm not sure we'll be able to—"

"We're not redoing it," Papa says, his voice a mixture of annoyance and confusion.

I hold on to the windowsill, the chilly breeze pinching my cheeks. I can't see the factory from here but imagine it relaxing as the rope went loose.

"When I was on my adventure, I saw Ron—twice," I say. "That's more than I've seen him in person in *ages*. But it was also the most I've ever done without him. Both those things are true."

I turn around, back to the window, and look at my parents. Papa, looking a little worse for wear after a weekend with pirates. Dad, looking so frazzled and unkempt he might as well have stuck a finger in a socket.

But their eyes are fixed on me, wide and attentive. All along, I've known I'm the reason we stayed. The reason they tied the rope and kept quiet about how business *really* was. I knew I had the power to end this, to let us all free.

But I never even considered it. Each time the thought bubbled to the surface, I squashed it down before it could become real.

They should be relieved. Leaping with joy now that the rope is gone, that I've told them to sell. But still, their eyes are on me.

That, I realize, will never change. And, really, that's all I need.

"It doesn't matter if we sell the inn," I say, "because it doesn't matter where we go next. The inn was our big adventure—but it ended a while ago. And I think we're all ready for a new one."

Dad and Papa exchange a glance. "As long as it doesn't involve space pirates," Dad murmurs.

"It won't." I straighten up and plant my hands on my hips. "Because Weston and I chased them into the central system and smashed their sacred, time-stopping amulet!"

Dad's jaw hangs and Papa's dark eyebrows pinch together. "Galaxy, what in the universe—"

Dad wraps an arm around us both. "Why don't we go downstairs, have some calming tea, and talk this all through. How does that sound?"

Papa and I nod and Dad directs us toward the door.

I tighten the cloak around my shoulders, snug and warm.

I wonder when Ron will notice the rope is broken. It'll probably be a while, since he's still out on deliveries. By the time he even notices I've cut our rope, Dad and Papa will be in negotiations with the royal family. There will be a SALE PENDING sign hanging, for the sake of no one, on our front lawn.

I don't know when my phone will ring with Ron's frantic call, or how long it'll take his mom to relocate their factory. I don't know where we'll go next, or when I'll see Weston again, or if I'll even, ever, reunite with Comet.

I don't know much about what my next adventures will bring. But here, beside Dad and Papa, I know that regardless of what I don't know, I will be okay.

ACKNOWLEDGMENTS

Galaxy and her universe lived in my head long before I found the courage to put these words to the page. I've always been fascinated by the metric expansion of space; although I'm no astrophysicist, I always believed the concept embodied much of what the young characters I write grapple with: from the inevitability of change to the challenge of forming identity in a world so big and complex that control seems out of reach.

Once I finally started writing Galaxy's story, I couldn't stop. I spent every lunch break down at Riverside Park sitting on a bench with my laptop on my knees and typing until my fingers went numb from the cold. I stood on the train with my notes app open, typing furiously between stops. *Galaxy Jones* quickly became the book of my heart: a love letter to the places and people I've lost to time and change, just as much as it was a celebration of the growth and beauty that comes on the other side.

I'm so grateful for the people who have supported me and this story over the years. Thank you to Nicole Ellul for your enthusiasm and feedback; I couldn't have asked for a better partner to work on this book with me. I'm grateful to the entire team at Simon & Schuster Books for Young Readers for their support, including Morgan York and Ela Schwartz for their editorial feedback and Camila Nogueira and Chloe Foglia for the lovely jacket illustration and design. And the biggest, heartiest thank-you to Jennie Kendrick, agent extraordinaire. Your encouragement, support, and advocacy are invaluable, and I'm endlessly grateful to both you and the entire Red Fox Literary team.

Thank you Mom, Dad, Shannon, and Grandma for your limitless faith in me and my work. I'm so grateful to my friends and family for always showing up to celebrate me and my books. Rex, thank you for keeping my life full of adventure and laughter, and for crawling on top of my keyboard to remind me to take writing breaks.

Coda: I wrote Comet in memory of you. While we'll never stop missing you, I hope that your boundless love and warmth can live on through these pages and the readers who enjoy Comet's story.

And Melissa. Thank you for being *Galaxy*'s biggest fan from day one, and for being my biggest fan always. I'm the luckiest girl in the solar system to have you by my side.

ABOUT THE AUTHOR

Briana McDonald writes diverse and adventurous books for young readers. She studied writing at Fairleigh Dickinson University, and her short fiction has appeared in several literary journals. When she's not writing, Briana lives and works in New York City with her wife and their dog, Rex. She is the author of *Pepper's Rules for Secret Sleuthing*, *The Secrets of Stone Creek*, and *Galaxy Jones and the Space Pirates*. Find out more at BrianaRoseMcDonald.com.